ASSASSIN'S CREED
MIRAGE

DAUGHTER *of* NO ONE

MARIA LEWIS

ACONYTE

UBISOFT

First published by Aconyte Books in 2023.

ISBN 978 1 83908 280 1

Ebook ISBN 978 1 83908 281 8

Cover art by Anika Mercier

Distributed in North America by Simon & Schuster Inc, New York, USA
Printed in the United States of America
9 8 7 6 5 4 3 2 1

asmodee ENTERTAINMENT

ACONYTE BOOKS

An imprint of Asmodee Entertainment Ltd

Mercury House, Shipstones Business Centre

North Gate, Nottingham NG7 7FN, UK

aconytebooks.com // twitter.com/aconytebooks

For Shohreh Aghdashloo, the OG

Chapter One

Fustat, 824

No one survived this prison.

That's what Roshan had been told from the moment she was brought here.

"You will rot," the bearded guard spat once he'd hurled her inside the cell and slammed the cell door shut behind him. She smiled at his back, a grim expression the man never saw.

Thankfully, survival was not the priority: escape was. As someone who had spent her whole life escaping prisons of numerous varieties, she was confident she could find her way out of this one if she just had enough time. That was the problem, as she soon learned.

There were very few women in this shared prison cell, and even fewer who survived more than a day. She was lucky her attire made it difficult to spot her as female and fortunate it remained mostly intact even after she'd been thrown in the cell with the other prisoners. The billowing layers of fabric made her seem like a slight street urchin at best. But male, critically. Despite this, she remained in danger.

Roshan had been there a week and, much to her chagrin, if she hadn't been constantly defending herself or running interference on attempts at her life, she would probably be breathing fresh Fustat air right about now.

Of course, the air of Fustat was anything but fresh. Amongst the hustle and bustle of the city markets and the intoxicating allure of various spices, there was always the underlying scent of manure. If you breathed in deeply, odds were you'd end up coughing and spluttering a mound of the fine, red sand that seemed to coat everything.

And yet, she missed it. Deeply.

She longed for the chance to run her finger along the edge of her windowsill, streaked with remnants of the latest dust storm. She hadn't loved the city when she first arrived, but compared to the bowels of prison, Roshan viewed the surface as a heavenly oasis.

Fustat was famed for the towering pyramids that stood tall on the outskirts, even though the rulers who'd made them had long since passed. The irony wasn't lost on her that she was in a monument just as great but built in subversion. Her prison was an inverse, pointing down and deep into the earth, which of course made that pesky escape concept even trickier. Not impossible, just… trickier.

Roshan knew that to get out she would need to navigate her way up, as she'd learned there were several levels below her going further into the earth, and several more above. She wasn't at the very bottom, which was the only positive thought she could muster. As far as she could guess, her cell was located five floors below.

Blood had been pouring from a cut above her eye when she'd been dragged down, down, down. Her vision had been obscured, so five floors deep was as much as she could gauge, but she trusted her instincts – while she might have been hurt and bleeding, she always kept track of her surroundings. She always found a way out.

While her arrest had been violent and caught her by surprise – she thought she'd covered her tracks well – her first order of business had been fixing her vision. She couldn't fight what was coming if she couldn't see. One look at the lumpy, brown water that was supposed to be their drinking trough told her that if a drop of that got near an open wound, infection was imminent.

She had navigated around the perimeter instead, with the cell being really more of a pit. The walls and floor were carved from softer clay from top to bottom, except for one main wall, which had a grate running along the bottom of it to bridge the small space between the prison bars and the clay floor. Roshan figured it maintained the structural integrity of this awful place. Two barred and ungrated ominous-looking doors sat in the middle of the wall.

At least one hundred prisoners were all crammed together in the space. Roshan searched for a pocket of space away from them, where she could slip into obscurity, and everyone would go back to doing whatever they were doing before she'd arrived as the shiny, new plaything. As she moved around the edge of the crowd, she ducked lower and lower until she was practically crouching. A sense of malice rolled off a tall, skinny man with a long beard that dangled from his chin like an insidious black snake.

It took a moment to establish him as the real threat. There were just so many people, it became challenging to sort through the various energies being projected at her before Roshan pinpointed his. Even in the dim light created from the flickers of torches fitted into the wall, his eyes were like bottomless black caverns that sliced through the distance between them.

As soon as she identified him, he disappeared in the crowd just as quickly.

Wherever he was, she needed to be somewhere that was *else.* Staying small and quiet were the first steps. Getting a wall against her back was next, as that meant she only had to look outward for danger. Then, as discreetly as she could, she patted her clothes for anything the guards may have failed to pick up. The benefit of wearing this many layers meant she was hard to search quickly, and she wasn't without resources.

A small belt at her waist had a pouch of spiced chickpeas, a flask with little more than a few splashes of an alcohol so strong she largely used it as a fuel, and a half empty canteen of water. The last item she would hold out on for as long as she could, but the other liquid she sneakily emptied onto the fabric of her headwrap and pressed it to the cut on her head. Wincing as the alcohol stung the wound, she held it in place as hard as she could while her eyes focused on the backs and legs of the people in front of her.

Yelling from across the cell, followed by the undeniable sounds of wet flesh smacking and bones cracking, meant there was already something more violent happening.

Pulling her knees to her chest with a snarl of disgust, she tried to take up as little space as possible as she searched for something, *anything*, that could help staunch the bleeding. She found help in the form of a tiny, almost imperceptible ant. With a yellow body and brown rump, they were jokingly called Pharaoh ants by the locals. She'd never been so grateful to see the pest in her life. Careful not to crush it, she gently picked one up as it trudged in a line behind its mates.

Squinting, she could see its tiny gnashing mandibles as she held it to the arch just above her eyebrow. She knew the second it made contact because she felt the pinch of the bite. Roshan left the ant to wiggle around there as she grabbed another, roughly estimating the size and length of the cut by what hurt. It took eight ants and as their jaws clamped shut between her flesh, the mandible acted as the stitch she would have preferred to make with a needle and thread. This was all she had.

Sorry, little one, she thought, snapping off the body of the first ant and then his remaining friends. They'd done nothing but mind their business, heading back to their queens entirely unbothered, and their last act in life had been to help heal her wound. Life was precious, and in the moment, she'd had to make a judgment about valuing hers over theirs.

Worth it. Especially when less than a few hours later, Black Eyes had come hunting for her. She'd known it was him even before the crowd parted. He cut through the sea of bodies, communicating his power and fear among the group. She stood and skulked along the wall, nearly tripping over the corpse of a man who, by look and smell, had passed weeks ago, in her attempt to not be where her foe expected to find her.

There was a chunk of the clay wall that had fallen away near the back and Roshan folded herself into the alcove left behind, using the dead man's body to shield her from sight. She watched from afar as the man lurked around, two larger prisoners following in his wake like they were waiting for his command. She guessed they were. She strained to listen as they exchanged words in rough Turkish, which told her they were lower class, probably career criminals, and terrible ones at that if they ended up here.

"Keep looking," he said, followed by something that sounded close to "bribe."

It wasn't until the crowd swallowed them again and Roshan, crammed in her hiding spot, finally comprehended what he'd meant: "with a woman, we can bribe." Roshan guessed he meant bribe the guards, and she didn't like the idea of that, either. Yet, if she analyzed the threat, it meant the guards hadn't seen through her disguise. Her cellmate had. She'd prefer to take on a foolish adversary than a cunning one.

She slept hunched in that position for as long as she could, using the alcohol-soaked rag to cover her nose so she didn't breathe in the full, nauseating scent of the rotting corpse that obscured her location. It had gone past the sickeningly sweet stage of decomposition to the retch-inducing one where even the maggots had moved on because there was so little nutritional value left.

So when Roshan woke with a jolt as she felt the dead man moving, a yelp escaped her mouth, and she scrambled out of her hiding place. She maintained eye contact with the rotting socket as the corpse's head moved back and forth ever so slightly. Roshan shuddered and refused to be reminded of another woman in another place, with her vision similarly marred. Yet the head wasn't really moving, something *behind* it was, and she squinted to see that it was… a child.

No, more of a young teenager. But it was hard to tell with his dirty face and long, dank hair. He was hunched over the bottom half of the corpse and as he looked up, he smiled at her. It was a toothy grin and for the first time, the idea of cannibalism crossed her mind. What *did* the survivors eat down here? There wasn't enough slop to feed everyone. In horror, she scanned the corpse for bite marks, and decided it was time to relocate.

She ducked and leapt over various figures as she tried to put space between herself and the potential feast.

The next few days were largely spent in a similar manner, one threat arising and Roshan doing her best to avoid it. She traded her headscarf for protection, only for that deal to become worthless when her freshly acquired protector had his neck broken in a brawl – a brawl he started with another prisoner – over food when buckets of mush were dispensed by the guards.

The teenager kept sniffing around, only dead subjects seeming to be of interest to him, so Roshan wryly concluded she could stay un-devoured if she remained un-dead. *Maybe he's just searching the bodies for items of use?* Such an idea had occurred to her, there being a few bones in the ribcage that could make effective shivs. Right now, however, she had other options, and she would utilize those first. She spared two sharp hairpins to clip layers of fabric in place like a hood to disguise her gradually healing face and then, with the other metal clips, she began twisting them together to make a weapon. It would have little structural integrity when it came down to it, but if she hit the right artery at the right time… she had done it before, just once, but she could do it again.

"They put us down here to kill each other," a man said in a thick, Grecian dialect Roshan hadn't heard in years. "No one lives. No one escapes. We just die one by one, and they throw more and more of us in here. If I knew–"

"You would have killed him anyway," his comrade snapped.

"Absolutely. But I would have made sure we never got caught."

Roshan smirked. She had committed so many crimes over so many years, but she'd always found a way to escape. Part of her was seething mad about finally being caught for one she didn't commit. Her mind flashed back to the gold that glinted in the hand of a soldier, gold she'd never seen before in her life, and in a form she would never have chosen to fence. She'd been set up. Her immediate assumption when the guards crashed through her door and dragged her out of bed was that she'd be punished for her most recent offense – destruction of property. What she'd wrecked had been precious, a beloved item sought by some Mamluk general who was the last kind of person who should have access to such a device.

When she'd obtained the device, Roshan had done what she always did to document such stolen oddities. She moved the item through various channels, created a clean path of origin, and fabricated ownership papers. Except this time she disconnected the hidden ignition thread deep within the design of the music box. Her vision had flared with the second sense she'd had since she was a child, showing her what mechanism needed to be disabled so the destructive contraption would cease to function as intended.

"Happens all the time with stolen wares," she imagined Dervis saying to placate the unhappy customer. "The nature in which we acquire these items means they don't always arrive in pristine condition, but that's the bargain you agreed to."

She wondered where the master of thieves was now, whether he'd heard about her imprisonment. Roshan was under no illusions about their relationship. They had worked together successfully for over a year now, yet when it came down to it, Dervis would protect his own neck and operation at all costs. He would never throw her to the wolves per se, but he also wasn't coming to rescue her.

That was why Roshan had concocted a plan depending on only herself, the pieces slowly snapping into place as she watched horror after horror in the cell. The plan was shaky. She'd needed to keep moving through the crowd of prisoners, slipping in and out of larger groups so that she stayed unnoticed. If she was alone, she became an enticing prospect. The teenager had sparked an idea and she began to do what she *hoped* he was doing, too. As other cellmates passed away in various skirmishes, or due to illnesses, dehydration, or starvation, she adopted something of theirs – whether it be a tattered blanket or a section of fabric. She swapped such items out for her own so that her appearance was never consistent, especially as Black Eyes kept up his frequent hunts for her.

Clearly, he hadn't shared his suspicions that she was female with anyone outside his little group: that piece of information being too valuable, as it meant almost every cellmate would be tracking her and he wouldn't get his chance to use her.

With the buckle of her belt – the chickpeas now eaten and the last of the water now drunk – Roshan dug. The clay-like texture of the ground was usually hard and tough, but the second it made contact with liquid it was tenable. She would never waste her last few precious drops of water, but the contents of the disgusting trough were ideal.

Night or day didn't matter down here. There was no natural source of light outside the dim torches fixed into the wall, but she still tried to time her digging for when most of the prisoners were asleep. Back to the grate, eyes on the cellmates in front of her, she dug at the clay underneath it. When she had cleared enough space, she let her route dry and covered her handiwork with the corpse of a freshly fallen cellmate. After all, nobody was picking at the bodies… yet. The guards only grimaced at the pileup of the dead when they visited. Roshan had hidden her work well.

Dinner time was the bloodiest of all, there being only one meal a day served. The guards needed their full attention fixed on the doors as the fray pushed forward to fight for their food. It was also when the prisoners would be most distracted. Roshan seized both advantages of the opportunity.

By the time she heard the metallic jingle jangle of the keys that heralded the guards' arrival, Roshan had her garments streaked as dark as she could get them. If she stood silent and still against the clay walls, she blended in. She needed to. As the two guards wedged open the door and the now familiar crush of bodies surged forward, Roshan made her move.

She slunk along one side of the grate, dropping low as she pushed the corpse out of the way and exposed the hole she had dug underneath. Roshan went in headfirst, and this was when she'd be most vulnerable as she gripped the end of the jagged iron bars and leveraged herself down, around, and under. Hopeful, she wiggled into a sitting position, ignoring the painful scratch that ran along her knee in her rush to get up and get out.

Her upper arm strength was critical as she soundlessly yanked herself to a standing position, wasting no time as she streaked to the side of the corridor farthest from the guards. With a leap, she used her old food pouch to put out the closest torch and plunge herself into darkness. She repeated the movement for the next one, the pouch fully destroyed now as the flame burned through it. She stamped it out with her feet.

She was in darkness and she had gone unspotted.

Roshan didn't look back as she ran, keeping a hand outstretched to her right as she used the wall as a guide. Up was instinctive and when she reached the first grouping of stairs, she took them two at a time. There were markings at each level and she was delighted to find that when she hit the next one, she'd only been three floors below rather than five. She kept moving, using the same method with spare pieces of cloth to extinguish the torches while staying hunched low along the wall.

Roshan was forced to slow as she encountered new guards, but prisoner feeding time seemed to be staggered at each floor, so the level above her had the guards emptying out buckets. She inched past them, careful, eyes locked on their backs as they made idle chatter at a cleaning station. The next stairwell came fast and as she headed up it, she paused. There was no sound, just the vaguest sensation that she wasn't alone.

She looked down into the dark as her skin prickled. There was nothing there. No one there.

Roshan pivoted and increased her pace, racing toward the next floor level when suddenly she felt the ground give out from under her. Her ankles were yanked and she fell hard on the stairs, teeth clacking together as her chin hit the floor. The progress she had made disappeared quickly as she was pulled down, gravity working against her as the curving stairs became a slide of doom.

There he was.

Black beard, black heart, and black eyes fixed firmly on her. She thought he'd given up. *Stupid*. It turned out he'd just been watching and waiting. Her escape had given him one too, and she could tell from the glint in his intense gaze that he deemed his freedom close enough for him to take his prize. He'd dispense with her and then he'd dispense with this place. Men like these thought they were such unique, special monsters. Yet Roshan had encountered them everywhere her whole life. The only surprise here was how unsurprising they remained.

They always went to pin the hands first, cowards. She was ready, kneeing him hard and fast with all the strength she had in the place that men valued most. He let out a pained grunt and an even louder cry as she hooked her thigh under his crotch, tossing him up and over her. Roshan let herself slide further down, flipping over as fast as she could and slipping the entangled, weaponized hairpins free from her sleeve. During the struggle, she'd registered the noises from down below: the shouts and the thuds of feet running and the chorus of prisoners rioting.

She might have been able to slip from the cell quietly enough, but it was obvious that he hadn't. The idiot had been seen, and Allah knew what was left behind in his wake. The guards were coming from the bottom up. Roshan was swift on her feet, but it would be even better if she was swifter than him. The guards were looking for an escaped prisoner and she'd give them one.

With her left hand, she reached upward and lifted the leg of his tattered trousers to reveal the skin. With her right, she slashed across his Achilles tendon. He screamed, kicking backward at her as the flesh became bloody layers. Roshan ducked the attempt, climbing over Black Eyes as he squirmed and wriggled beneath her. She spared a second to look back down at him.

"You wiiiiiitch!" he howled, words flying from his mouth like spittle. He tried and failed to crawl up the stairs toward her, the blood leaving a trail behind him. It would have been so easy to lean down and stick him one last time in the jugular. She clenched the sharp and twisted hairpins, and crouched so that she was at his eye level.

"You're lucky I need you alive," she whispered.

His hand outstretched, he snatched at her, managing only to get a handful of dirty garments. She twisted free and made a run for it, dashing into the final corridor that was lit by not just torches but – mercifully – real sunlight. The light shone through tiny, circular holes cut into the walls, slicing through the gloom in beams of white. It distorted her vision somewhat and she dashed around the sunbeams, trying to keep her gaze focused on the end of the corridor.

The end. The end. The end.

It had to be somewhere up ahead, all she had to do was just keep running until – *ooft*. Roshan was flung backward, colliding with an immovable object. Her head hit the ground and as she tried to blink away the stars from her vision, she thought she saw something descend from the heavens.

"Angel," she groaned, struggling to sit up.

As the seconds passed, she reconsidered her statement. They had come from above, but not like an angel. It was as if the person materialized in front of her, their face hidden from view under the shadow of their hooded cloak. She could hear the guards coming, she could hear the shouts of the man she'd left behind, she could almost taste freedom and yet… she couldn't move. She was frozen as this stranger walked toward her, lethality in their every step.

Demon, she corrected in her mind. This was death incarnate.

"I'm no angel," they said.

They reached down to her, extended a hand that she should have interpreted as an offer of kindness. Yet beneath the sleeves, her senses told her there was something else. A weapon. A threat. She knew it deep within her bones.

Even then, Roshan felt her fingers give the slightest, most imperceptible twitch, as if her body was willing to reach out and take a firm grip and make a deal with a devil such as this.

Chapter Two

Baghdad, 819

Roshan was covered in blood.

More blood than she had ever seen in her life. She was dripping in it, drenched in it, desperate to be rid of it. The sound of a scream shook her out of her temporary horror. In the moment, she didn't even remember doing… *it* as she dropped the weapon and ran. Blood made her path slippery. Her shaking hands gripped the railing of the wooden ladder and she climbed upward out of the berth, frantically searching for the night sky she only ever got to catch in stolen glimpses. Searching for freedom.

One of the wives was screaming even louder now. It had looked like Halima when the flash of dark hair had come sweeping into the room. *Funny,* Roshan thought. She had always considered her one of the quiet ones. Roshan didn't think she'd heard the girl say more than a few words the entire time she'd known her. The singular scream became a chorus of desperate cries that accompanied her as she climbed up and onto the boat's main deck.

It was a clear, cloudless night.

The sun had set hours ago but the air was still hot on her skin as she paused to look up at the moon. She gawked at the waning gibbous. It had been so long since she'd seen the full sky. She had imagined this moment every day since she was first sold to the Persian Harbor Master on her fourteenth birthday. He had wanted her sisters instead.

"Either will do," she remembered him saying to her father as she eavesdropped, pressed to the door. Her parents were kind but unlucky people, cursed with three daughters and no male heir. Not that there was much to inherit, as they had always been a breath away from poor their whole lives and any dowry they could offer prospective suitors was pitiful. The Harbor Master – *don't say his name, don't even think it* – had presented himself as a gift, forgoing a dowry for a bride price instead. "A generous suggestion," her mother had said, voice hushed as if she couldn't quite believe it. Yet Roshan had seen him for exactly what he was the second he returned home with her father.

She had offered herself. Her sisters were sweet, innocent girls and the thought of either of them being trapped with that man made her sick. Not that she was enthused by the idea of it for herself, but her options were limited. Several girls her age had already been married off to worse husbands in worse deals. At least with the money from her, both siblings stood a better chance at finding more suitable pairings. The idea of a love match was a fairy tale, so too a husband that was handsome. All she wanted for her sisters was someone that was financially stable but, most of all, benevolent.

That went further than a full set of teeth in her books, which the Persian Harbor Master did not have. Of course. Her sisters had cried for her when she'd left, pressing necklaces and bracelets into her hands that they'd made her, which she promised to treasure forever. Her new husband managed to destroy all but one within the day and the jewelry became just an item on a long list of precious things belonging to her that he set out to destroy.

Roshan's fingers curled into a fist, brushing the colored beads looped around thin bands of metal that hung from her wrist. It was the last thing she had of her family, the last thing reminding her of who she was and where she'd come from. And, brutally, how she could never go back. The sound of the other wives stirring below her grew louder, their voices mingling amongst Halima's cry, and she could hear someone try to shush her, stifle the hysteria.

After all, if he was dead then it wasn't just Roshan who was free. They all were. Yet the damage had been done. Already she could see lamps being lit on the surrounding boats in the harbor where they had been docked, the wooden jetties sectioning off the vessels in some kind of order. Only at the far end of the port could she see the Tigris river leading away in two directions as it cut through the city she knew was out there, but never had the freedom to visit. A bell rang out, the sound slicing through the Baghdad night like a blade. Soldiers were being called. And Roshan was guilty, not just literally but visually. She caught a fleeting glimpse of herself as she peered overboard at the still water; the only part of her not blood-soaked were her wide, white eyes blinking back at her.

She wasn't horrified by what she saw. She was simply shocked that she had done it. She felt calm in the moment, but as the seconds ticked by, that sensation ebbed away only to be replaced by panic.

"Roshan."

She whipped around, grabbing the edge of an oar that was strapped just under the gunwale beside her. If she thought she had needed a weapon, she was wrong as she met the piercing gaze of Talâyi. The oldest wife. Not the first, nor the second, but the third. Her predecessors had been stubborn and not survived long, Roshan had been told. Talâyi was stubborn too, but she was also smart. Those older wives had taught Talâyi plenty, so she hadn't lost her life to *him,* yet he had taken an eye. She refused to wear a patch that would disguise the wound and bring him comfort. Instead, the left side of her face remained scarred, the eyelid sealed shut.

"I…" Roshan didn't know what to say, what she wanted to say.

"We have quietened Halima. Nai gave her the sleeping tea. But it's too late, you heard the bell."

Roshan sank to her knees, despair washing over her. "What have I done?"

"What you had to," Talâyi said, her voice neutral and unfeeling. "What others wish they had the courage to do."

"Have I doomed you?" She looked up as tears streaked from her eyes and cut a clean path through the blood covering her face. "Have I doomed you all?"

The older woman shook her head, face grim. "No, dear. Only yourself."

Execution. That's what awaited her. There would be no trial, no hearing, probably not a single question asked. Men like *him* could do what they wanted to their wives and the only consequences were felt by those with no power. Probably torture first, then execution, perhaps even a brutalist brothel if she was lucky. She did not want that kind of luck.

For a fleeting moment, she let herself hope. *Home.* She could go home! She could see her sisters again, enjoy the tang of her mother's spicy soup on her tongue, kiss her father on the side of his cheeks, hug–

"You cannot go home," Talâyi snapped, her sharp tone cutting into Roshan's happy thoughts. "Don't dare even think it. I know you miss your sisters, your family, but you wouldn't just doom yourself then, you would doom them."

The woman she had come to know had correctly anticipated what Roshan's wildest dream was... because it was hers too. All the wives yearned for home. The shouts of men could be heard off in the distance, but still closer than she would have liked. Roshan's resolve hardened. She wiped away her tears, angrily getting to her feet.

"I accepted my fate back then," she said, returning Talâyi's hard stare. "I welcomed it willingly, not knowing how truly cursed each day from then out would be living in his presence, on this cage of a boat, not setting foot on land for three years."

"And you got your vengeance," Talâyi replied. "Not just yours, but all of ours, all our sisters, but you knew it would come at a cost, Roshan. You are clever, do not feign otherwise. The most you can do now is to be happy with what you have given all of us and accept your fate bravely, boldly, graciously. What more could you want than that?"

The thrum of marching footsteps filled the air, approaching quickly. Soldiers running from somewhere, toward the sound of the earlier screams and trouble. Roshan could just make out the shape of their helmets as they sprinted down the jetty. Her gaze cut back to Talâyi, who had seen and experienced so much, worse than she could probably ever imagine. Yet she was disappointed that this woman couldn't see the possibility of what she wanted for herself.

"What more could I want than that?" Roshan repeated the question. "I want to *live*."

She had but seconds to make a choice and she committed to it fully as she spun around, sprinting away from the oldest wife and her former life. She heard Talâyi's surprised gasp behind her as Roshan darted around all the remnants of her world for the past several years. The Persian Harbor Master refused men on this boat – it was just for them, the women – and she was glad for it as it meant there was no one in pursuit of her. Yet.

Yanking the many layers of her dress free as she ran, Roshan kicked off her shoes and pulled away her belt which jingled with her movements. Sparing one more glimpse upward at the moon, she grabbed the edge of a sail as it hung off the side of the boat and used it to steady herself. Climbing higher, her toes curled over the edge of the bow. The wood underfoot was comforting as she braced herself.

Taking a long, deep breath, Roshan dove into the water.

The blood that had been drying on her skin was instantly wet again as she plunged into the depths, the cool water a relief from the warm air of the surface. She kicked, urging herself deeper as her hands pushed the black water aside. Since becoming a better swimmer than anyone else on the boat, she could move like this for a long time and was grateful for the hours she had spent languishing in the waters of the harbor on their daily supervised baths. When she finally broke the surface, she was far, far away from the boat.

She bobbed there for a moment, watching silhouettes like she was viewing one of the shadow plays she loved so much as a child. Soldiers were trying to board the boat, yet Talâyi blocked their path. She was screaming in a hysterical fashion Roshan recognized as distinctly unlike her. Four of the other wives had joined her, all of them clutching at their skin, pulling at the clothing of the soldiers around them, yanking one to his knees even.

She felt a flash of affection for the women, many of them like Talâyi who probably thought she should have stayed and greeted her death with honor. Even though she had made a different choice, they were helping Roshan anyway. They were buying her time, creating a distraction, and giving her the window of opportunity she would need. She would not let it be wasted.

She paddled away as quickly and quietly as she could, only throwing her hands over her head into a faster stroke when she thought she was far enough away that the splashes wouldn't be heard. Roshan avoided the boats, *hundreds* of them, as they contained people, and people could tell others that there was a bloodstained girl flopping about portside.

So she kept swimming, her goal in sight, and after an hour or so she was at the farthest end of the harbor.

There were stone steps that led up from the water and were frequently populated by fishermen cleaning their catch and preparing for the busy daily market. Her route there, however, was in clear view of a group of drunks loitering on the jetty nearby. She hid directly underneath them, using one of the wooden pillars to rest against as she waited.

As they laughed and hollered above her, Roshan watching their feet dangle over the edge with trepidation, she worried about the fresh problems she was about to face. She had stripped away as much of her attire as she could, ditching the bloodstained fabrics that would slow her down and hold her back when wet. Yet now her exposed skin made her an obvious target while navigating the city streets of Baghdad. She had no food, no water, no money, no contacts, and not a single person she could get assistance from. Even if she did, she'd never stepped off the boat except for observed plunges into the harbor.

The wives had been forbidden from anything else and beaten if they tried. She had lived in this city since leaving her home village with her newlywed and yet she had never walked a single street. She had no sense of direction. No clue about where to go or what to do. Panic rose and she took a steadying breath, sinking under the water's surface where everything was calm. Quiet. Still. Safe.

When she re-emerged, she tried to still her mind. Panic would do her no good. What she had to do was focus on the problem in front of her. Overcome that. Then begin working on the next one. Her world had been the size of a pinprick and now it was massive. Expansive. Full of possibility. Danger too, of course, but that was everywhere. The potential was worth the risk.

So she waited. The water's coldness crept into her limbs, making them numb. She shivered and tried to push her discomfort aside. Despite this, she waited for the right moment. Eventually, two of the men stumbled home. The lone remainder of their trio fell asleep, an empty bottle rolling off the platform and landing in the water with a hollow splash. Roshan swam forward quietly, leaving the safety of the jetty's shadow and making for the huge steps that led to street level.

She reached out in front of her, hands searching through the water for the surface of the first ledge and when she found it, she pulled herself upward. Moving as quickly as she could, she briefly smiled in victory once she was fully out of the water. It was a gesture that felt foreign given it had been so long since she'd had cause to smile, and she prodded at her cheeks uncertainly.

The loud neigh of a horse snapped her out of the brief celebration. The sharp echo of hooves against the hard ground soon followed and she swerved toward the nearest alley she could see. Roshan tripped and barely made it to the safe hiding place. The rider swept by quickly and when Roshan set off again, the same issue presented itself: she could barely stay upright. It was like she was poisoned. She struggled to find her footing and gripped the walls of buildings around her to stay standing. At one point she dropped to all fours and vomited up the contents of her stomach. *I desperately needed that last meal and now it's gone,* she thought angrily as she wiped her mouth. What was happening to her?

The answer came soon enough and with a thud as she sat, taking a moment to recover. She had made it several blocks into the city, but as the population got denser, she'd be in more danger. Whole pockets of city life operated twenty-four hours a day and it was getting harder to avoid people. It would be additionally challenging if she couldn't stay steady on her feet but, well, of course it made sense why she couldn't.

She'd been confined to that boat since she was fourteen. Now, at seventeen, she had spent years on the water. Even if they'd been docked for large portions of that time, she had her sea legs and had grown used to the constant rocking. Yet it had been so long since she'd been on land, she'd lost the knack for steady ground underfoot.

"Get. Up."

She grunted the words to no one but herself… or so she thought. A street cat treading past her paused at the sound of her voice. Roshan struggled to her feet once more and as it scampered off, its path drew her eye to another alley. This one was packed with clothing, fabrics in every color and style swaying in the warm, night breeze as they hung to dry.

She stumbled forward, reaching the first line just as she felt like she was about to topple. She gripped it for support and her weight caused it to snap, the damp items sliding down into a pile at her feet. Whether they were dry or not didn't matter to Roshan. She sorted through them quickly and found a rich, brown kaftan closest to her size, trousers, shirt, and undergarments to match. She stripped out of her soaking dirty clothes as fast as she could, tying a sash of rust-colored fabric at her waist and another in a matching shade around her head so that she was hooded.

It was preferable that these were men's clothes, and she took a moment to relish in the range she had as she moved her legs, shaking them out. Roshan slinked closer to the window of the first home she could see; the residences were stacked on top of each other to fit as many families as possible. The window was unlatched and she gently pushed it open, peering inside.

The kitchen. She lifted herself up onto the ledge, reaching inside as she snaked a half-eaten load of lavash flatbread. She was going back for what looked like rice in the dim light when somebody cried out.

"Oi! You!"

Her heart leapt into her throat. She froze, hoping it was a different "you." Tragically, it was not. As she turned her head, she met the gaze of what appeared to be someone's drunken father stumbling home from a nearby tavern.

"Thief!" he screamed. He pointed and shouted repeatedly, and soon candles were aflame as the residents started waking up and people began peering out windows.

Thankfully, she'd been seen by the one person who was just as useless on his feet as she was. Even as she stumbled away, she still made better progress than he did as she put distance between herself and the growing disturbance.

Roshan soon realized she was lost and had become turned about amongst the city's infrastructure, so she rerouted to what she knew: the water. She'd come quite far from Baghdad's inner harbor, which was a relief, so she used the Tigris river to continue navigating further. When she came to a bridge, danger presented itself. She could get a proper view of the horizon and along with it, dawn. Sunrise was still an hour away at least, but daylight was coming. The advantages she'd gained in darkness would soon be lost. Even the foot traffic crossing the bridge was hazardous, with the number of people hustling and bustling to their early morning tasks being a challenge.

Or an asset…

Slipping out from behind a loaded cart, she joined the largest group she could see. Someone had left their walking stick leaning against a series of barrels and she snatched it, the added assistance coming in handy as she limped over the rise of the bridge and down to the other side of the city. It was a good thing to be dressed as a man, but being an elderly man was even more beneficial as she hunted for somewhere she could hide.

The group she was with were slow moving, so she hung at the rear, following where they were going with the intention that she would peel off when an opportunity presented itself. Yet the longer she walked with them, the more others joined their number. Many of those, too, had walking sticks and she accidentally but rather seamlessly blended into the fold. She would have to follow where they were going, so she kept her head down and her face hidden as best she could as they shuffled up steps and into what she assumed would be a mosque.

The prayers she expected to hear did not come. Instead, the chatter around her was a mix of not just the language she knew and spoke, but others she had never heard before. The voices she discerned talked about numbers and stars and other things that may as well have been another dialect. She was inside, however, and that was critical.

Carefully, she peeled off until she was at the edge of the group. She risked a glance upward, and her breath caught in her throat. If this was some kind of temple, she had no idea what they worshiped. But it was *beautiful.*

The stars were painted on the ceiling far, far above her with prophets of old illustrated alongside them as they moved through time, through history, through space. Gold glinted off seemingly every surface, the various candles reflecting against the metallic sheen and creating even more of a glow. Men threw back their hoods, greeting each other with hugs and handshakes warmly.

They knew each other, they knew this place, and sooner or later she would be the odd one out. Cloaks were being folded and placed away. She tracked what looked like a lesser worker with her eyes, mimicking his activities as she scooped up a stack of scrolls and limped after him. He pushed through swinging doors and she did the same, neglecting to grab a candle so she could remain in the dark.

The view that greeted her through the doors was just as daunting, with a cityscape of shelves stretching before her in an endless row. *Library.* She knew what one was in theory, but she had never set foot inside a place like this in reality. It looked like a mini-city made of books. She retreated deeper into the bowels of the place, moving further away from the opening. She trod away from the bubble of voices, eventually placing the scrolls she carried, yet couldn't read, down gently on a table. Then she sought the quietest section of the library where the volumes would be coated in dust and where the squeak of a rat would tell her that visitors rarely came here.

Checking over her shoulder, she saw that no one was following her. Why would they? She looked like she belonged here and as she turned down an aisle, she leaned the walking stick against the shelves. Her feet were sore and raw, and she slumped down onto the ground.

Clutching the stolen lavash she'd rolled up at her side, it felt like her only lifeline. If she was careful, she could stretch this for a week. And then… she had no thoughts after that. No ideas. No solutions. She was alone. Yet for just a moment, that could be enough. As she bit into the bread, she chewed with relief and closed her eyes. She was alone, but for the first time in what felt like forever, she was free.

Chapter Three

Fustat, 824

Roshan didn't take the cloaked stranger's hand. She watched the faintest frown of discontent mar his features – for she could see now, just underneath the hood, that this was a man before her – but it disappeared so quickly she questioned whether it was imagined. It turned out there was a lesson there she needed to learn. The consequences of her rejection became apparent.

The guards crashed down the corridor behind her, pouring into the tight space like water erupting out of a funnel. They were on her in a flash, hands grabbing her, feet kicking her, voices yelling and overlapping as they picked her up off the ground. They hauled Roshan back into the bowels of the prison and as she feebly tried to fight them, she managed to twist back around and look for the mysterious man.

He was gone.

Only darkness punctured by the shards of natural light

remained. As two guards crossed paths exactly where he had once stood, it became clear that she had been the only one to see him. It felt like he had never been there at all except… even through the chaos as Roshan was dragged away, she could still sense him there. Watching. Waiting.

A swift elbow to the ribs snapped her back to more pressing concerns and a bag was shoved over her head, blocking out anything else, and she was dragged over the steps leading downward. Her one chance at freedom rapidly disappeared. She had been so close. Anguish filled Roshan as she was pulled away from her goal, away from hope.

She wasn't returned to the pit with the other prisoners. Instead she was dumped in her very own cell, slapped a few times for good measure, then left in the dark. When she pulled the sack off her head with her restrained hands, it didn't matter, such was the level of penetrating darkness in the space. She blinked, waiting for her eyes to adjust, until she was able to make out the faintest outline of what looked like a cot in the corner. As she slumped down onto it, she realized it was made from unforgiving stone. Still, at least it was something.

Back against the wall, feet curled up underneath her, she peered closely at her restrained hands. Nothing but a pair of rusty, old manacles at best. She could get out of those, no problem. And then be… where, exactly? With free hands even though every other part of her was still a prisoner? Contained. Fatigue washed over her as despair really set in. Her throat clenched as she felt a pained sob forming, but she swallowed it down. It would do her no good.

You will rot.

The words came floating back to her as she lay down, trying her best to ignore the hard stone ridges that dug into her back. *We'll see,* she thought, less optimistic and more eternally stubborn. She let the heaviness of her bones pull her under, her various aches and pains fading as she slipped into unconsciousness.

When she woke, it could have been hours or days later. The stiffness in her neck suggested the latter, but the lack of fresh injuries inflicted by the guards suggested the former. Roshan groaned, struggling to move back into a sitting position as she felt various hurts flare to life. Her neck was the worst and as she sat, she patiently stretched it out to the left, to the right, to loosen the muscles.

She shivered slightly, the drop in temperature telling her it was evening. It also suggested she was deeper in the pyramid than before. Fustat was famed for its heat, but when the sun dropped, the conditions could be just as unforgiving. Roshan unwrapped part of the fabric that had been cloaking her face and head, using it as a flimsy but additional layer of warmth. Draping it around her shoulders, she reached up, fingers sliding through the thick braids she had pinned under the ill-fated scarf.

Her hair was long and heavy, yet even though she'd removed several of the pins to create her weapon, she knew she'd find more still buried in her locks. It was more challenging than she would have liked with her restraints, but she let out a hiss of elation as she slowly extracted a pin from deep within her hair. Slipping it between her teeth, she bit down as she reshaped it into the most useful tool. She tried to position the hinges of the manacles in front of the hook she had fashioned as best she could with both mouth and hand.

It was challenging given the lack of light, so she worked off instinct and what little of the design she could feel. She could never count on her secret skillset, the one she'd had for as long as she could remember. That second sense was unpredictable and uncontrollable, with objects and pathways brightening in her vision at random moments. However, the moments only *seemed* random, especially because they appeared like a direct message from her very spirit, guiding her when she needed it most. When she was a child, she assumed her sisters could also see the triangle shape illuminated as her chubby hand had hovered nearby with a wooden block that needed to fit the right hole.

They had not. When she had brought the ability up with her mother, the reaction had been… significant. She'd urged Roshan never to speak of it again, forcing her into extensive prayers Roshan did to appease her. Her second sense became one of those things Roshan inherently understood as something she was supposed to pretend wasn't happening, even when her mother asked her about it or took her on visits to the lady in their village who "cleansed her" with a combination of smoking scents that made her wheeze.

Roshan learned to lie about the golden glow then and had lied about it ever since. Yet she had relied on it in the same way she relied on her cunning and physical abilities to keep her alive. Looking down at the restraints, the outline glowed ever so slightly, giving her a pathway to work the lock. She heard a sharp *click*.

Suddenly the cell was cast in a small, warm light that felt

blinding. Roshan nearly choked on the pin in shock. She had no idea anyone else was in the cell with her. There had been zero indication of it. Not a sound, not a scent, not a clue. As the light flared down to a dancing flame at the end of a freshly lit candle, Roshan knew it was the mysterious stranger in front of her.

"I thought the light might help," he said, voice low as he sat perfectly still. She couldn't see his gaze under the peaked hood, but she could somehow feel it penetrating right through her. It was so intense; it was a wonder that she hadn't sensed it earlier. He had been completely invisible to her again, in a way that wasn't just disconcerting but entirely new and rare. Such a thing had never happened. Her senses never let her down like this. And yet…

She tried to maintain her composure, offering the stranger a firm glance as she resumed her task. The light did actually help. A few moments later, she identified the weak spot in the bottom bolt of the manacle and unpicked the hinge completely. As the restraints dropped away, she moved the metal to her side where it could be reached at a moment's notice if she needed it.

"I'm not here to hurt you," the stranger said finally, having silently watched Roshan free herself. Roshan had gathered that much, given that she had no idea how long he had been there, maybe even watching her sleep, completely unguarded and vulnerable.

"I know who you are, *Bint la-Ahad*," he pressed, the words causing a chill down her spine. "And I do not care."

"Don't call me that," she growled.

"Ah, she speaks."

Roshan immediately swallowed her next words, remaining as stubborn as ever.

"What would you prefer I call you?" he continued, the hint of a smile dancing on his lips.

She said nothing, dropping her gaze and rubbing at the raw skin of her wrists.

"Daughter of no one doesn't sit right. How about… Roshan?"

Her head snapped up. She knew exactly how many years, months, and days it had been since someone last spoke that name. The name of a murderer. She closed her eyes, trying to quell the fear and worry curdling up from the core of her being.

"Put me back in the pit," she whispered.

"It means light. You weren't the daughter of no one."

She shook her head, trying to dispel the words as he continued to talk.

"You were someone's splendid light."

"Put me back in the pit!"

Roshan's shouted words echoed around the cell. She was on her feet, manacles clenched between her fists as a weapon. Her chest rose and fell quickly, breaths coming out in rapid pants. The stranger didn't flinch, didn't react, barely blinked. All he did was lean back slightly in his chair, his neck arching upward as he studied her with consideration.

"Don't worry," he said. "I'm not here to expose you."

His voice was flat, neutral, impassive. He was either the greatest actor she'd ever met, or he truly meant what he said. Yet still, there was a threat there. She just couldn't work out where or why. Roshan slumped back down onto the hard ledge. In this moment he had all the power. She had none. This was a position she was familiar with.

"What do you want?" she spat, hearing the despair in her own tone. "You're not here to expose me, just to let me know that you can. You're not here to kill me, just to let me know that you could with whatever you have hidden under that cloak. So what *do* you want?"

"I'm here to offer you your wildest dream," he replied. "Freedom."

She snorted. "Never trust a jinn."

Yet she couldn't deny the thrill that ran through her at that word. *Freedom.* That was what she wanted, wasn't it? She wanted out of this place more than anything. Her escape hadn't worked. The guards would be watching her closely now. She was confined to a cell she couldn't dig her way out of. She wouldn't get another chance.

"What's the price?" she asked.

"Clever." He nodded.

"There's always a price, one way or the other."

Roshan was twenty-two years old, but she had learned that truth from childhood. Freedom sounded lovely in theory; after all, it was what other people lived and died for. But it was a lie for people like her. The price was often higher than she could pay, and in reality, she never stopped paying. And yet, that didn't prevent her from asking.

"What is it?"

He tilted his head. "I hear you're good with objects."

"*Good with objects,*" she recited.

"Finding them. Rehoming them. Tracking them. Destroying them."

Roshan went to reply but bit her lip. This stranger knew entirely too much about her. If he knew who she was, who she *really* was, then he knew what she'd done. Then and now. The objects were the least of it.

"I'd be interested to know who you heard that from," she finally said.

"If it's any comfort to you, they did not disclose that information willingly."

"Ah yes," she replied drily. "Very comforting."

"There was a particular object an associate of mine was trying to locate," the stranger offered. "He had spent months looking for it, actually. It was exactly what I had trained him for and after much hard labor, he managed to infiltrate the Turks that had purchased it. However, when he went to obtain it–"

"To steal it," she guessed.

"It had already been stolen. But I think you know that."

Roshan narrowed her eyes. "I'm not a thief. But I think *you* know that."

He let out a long, slow exhale and she watched as the candlelight flickered, creating dancing shadows in the dark. Her eyes tracked the dripping wax as it melted, landing on the filthy floor. Perfect, white droplets: the only clean thing there.

"The object had already been stolen and resold," he reiterated. "Except when my apprentice traced it to the buyer, it turned out this precious object had ceased to work. The very purpose for which it was designed was left… unfulfilled."

She felt the smallest spark of victory at that. Ah. Now she

understood. She had gotten caught regardless, but at least she'd been successful in one aspect.

"Sounds like your apprentice is terrible at their job."

The stranger surprised her then with a raspy laugh, the sound a throaty baritone and somehow scarier than all the loaded silence and sharpened words that had come before it. A truly and utterly terrifying sound.

"Perhaps," he said, once the laughter had abated. "But the buyer led me to this prison, so it wasn't an entirely wasted exercise."

He got to his feet, taking the light with him. Holding the candle up to the wall, he revealed a tapestry of stories. There was a blood smear down one side. Someone had carved a brief love note to a lost someone. What looked like scratches in a set of three shredded into the hardness, what might have been a fingernail still embedded in the deep grooves. One symbol had been drawn more than anything else, however, repeated over and over again and etched by various prisoners across time.

"Hieroglyphs," he said. "Can you read them?"

She shook her head and there was a flash of disappointment there, as if he *knew* that she was lying.

The man clicked his tongue. "It's rare to find a woman who can read. Even rarer to find one who can write. For you to survive this long, to have gotten this far, it's my understanding that you can do both across many languages. I'd be interested to learn how you acquired that skill."

The verbal trap had been laid, and Roshan deftly avoided it. Depending on her location and company, even admitting that she could read and write would carry a death sentence.

She wouldn't allow him to outmaneuver her. However, if the stranger intended to kill her, he'd had plenty of opportunities

"The same way you acquire any skill," she answered. "With dedication and patience."

"Mmm," he mused. "Valuable attributes."

His finger brushed the shape of the most dominant symbol, which looked somewhat like a thinly limbed star set inside a circle.

"Duat, home of the gods," he said. "Also known as the underworld. Hell."

"That's what they call this place," Roshan mumbled, understanding more clearly now.

"You will not get out of hell without my assistance. And you will not get my assistance without completing a task."

"What kind of task?"

"Agree first."

"No."

"Stubborn."

"Suspicious," she snapped. "What kind of value could I be to someone like you, who can dance into hell and back out again anytime they want?"

"Dance?" he questioned, amusement clear in his tone.

She narrowed her eyes. "I will not kill."

He looked intrigued by that, moving away from the wall and closer to her. "Why not? You've done it before. Many would say, in that particular instance, it was justified."

Now Roshan really did shut her mouth, sealing her lips tight. Another question which felt like a trap and there was no safe way for her to extricate herself from it. They stayed in silence for several moments. The stranger considering her, Roshan refusing to budge. Eventually, he broke the peace.

"I'm not asking you to kill. Killers are easy enough to find. You will have to work with many of them, in fact."

She let the silence hang between them again, her "and?" not verbalized. She wanted the details.

"There's a stolen package," he continued.

"That sounds familiar."

"The group who stole it are traveling along the Silk Road."

"Toward where?" she asked.

"China. The task is to intercept them and obtain the object. No killing required if you do not see fit."

"Because you have other killers," she mused.

"Correct."

This stranger knew that she didn't have a lot of options. In fact, after her failed escape Roshan had just one: accept this task, come what may.

"If I say yes, you will get me out of here?" she questioned, wanting to be crystal clear on the specifics.

"Yes."

"Forever. Not just for the duration of this assignment or–"

"Your crimes will be expunged, you will never return to hell. Although I would recommend avoiding Fustat until the inevitable change of regime."

The word *inevitable* stuck out to her, as if this stranger knew things that he couldn't possibly, things that were already in play, plates that were already being spun.

"But you must bring me this object. Otherwise, you'll be free until the next time you're caught. And trust me, they have been kind to you so far."

"If I say yes, if I agree, then how do I know if you're good for your end of the bargain?" Roshan questioned. "And do not say 'trust.' It's a word I do not like and rarely see used in action."

"I trust," he began, smirking, "that now would be a suitable time to leave?"

The sting above her eye told her that her eyebrows had shot up rapidly in surprise, agitating her healing cut and giving away her eagerness. In the moment, she was grateful for her many aches and pains as it prevented her from leaping off the cold, concrete bench in gleeful excitement. The stranger watched all of this play over her face and then he gestured her forward with a simple bend of his fingers.

Roshan swallowed down the groan as she got up, taking a moment before limping after her new broker toward the door. He had not removed his hood the entire time he was there, but he readjusted it slightly so that more of his face was covered. He paused at the cell's door, hand braced on something she couldn't see and the other still gripping the final remnants of the candle.

"How did you know I have a weapon?" he asked, turning to her.

The question took her aback, the tangible possibility of freedom so close Roshan felt like she could almost smell it.

"No one would willingly come down here without one," she supplied, before rethinking her answer. "Without several."

"Yes, but it wasn't a theory. You verbalized it like a statement of fact. Your eyes even looked toward a certain area on my person, as if that's where you were expecting it to be."

Roshan had liberated the last of her hairpins from her scalp, retwisting and contorting them until they resembled that same, flimsy blade from earlier. She held up her wrist, demonstrating as she slipped the makeshift weapon between the sleeves of her own garment.

"That's where mine would be," she said simply. The stranger was less than a few inches away and he towered over her, his muscular frame almost hunching. Roshan couldn't read what was going on behind his neutral expression, but she wondered if he had picked up her lie wrapped within a truth. She hoped not. As he leaned forward she tensed, wondering if she would have to fight him, only for the man to blow out the flickering flame.

Immediately, they were plunged into darkness. She heard a metallic scrape and subtle creak as the stranger opened the prison cell's door. A hallway awaited them, bathed in only the most subtle of brown light from lanterns that were quite far off.

He stepped out first and she followed him, staying close. Nearby, a guard slumped in their chair, fast asleep. Their head was arched backward at an impossible angle, snores blasting from their open mouth. The stranger moved past them unbothered.

The hallway wrapped around in a long arc as they passed cell after cell. The various scents emitting from under the cracks of each door told Roshan much about the state of those inside. Many were dead. Others were probably dying. Her fate was tied specifically to the person in front of her, whose name and identity she knew nothing about, but who knew more about her than she would like any individual to know.

Bile stung the back of her throat at the very idea. Hell or restrictive freedom. Those were her choices. As the stranger pushed through a door to his right, revealing a staircase so narrow she had to turn sideways to ascend, she told herself to feel comfortable in this choice.

She had been imprisoned much deeper in the prison than before, with two levels passing before she started to recognize some of the features she had dashed past in her first clumsy attempt at freedom. How the guards worked here without getting lost in the maze of dimly lit corridors and intertwining stairwells she had no idea. Roshan was hyperaware of the fact that without the stranger in front of her guiding the way out, she would never have made it. One level, maybe. At best two.

She would have died down here, exactly like she was meant to.

It was at the final stretch toward freedom, slinking through the shadows, where they encountered a problem. Specifically, the kind of problem of five guards blocking their path to the outside. They had been marching forward when she and the stranger stepped directly into their path.

Even before they shifted their stance, Roshan knew she would have to fight her way out. Her grip tightened on the manacles doubled up over her left hand, her knuckles gripping the harsh metal that would add *oomph* to any punches she swung. Her hairpin blade was out and brandished forward as she readied herself.

Perhaps the most surprising element of all, however, was that she didn't require either. She didn't even get a chance to inflict a wound as the stranger simply extended a hand and pushed her to the side, out of the line of sight. He calmly and coolly strolled toward the guards, his posture telling the five men they had nothing to worry about. That was proven to be fundamentally untrue.

The blur of movement came so fast the first guard didn't even have enough time to get his hand on the hilt of his sword. The stranger leapt up and around them, bringing the guard to the ground and rendering resounding unconsciousness in a swirl of fabric. The feet of another were swept out from under him, an elbow awaiting his descent as the stranger quickly dispatched him.

Of the three remaining guards, one ran. The other two attempted to fight, but it was futile. The stranger ducked the jabs of their swords like he was bored, dodging mere moments ahead of each thrust. The two guards thought they had him backed into a corner, but he used the environment around him to get the upper hand. He sprinted up the wall, feet moving so fast they were a blur as he gained height and used the shoulders of the man trying to kill him as a brace to somersault over both their heads.

As he landed behind them, the guards stood staring at the place where their target had once been. Roshan's eyes caught the silver glint of a hidden blade that was dislodged from his wrist with a soft *shwick.* Two quick outward motions with his arm and the guards were dead, dropping to their knees with a final gargle. He looked down at them, almost with regret, before a shift in expression erased such sentiment. He quickly wiped his blade free of blood. *Necessary,* the gesture said.

He looked up, meeting her gaze. With the tilt of his chin,

he told her to follow him. At first, Roshan didn't think her legs would obey. Yet her soul's desire for freedom had other plans and she soon found her feet taking off while her mind struggled to catch up. As she stepped over the bodies of the guards, she couldn't help but spare a look down. Two dead. Two incapacitated.

She gulped and focused ahead. Forward. Yet the broad back of the man she was following had the faintest spray of blood splattered across it as a reminder of what she had just witnessed. The fight had confirmed everything she had known in her bones about this person, everything she had feared about negotiating with him. Roshan had never seen *anyone* move like that, let alone emerge triumphant against such numbers with so little cost to themselves.

She should have been horrified by it, but envy overwhelmed her instead. She did her very best with the skills that she had and the circumstances she had been dealt. Yet what a gift it would be to have that kind of mastery over the world around you. To know that whatever threat came, your body could be your greatest weapon. Her whole life she had felt like her body was her weakest link; such was the curse of all women.

The door ahead was kicked open and the swift thuds against wood pushed the thoughts from her mind. She spared only a second to cast a look up at the man beside her. She might have just escaped hell, but at what cost?

Chapter Four

Baghdad, 819

Roshan soon discovered that she had hidden in the House of Wisdom.

Those words meant nothing to her at first, just that she heard them spoken over and over again. The Grand Library of Baghdad was a place she had heard *him – don't think his name, never think his name* – speak about. Not that he had ever attended, but that he loathed those who did.

"They just let anyone into the city," he had hissed. "Disbelievers, pagans, women, all if they carry some little manuscript of importance. They believe in no god, only what's on the page. It's sacrilege."

Roshan eventually realized *that* place and *this* one were the same. He didn't plague the realm of the living any longer, but just knowing that her sanctuary was somewhere he would never haunt comforted her.

And it proved the perfect place to hide. The city was a trap until she could learn to navigate it. Even worse, the murder of the Harbor Master remained searing hot news. It consumed every whispered tale and hushed story she overheard as she hid in the aisles, still bundled in her nondescript clothes. They may have been scholars, but even great men liked to gossip.

"By one of his wives?"

"That's what I heard."

"He was a huge, portly man – don't you remember? There's no way one of those tiny

girls could have done it."

"What happened to her?"

"I heard she was killed."

"Killed? No, they must be saying that to save face. Who else are they tearing the city apart for?"

"Definitely not a small woman."

"His brother is a silk trader, the boats were a critical part of that operation. Both of them were powerful businessmen as a pair. Without the other half..."

"His reign is in jeopardy."

"Her family should hope she's dead. What would they do with her? I shudder to think."

"Brutal, brutal men."

While hidden, she had watched them swap this information about her life idly as they picked through the scrolls they sought. It made her decision to stay exactly where she was that much easier. The streets of the city were the most dangerous place she could be. For now, the walls of the House of Wisdom were the safest cocoon she could be encased within.

Mercifully, it was exactly what she needed. The world outside was an overwhelming prospect. Yet expanding the aperture of her universe slightly from that of the boat to this library was manageable. It took her days to get steady on her feet and when she regained her land legs, she began to feel a little bit safer. A little bit more capable. Not that there were guards patrolling the aisles. There were a few stationed outside, she realized, but this was not a site for frequent violence and their presence was more to protect the priceless volumes.

Since she had already fumbled her way past the guards as an incidental older man, they now protected her without even knowing it. The only thing she had to avoid were the administrators as they returned huge books, piles of parchment, and restocked pots of ink. The occasional cleaner would come her way, maybe once, twice a week. Roshan just had to be up on her feet and hiding any sign of permanence when that happened.

To do that, she climbed. Roshan turned the highest of shelves into her home. She created her nest from cloaks stolen from those visitors seeking information and the odd pillow she slipped from the reading rooms. At first, food was a problem. Where she had felt safest, the occupants rarely brought anything with them except water and wine. Each of those she could steal for a time. But once the lavash was gone, she had to learn other methods.

She hunted rats. The very thought made her sick, yet there was nothing respectful about starvation. She got good at it. Trapping them, snapping their necks, cooking them over the small open flame of a stolen lantern in the darkest corners of the expansive library. She had managed to steal a knife that was more ornamental than it was useful, but she made do.

The other thing she was left with was time.

She became a ghost of the library. She set out to learn every inch of the place if it was to be her home for the foreseeable future. Roshan learned every tile, every arched window, every shelf, every doorway, every table and exit of the wing she lived in. Ideally it was best if she wasn't seen at all, because when she had pulled up her hood and tried to use the walking stick to explore the library further, she had been accosted. By kindness, of all things!

Assistants who offered to help, a cleaner who cleared a space for her to sit, even an administrator who Roshan, shocked, realized was female. She shook them all off, hiding her face beneath the fabric folds until they left her alone to retrieve a glass of wine that she hadn't asked for. When they returned, she was gone. Yet Roshan had learned an important lesson.

Women were allowed here. Young women, even, so long as they were dedicated to serving the House of Wisdom and its relentless pursuit of knowledge. That was all that mattered. Occasionally, she would even see a female scholar, usually an older woman, always accompanied by men, but she was never treated like their wife. She was treated like a colleague. Like an equal. Like someone whose thoughts and opinions and ideas mattered.

Roshan would go to bed at night, scaling the shelves until she reached her lofty position, and she would lay there in wonder. Often it took hours for Roshan to fall asleep, some nights never at all. Yet she wasn't tired. Her mind raced with wonder and possibility and hope. This building had existed in her city all along, but it was like she had stumbled into another dimension.

No wonder the Harbor Master had forbidden his wives from leaving the boat. If any one of them had understood what was out in the world, the promise of what they could become, it would have made his goal of keeping them suppressed and repressed even harder. She spared a thought for the women she had known, wondering what had become of them now and what their new lives might look like. Those memories caused her pain, so she pushed them aside.

Instead, she focused on the present. The House of Wisdom was supposed to be a temple of learning, after all. So she decided to learn. The Harbor Master had forbidden any of his wives from reading or writing, although a few of them had secretly learned. His second wife had taught some of the others and that was what had got her killed, Talâyi had said. The one word Roshan could write was her name and that was useless to her now. Speaking it or writing it was a death sentence.

She grieved for it, for herself, for the family she would now truly have to leave behind forever if she was to spare them the dark mark of her actions. Roshan had to die on that boat along with everything she'd been: a daughter, a sister, a reluctant wife. What was left? Well, what she could create for herself.

It wasn't hard to sneak a set of administrator's robes so that she could blend in seamlessly as she watched and listened to the scholars she could understand, those speaking Arabic and Farsi. When they were gone, she inspected their work. Roshan's fingers ran over those marks, tracing their outline and their shape as she fought to learn them. She pinched pieces of parchment, attempting to recreate what was written by others before making her own combinations. Soon, they began to make sense, and she felt a new kind of hunger within her. Hunger to learn. While the men and women studied, she studied them.

She picked her favorites, the ones who had jolly laughs and were kind to the younger scholars who worshipped each word they uttered like it was a precious jewel. Most of them were working on a grand translation project, arriving with hundreds of manuscripts that she overheard had been brought by camel. She couldn't fathom how many of the animals that would take, but it would have been a grand sight. It was their job to convert the great texts of Roman and Greek minds into the various dialects of their language, all the while debating what was contained within.

Many of these stories were about saints and martyrs she'd never heard of. As the scholars debated about whether these tales were real or metaphors for morals, Roshan would stick to the shadows and listen with rapt attention. They would draw through lines to their own prophets and shared value systems, connections she was surprised by but ones that lingered with her long after the sessions died down.

Even more shocking was that they were being paid for such debates and translations, drawing scholars from faraway lands outside the city. There was one in particular she was quite fond of, a man with a bald head that seemed to shine like the moon as it reflected the library's illumination. He had the darkest skin she had ever seen, with colorful robes contrasting against the pigment and layers of necklaces *click-clacking* as he shuffled around the library like an elderly wind chime. He didn't come as often as she would have liked, but it would always be late in the evening, when so few others would be there and hours after the last calls of the Isha prayer had ceased to echo throughout the city.

It was like he was intentionally avoiding company as much as she was. He would hunch over scroll after scroll of what looked like complicated mathematics, numbers that she was only just beginning to understand shoved together into formulas she could not yet fathom. He made notes of his own in a small, leather-bound notebook that he took with him when he left. Always comparing what he had jotted against what was on the scrolls, she even sometimes saw him make corrections to the library records. A small annotation here, a note there.

She particularly liked him because he always brought food, happily sneaking a bite of kotlet between visits from administrators to ask if he "needed anything else" or whether he'd like "another text to translate?" He always said no, and when he exited, he left scraps behind. Roshan would sweep in, partly because she was desperate for any meal that wasn't the rats, which were getting rarer the longer she stayed, and also because she worried he might get in trouble, meaning her opportunities to observe the unusual old man who hummed while he worked would be gone.

She saw plenty of other scholars sneak in handfuls of nuts, the occasional date pit bundled up in a square of fabric and tucked away when they left so as not to leave any evidence behind. Only this man soon started to bring entire meals with him, which he consumed bite by bite until he left at the first prayer of the morning. He never joined in, just used the beneficent and most merciful exclamations of Allah's name like an alarm for when it was his time to exit. Then he started coming more regularly, the visits shifting from once every two weeks to twice a week, then three, and her reliance on rats became practically nonexistent.

She was so delighted by parcels of food left behind that she didn't spare a moment to think that they may have been intentional. It wasn't until she swept in one morning as Fajr rang out that she realized her presence had not gone unnoticed. Instead of the usual half-eaten falafel that she could ration over a few days, she found a full-sized portion along with a bowl of aromatic sholeh zard. As she lifted back her hood, it smelled *so good* her mouth watered. At least, that was what she put her distraction down to, as she didn't realize the scholar had returned until it was too late.

"It was a test."

Roshan froze at the words that were spoken behind her. She dared not move. She had spied on the scholar enough times to know the exact tone and lilt of his voice. She thought he had gone.

"I wasn't sure if you had a sweet tooth or not, so I had my chef prepare something special."

She turned around slowly, a lie on the tip of her tongue before he held up a hand to stop her.

"There's no need to pretend any further," he said. "I mean you no harm and, frankly, I have enjoyed the company these past months."

Roshan had no words. She had watched him pack up his things in exactly the same fashion every time, giving away no clue that he was aware of her presence. She cursed herself for a moment, cursing the comfort she had so gladly welcomed and cursing the laziness she had fallen into. She should have stayed on her guard. The stakes were too high for anything else.

"Now, now, there's no need to look like that."

"Like… what?" she managed.

"Words!" he laughed, clapping his hands together with delight. "Stop looking like you're about to drop the best meal you've seen in your life and run for the high heavens."

Roshan needed to get better at masking what was on her face.

"Come." He gestured, turning on his heels and returning to his desk. He plopped down on the cushioned seat and faced her with an expectant expression. She *should* oblige him. Keeping a seat between them, she took the spot across from him at the table.

"Eat, eat," he exclaimed. "You're far too skinny."

Clearly he'd noted the way she looked around, cautious of any additional company that may be joining them. Roshan took a hesitant first bite, feeling awkward as he watched her. This was the first time since she fled the boat that she had been engaged in a conversation. Trapped was probably a better word, which only increased her discomfort.

"We're alone for the next thirty minutes at least," the

scholar continued. "Although I suspect that you know that, given things don't really get busy here until after sunrise."

She did know this. Roshan swallowed before taking another bite, slightly less hesitant now.

"While you eat, I will tell you about myself and hopefully by the end of your meal perhaps you might look less like a rabbit caught in the snare of a hunter," he said.

She nodded to communicate that she understood but said nothing further. She just ate and listened.

"My name is Bakhit, which means luck where I'm from in Sudan. In your particular case, it means you were lucky to find me. I'm an engineer of sorts, but most of the others here call me an inventor."

"What's the difference?" she questioned, her voice barely above a whisper. He looked delighted that she'd asked.

"Well, as I'm sure you've observed over many hours watching not just me but the others, the relentless pursuit of knowledge isn't as holy as they would have you believe. Just like there are class lines out there, they also exist within here but are drawn up via the paths of educational pursuit. The mathematicians stick with the mathematicians, the scientists with the scientists, the astronomers with the astronomers and the engineers–"

"They come during the day," she interrupted. "Usually."

"That they do." He smiled, pleased that she had noticed. "Which is why I come at night. Fewer people to bother me. Fewer people to ask me what I'm working on and why. Fewer people who understand it."

There was a glint in Bakhit's eye that hinted at something more nefarious, something dangerous. It was like he wanted her to see it and when she didn't shy away, he pivoted to a topic in safer territory.

"Can you read?" he asked.

Roshan was busy licking the sweetened rice off her fingers from the sholeh zard, dispelling all notions of civility as she dug into the bright yellow dessert with delight. She paused. "Yes," she replied, cautiously. "Not well but–"

"Write?"

"Some words."

"What's the most challenging for you?"

Roshan thought about it for a beat. "Numbers."

"Ah, that won't do."

He reached across, snagging the parchment that was peeking out from her top pocket. It was where she had made several drawings and diagrams that day. She was self-conscious as he inspected it. He focused on one of them, grunting with approval.

"You see here? You understand an angle, yes?" He tapped at one of the drawings she had imitated with a charcoal pencil. Roshan

nodded enthusiastically.

"Use the angles to count, they tell you the number," he continued. "Look, one: one angle. Two, two angles. Three..."

He trailed off, showing her the angles he was drawing inside the shapes that made individual numbers.

"Try that one," he suggested. She took the pencil from him, looking at the shape that had a square and a long, sharp tail. Roshan began drawing the angles, stopping when she reached the maximum amount.

"Nine?" she offered.

He grinned. "Exactly. And how many on the circle?"

"Well, it's curved so… there are no angles. It's zero."

"Do you see? The clues are right there in the design."

She smiled, greatly appreciating the lesson because it helped click things into place for her. It was one thing to mimic the work of others and attempt to study on her own, but it was another entirely to be shown and to be taught.

"Would you like to learn more?"

"Yes," she replied instantly. It was an impulse. She didn't think deeply about the how or why. She just knew that this excited her. A door had been opened and through a tiny crack, she viewed a world she never knew was there. And she wanted to explore it.

Bakhit smirked, as if this was the reaction he had expected.

"Properly," he added. "Not just trying to decipher the scraps others have left behind."

Roshan nodded enthusiastically. "Are you offering to teach me?"

"No, I haven't got time for anything like that. But where I'm from, women aren't just allowed into places like this. They thrive in them. They can learn anything. Everything. All that they want to."

She felt her mouth slip open in surprise, the smallest sound of shock escaping from her lips.

"They can own property, buy property, inherit property," he continued. "They are heirs to the crown."

"Why would you ever leave?" she uttered, hearing the wonderment in her own tone. A chuckle rumbled up from deep within his core.

"My point is," Bakhit grinned, leaning forward, "that

attitude is catching. Every Tuesday and Thursday, there are free lessons in the east wing and *all* are welcome to attend."

Roshan frowned and he picked up on it immediately.

"Do you know where that is?"

She shook her head.

"My girl, how can you attach yourself to the walls like a breathing mosaic and not know the east wing? It's just through the doors–"

"I don't leave," she cut in. "I don't go outside this building."

"Ah," he sighed, something like understanding crossing his features.

"It's not safe."

"Mmm," he mused. "You are dressed like an administrator. If you were to perhaps accompany me through to the east wing, it would not look at all out of place or unusual. Until you get your bearings, that is. Would you consider it?"

Roshan would. She nodded, cautious. "Why would you help me?" she asked. "Why would you feed me? If you've known I was here this whole time…"

"Very few beggars have been clever enough to get in here undetected," he answered. "Even fewer have been able to make it their home permanently."

She didn't correct him about the beggar part. It was better to let him think that.

"Yet you have managed to do so for… how long?"

Roshan didn't answer his query.

"I see." Bakhit nodded, like that was exactly what he had expected. "You have managed it, found food, although clearly not enough, found garments that allow you to blend in, found a place to sleep and a way to keep yourself clean and presentable. There's a level of resourcefulness there that I respect. That resourcefulness always has value in my line of work. How old are you?"

"Seventeen," she responded. "Almost eighteen."

"Very resourceful."

He got to his feet. "I shall return on Thursday. The lessons start after Salat al Zuhr. I will meet you here just before and accompany you."

He was about to leave when he stopped, considering her for a final moment. "Do you have a name? Do you feel comfortable sharing it?"

She shook her head sharply, her gaze cast downward.

"Come up with something."

And with that, he was gone. Roshan was left sitting there in both shock and delight at all that had transpired. She had been living in the House of Wisdom for almost five months now, comfortable and content yet knowing it couldn't last forever. But with no resources outside of those walls, she hadn't been able to come up with a solution. Now, she might just have one. As an added bonus, she might just have a friend as well.

Bakhit was waiting for her exactly when he said he would be that Thursday and Roshan tried to project an air of confidence that she didn't feel as she walked alongside him. He led her out the doors of the main library and through a courtyard she'd been too afraid to explore on her own. It was open, it was exposed, it was *beautiful*.

There was a fountain at the center of it and sparrows chirping happily as they dove beneath the surface of the bubbling water there, taking a quick bath. She noted it as a possible location where she could do the same if the main bathrooms in her building ever became unusable. There were scholars collected here, too, sitting on benches amongst the garden and some hunched over in heated conversations with their colleagues. Roshan gawked and she tried to school her features and bury the wonderment she felt inside from showing on the outside. She needed to look like she belonged here. Like everything was perfectly normal and not a marvel occurring before her very eyes.

Bakhit was right: dressed as an administrator, no one cast her a second glance and if she saw the occasional frown, it was probably because of her perceived age. For the lesson, he handed her a small, blank notepad and a pencil. She took them both, open-mouthed with surprise. Roshan couldn't even mumble a thank you at him before he gave her an amused nod and left, leaving her no choice but to join the others as a man with beads woven into his braids called everyone to order.

She wasn't the only administrator there, nor the only woman, and she realized that these lessons might be part of the appeal of taking a job within the library. It was the last thought she had for a while, her mind soon occupied with the structures of what she needed to learn and why. Her path wasn't a linear one, with Roshan already having a grasp of some quite complex combinations thanks to her time spying behind the shelves. The simpler, more basic exercises proved challenging.

Yet not impossible. Her fellow students had lives and loved ones to occupy their days in between lessons. She just had the library. So she practiced and studied and rapidly began to excel so that after just three months, her teacher quietly pulled Bakhit aside when he came to collect her and suggested she find a more advanced class. Such a thing didn't exist for women of her stature, even ones who seemingly had a patron in an eccentric Sudanese engineer.

She became his notetaker instead. At first, Roshan didn't feel like she was very good at it, there being a sense of detachment from the work when she couldn't fully understand it as Bakhit dictated phrases and sentences to her during long hours at the library overnight. Yet it helped her pick up speed, her handwriting and quill strokes soon growing in confidence as she did so.

He kept bringing food and, on the days in between, she no longer had to resort to the rats that were basically nonexistent now, as if word had gotten out about the teenage girl hunting them for her supper. Her lessons and her companion meant that Roshan's confidence had grown, and she dared to explore other parts of the library, the other wings, even the famed observatory that was under construction when she thought it was safe and she could comfortably stick to the shadows.

Most importantly, however, she discovered a kitchen she had no idea existed below ground. It was small and not designed to facilitate many people, yet the chefs there did an impressive job at pumping out several fairly basic dishes to keep some of the more notable attendees satisfied during long lectures or academic meetings that seemed to stretch for days in some instances.

Roshan became a familiar face there, volunteering as one of the administrators who helped with catering. She didn't even need to slip portions for herself into her pockets, they were often freely given from the leftovers at the conclusion of these functions. As her mind grew sharper, her vocabulary expanding and her comprehension growing, so was her body.

The skinny comments Bakhit had once made no longer applied. With an expanded and frequent diet, she could feel herself filling out to one of the figures she so greatly admired among the other wives. There were curves mixed among the muscle, both hinting at an abundance she had rarely experienced in her life even when she had lived in a loving home. Now she was full. Frequently. And her body was growing toned from the time spent climbing up and down shelves to her self-made quarters.

When she caught glimpses of herself in the mirrored reflection of the bathroom, Roshan wasn't sure who was looking back at her: less a girl and now a woman of eighteen, who had color in her cheeks and a lightness in her heart. It had not gone unnoticed to Bakhit, who made remarks about her looking very well every time he saw her now.

"Still not enough sunlight for this indoor cat," he would say. "But progress."

It was during one of their evening sessions that he made an offer to Roshan so casually she had to ask him to repeat it.

"My assistant," Bakhit repeated. "Would you like the job?"

"Isn't... isn't that what I'm already doing?" she questioned.

"No, right now you are note taking. Occasionally you make thoughtful queries about what you don't understand for free, while I'm paid in gold equivalent to the weight of each book I translate by Caliph al-Ma'mun."

"Not free," she corrected. "You bring food every time you visit. Notebooks–"

He made a *tut-tutting* sound at her evaluation of the exchange. "A salary," Bakhit offered. "I could pay you a weekly wage plus provide housing if you took over as my assistant. Hmm? What do you think?"

That would mean leaving the House of Wisdom. That would mean taking another small but significant step to expanding her world once more. She had lived there for a year, would happily live there for several more, but the longer she stayed the more likely it was she would get caught. People knew her by sight now, recognized her, and she had been so pleased by the familiarity that she had pushed the niggling worry about which would come after that to the side. Now Bakhit was offering a solution.

"What happened to your last assistant?" she questioned.

"Oh." Bakhit shrugged. "He blew up. So… do you want the job?"

Chapter Five

Fustat, 824

Roshan silently wept as she sank down into the simmering heat of the bath. The sensation was such a relief to her after the experience in the prison that she didn't care about the outward display of emotion even though there was no one to witness it. If it were seen, it would be considered a weakness. In private, she could allow herself to be soft as she slipped beneath the fragrant waters.

She guessed it was the stranger who banged on the door sooner than she would have liked, telling her she was taking too long. Roshan didn't care, but she obliged after an additional minute in what felt like the greatest and most important bath of her life. Wrapping herself up in towels, she stepped from the bath to an adjoining room to find fresh clothes laid out for her. They were plain, but they were not simple.

At first glance – and even first touch – they looked like

linen. That in and of itself should have been remarkable enough, but as she slid into the pair of tunic pants that were tight to her knee and then flared out for optimum movement, she realized the fabric was something much more advanced. She wanted to study it, understand what kind of fibers had created this stretchy yet firm series of garments that felt like they were made specifically for *her*.

She had the misfortune of being quite well-endowed, so when she was trying to pass as a man or even just downplay her femininity it required extensive and serious binding. The top half of her garment was in layers, the first without sleeves but featuring what almost felt like boning under her breasts. Once she was wearing it, she bounced on the edge of her toes and was unsurprised by how little bounced with her.

The final layer was longer and more conservative, yet still flattering to her figure. It told Roshan that wherever she was going and whatever she'd be doing, her gender would not be an issue. There was a belt that looked almost exactly like the kind she preferred, except better: it had loops and pouches and sheaths all designed for optimum efficiency. Not that she had anything to put in there right now, but she knew that she would soon.

Over the top of her gray clothing, she threw on a cloak of even darker gray, the texture of that also unusual to her. It was slightly reflective when she ran it under the light shining through the bedroom window. Grabbing the jug of water nearby, her suspicions were confirmed when she attempted to pour a few droplets on the cloak. They didn't soak into the threads like normal clothing. Instead, the water stayed grouped together, unbroken, until she let it run off and onto the floor where it splashed to finality.

It felt like the material of a tent, stiff as she moved her arms and checked her range of movement. Yet also, just like a tent, waterproof. Probably warm, too, even though it didn't feel that way in the moment and the Fustat sun would be sweltering as soon as they stepped outdoors. Roshan took off the cloak and folded it into a neat, tight square before she placed it inside the canvas satchel that had also been left for her. She slipped the strap over her head so that it sat comfortably along the length of her body. Her hair was still drying and she left it for now, striding from the room as she looked for her unfriendly host.

She was under no illusion that this small but neat apartment didn't belong to the man she had bargained with for her freedom. It looked ready for his appearance regardless, showing signs of regular upkeep with fresh blankets and a bath waiting for her when they arrived. She saw no mark of anyone else, but she was grateful for their labor, whoever they were.

The stranger had entered the prison clean and unshaven. Only the latter remained true on their return, but in the time it had taken her to bathe and change, he had removed his bloodstained clothes and replaced them with new ones. He'd also washed any additional gore free from his person, leaving a bowl now full of dirty water sitting on a table nearby. He stood, hands clasped behind his back and a calm expression on his face as he tried to project patience. She sensed nothing but impatience, however, as his eyes ran over her.

“Everything fits,” he noted. “Good. Let’s go.”

“Go?” she huffed. “What about a meal? Some rest? Your name wouldn’t go astray and, while you’re at it, I’d love one of those blades triggered by a projectile mechanism at your wrist.”

A smirk settled on his face at her outburst. “Did you drink water in your room?”

“Yes, most of it, b–”

“Then food you will get at our destination. With the others. The rest, I cannot guarantee. Any name I give you would be a lie, so why bother? And the blades, as you called them, are not freely given.”

“Is anything?”

“Time to leave.”

He spun around and walked straight out the front door. Roshan let out a cry of exasperation as she rushed to follow him. He had disappeared, and she leaned over the railing of the stairwell, looking down toward the street where she guessed he had gone. She saw the faintest flash of his own black cloak several floors far below, as if he had dropped from the very level she was on and plummeted straight down unharmed.

“A demon,” she whispered to herself, taking the steps two at a time as she descended rapidly. She burst out onto street level and right into the thick of a busy marketplace. She swore, spotting his tall frame far ahead and moving out of sight. She took off after him, jogging to catch up, elbowing others out of the way and ignoring the annoyed cries that followed in her wake. When she reached him, she let out a deep sigh of relief as she was able to slow her pace.

The day had barely begun, yet already the heat was beyond comfortable. She wiped the sweat from her brow as they walked quickly, cutting a path through the stalls and the barterers and the dangling delicacies. She was elated regardless. Roshan rarely had the opportunity to move through the world like this, her hair out and flowing behind her as it dried in the natural air. Her face uncovered, her gender unhidden, her safety all but guaranteed as she had seen what this stranger could do.

She made a point to minimize risks wherever and whenever she could. Roshan didn't need to worry about that here. Any threat to her would have to face this individual first. He was the most brutal and effective fighter she had ever seen. Even more importantly, he had bought her freedom with bloodshed and there would be more if anything prevented her from fulfilling the task he had for her.

"I've gone by a lot of names," she said to him, as they moved through the masses shoulder to shoulder. "The one you called me by earlier… don't."

She felt him cast her a sideways glance, but she kept her gaze fixed straight ahead. There was a small group of street thieves assessing their progress and Roshan started to take a guess at which one would be bravest. The youngest kid, she guessed. He'd be mad to attempt picking their pockets and sure enough, his mop of dark curls bounced off into the crowd as he prepared to do a wide loop.

"Bint la-Ahad will not do amongst your colleagues," he replied.

Roshan considered an alternative as her hand locked

on the wrist of the child reaching for the inside flap of her satchel.

"Isun," she told the stranger, going with a pseudonym she hadn't used in a long time.

The kid she'd grabbed let out a pained grunt and she gripped his limb harder, looking down at him. As they walked, he was forced to be tugged along with them.

"The first rule of thievery," Roshan said, leaning down to make sure she had the boy's attention, "is to pick better targets."

She released him and he squeaked off into the chaos of the Fustat morning, Roshan smirking as she watched him go. He wasn't one of Dervis' thieves. They were trained better. The stranger had watched their interaction closely and she raised a single eyebrow at him.

"The punishment for theft is–"

"I know what it is," she said, cutting him off. "If you'd like to chase after him for a hand, be my guest."

Roshan said the comment offhand, yet her mind flashed to the prison hallway. The dead guards. The injured ones. The one who'd run. This man didn't make idle threats.

"Besides," she said, trying not to make her comment seem too hastily applied, "the young one didn't technically steal anything. I have nothing to steal."

"Hmmm," was the only response.

They were silent for a few more streets before Roshan started to prod, wanting to know what answers she could get before he shut down again. "I suppose going to my villa is pointless?" she questioned.

"Ransacked, last I checked."

There was something inside her that chipped off with that news, heartbreak that she tried to pass off as crushing disappointment with a huff. She had taught herself not to get attached to any one place for too long and as hard as she tried, she still had to fight the urge to nest. Plants she grew. Knick knacks she collected. Pillows she coveted. Nothing truly personal that could hurt her, but silly little creature comforts that made up the difference between a house and a home. There were exactly four things in her villa that she really wanted, but she would have settled for two because they went together as a pair. If they were gone, then a key part of Roshan and a key part of her past was gone with them, buried here in the sands of Fustat.

"Your stash, however, is undisturbed."

She snapped her head up to look at him, his face expressionless as he took a sharp right, and she was forced to follow him. In every place she based herself, in every city she'd been, she kept a small collection of items stashed for safe keeping. It was usually money, clothes, identity documents she might need and some simple weapons. All things necessary to start a new life if she had to move and move quickly.

She couldn't even remember what had been in this stash, yet she had been certain that she was the only person who knew where it was: on a docked felucca and protected by a rather prickly elderly couple who had no idea it was there. This man had been watching her for a while, she guessed, suddenly uneasy. Perhaps much longer than he'd indicated.

Idiot, she thought, scolding herself. Every time Roshan started to feel a little comfortable with the man, the stranger would make a comment exposing her guarded secrets that would cause her to internally panic about what he did or didn't know about her. It was his way of saying "I have all the power and you have none." Which should have worked, she figured. It probably did on many others. Yet she had spent most of her life powerless, and finding ways to thrive and survive in such a position was what she was good at.

Instead, Roshan identified the technique. Respected it, actually. And said nothing. She stayed quiet for the rest of their journey through the winding city center and then eventually along the banks of one of the many canals that branched off the Nile. The areas that she passed, with their crumbling structures and stray dogs fighting over scraps out the front, told her they were moving toward the worst part of town. She hastily braided her hair as they walked, her fingers expertly pulling through the golden-brown strands and weaving them together. She could do this without a reflection and regularly did, knowing her way by feel as she tucked the long length over her shoulder and wrapped her face so that a woman amongst a growing number of bandits, beggars, and belligerents wouldn't be so starkly obvious.

Roshan had enjoyed the brief reprieve of leaving her face uncovered and let such a feeling go as the sun pressed down on her and she breathed in the shifting smells through the thin fabric shielding her. All slums had the same rough scent to her: piss, blood, excrement and animals. She stepped around the huge rump of a camel as it was led across her path, cutting her and the stranger off from each other for a moment. She had the impulse to run and ditch her promise since he'd already delivered his side of the bargain and –

historically – men who made promises always broke them with disastrous consequences.

Yet two things prevented her from doing so. Firstly, she had seen what this man could do. She could not overcome him in combat by even the wildest stretch of the imagination. She assumed that she knew this city and streets better than he did, but she had assumed a lot of things about him already and been proven wrong. *Except for the demon part,* she thought. Secondly, she had agreed. She had promised. And her words meant something even if it was just to herself.

The stranger reappeared, lingering on the other side of an orange dust cloud kicked up by the animals and looking like a foreboding apparition. He braced, as if he was about to take off after her. Maybe he'd expected her to run as well. Instead, the faintest flash of surprise crossed his features. For better or – much more likely – worse she would follow through on this. He jerked his head to the left and they took an alley wider than many of the others, giving them enough space to walk side by side as if he was testing her compulsions.

"Your colleagues are in the tavern up ahead," he said.

She scrunched her nose. "Colleagues?"

"People like you."

"Expendable?" she countered.

He huffed a brief laugh. "Skilled. Specifically gifted for the kind of task I need executed, but that does not mean you should trust them."

Roshan cast the man a confused look at what sounded very much like a warning. She only had value to him if she fulfilled her end of the bargain, so a concern for her welfare didn't quite fit the equation she had calculated on her end.

She had no more time to think about it as they slowed at the entrance to said tavern. Barrels were piled up out the front and a young man was slouched on top of them. He immediately straightened when they neared and with a stiff nod to the stranger, his eyes cut to Roshan and widened slightly. Then narrowed. He recognized her and was… displeased.

"Your apprentice, I take it?" she asked as she stepped through the door held open for her.

The stranger didn't reply, but the slight frown he offered said a lot. *Perhaps not for much longer,* she thought. She blinked, adjusting to the sudden gloom inside after leaving the bright light of day. Soon, her gaze drank in what was in front of her. Her pulse quickened as she now understood the stranger's earlier warning. Danger. Every single one of the people gathered in front of her represented danger in some form or the other.

"Good," the stranger mused. "Everyone's here."

He moved to the head of the group while Roshan tried not to be alarmed by the various sets of eyes she felt assessing her, judging whether she was a threat to them just in the same way she was considering whether they were a threat to her. There was no one else in the tavern. Clearly the absence of customers and staff had been paid for, yet that didn't stop some of their number from crowding the bar where they helped themselves to whatever they liked.

The whole tavern had been constructed from the remnants of barrels used to transport the venue's most precious wares. The walls were the weathered wood of alcohol containers, sliced in half and arching outward so that no surface was flat but rather curved.

The bar had barrels stacked on top of each other, a wooden plank hammered down on top of them to create a wider surface area. Even more barrels made up the seats that were positioned along it, varying in height and width depending on the region they'd come from.

Roshan's vision flared with the golden glow of her ability toward the center of the room where tables constructed from flipped and fastened-together boat wreckage were stacked with items of value. So many, in fact, she couldn't focus on any of them as they each brightened, dulled, and overlapped each other. Finally, she discerned food, stacks of weapons, supplies, all vital goods that were setting off her senses.

Roshan turned at the sound of a door being shut behind her, the apprentice casting her another displeased look as he made his way to the side of his mentor. The stranger tossed him a rag as soon as he was in range, and she watched as the younger man quickly got to work rubbing a crudely written menu off a blackboard.

"If I can have your attention," the stranger said, his tone indicating this was not a request. "You have all been brought here because you are being handsomely rewarded to perform a vital task."

"Some of us are being blackmailed into being here," one of the men near the bar mumbled, a dangerous sparkle in his eye and his golden hair glinting even in the low light. When Roshan looked his way, he winked. The stranger shot him a look and the man's lazy smile disappeared.

"Carry on." He ushered, waving a hand. Her eyes studied the scars there and the tan. A man who spent time at sea.

Roshan thought for a moment that hand might end up broken, but the stranger continued, a dark cloud simmering in his expression.

"The nine of you shall be working together until this task is completed." He snatched up a piece of chalk, drawing on the blackboard as he spoke. The shapes were jagged and vague, but the longer he drew the more Roshan was able to recognize.

"There's an object being transported along the Silk Road," he began, sketching a rough line that indicated a solely land-based route. "We believe toward China, although that information is yet to be confirmed."

"What kinda object?" a woman with a thick, Welsh accent asked.

The stranger looked annoyed at being interrupted, yet the flame-haired woman looked unchastised and – if anything – more defiant as she dangled her legs over the bar.

"The 'what' is not important," the stranger continued. "It's the 'where' that's vital and where it isn't, right now, is in my possession." His hard stare met hers, as if daring another question. The group remained quiet as he pointed back to what he had drawn on the board.

"It is contained inside a large, wooden case that has these symbols on the front. It will only be inside that case, no other, so if you obtain the case, you obtain the object."

"What are those exactly?" someone asked, a young, pale man who looked barely older than a boy.

"They are the symbols on the case," the stranger supplied, shutting down any further questions.

Roshan swallowed the laugh bubbling in her chest at his

abrupt response and tried to focus on the symbols instead. As she did so, she realized she knew what they were. She had studied and learned and consumed enough languages to know a foreign alphabet when she saw it, the words clearly spelling out something no one in the room except the stranger could understand. Probably. They were unlike any letters she had seen before, their shapes not dissimilar to the hieroglyphs that marked this city but also… not. Their construction was simpler, bolder, less detailed, with lines and curves repeated in a way that made her think each letter – or combination of letters – could mean different things depending on the context.

At the center of the words was a shape that resembled one of the many pyramids of Fustat except the third side was slightly disconnected from the others. The stranger continued talking but Roshan couldn't pull her eyes away, unable to resist the temptation to focus on the repeated letters as if she could use those to start filling in what was missing in this mystery alphabet.

"The case is being transported and defended by a group calling themselves the Martyrs of Agaunum."

That got her attention.

"They're dead," she said, before she could stop herself.

All eyes in the room cut to her.

"Sorry," she pressed. "But the Martyrs of Agaunum were killed hundreds of years ago. Martyred together after leaving this very city, all six thousand, six hundred and sixty-six of them."

"Hence the name," the apprentice said, dryly.

"A group *calling* themselves the Martyrs of Agaunum," the

stranger repeated. "I didn't say that they were. Their caravan will pass the northeast border in two nights' time. That's where you will need to be to intercept them."

"And if we fail?" the young boy asked.

"Then you try again," the stranger offered. "And again. And again, until you succeed. Success on this mission will not be defined by effort, but only one metric–"

"If we get the case," the blackmailed sailor interrupted, sidling up to the redhead. The pair of them were stunning together, his sunshine hair and bronzed, weatherworn face in perfect contrast with her inferno of curls and pale, freckled skin. Their chemistry was undeniable, although Roshan suspected they'd known each other about as long as anyone else here.

"To help you in this task, you will find weapons of any and every kind you desire," the stranger offered, gesturing to the table that was practically overflowing with them. "There are food and supplies here for you to select as well."

"What about money?" someone barked. "Gold?"

"As you can understand, that won't be provided outside of the individual rewards each of you have either already or partially received."

Roshan understood why. Many of these people – if not all – couldn't be trusted. If they were given a means to fund the mission outside of practical, physical tools, it would never be finished.

"When the mission is completed successfully, I will be in touch."

"How will you know?" someone dared to ask.

That question was stupid and met with the adequate

response: silence. Among the other strangers gathered, almost half of them were women, which should have brought a sense of relief to Roshan. Instead, she remained concerned.

"Every single person here has a rare set of skills," the stranger said, voicing her worries. "You have been recruited for this mission because of them. Although many of you are not used to operating in larger groups, might I make one suggestion: work together. Underestimating your enemy in this instance will not serve you and the only pathway to success and the reward you all desire is in unity."

There was a high-pitched cackle from someone Roshan couldn't see, along with more than a few snorts of derision. As the group broke apart to inspect the weapons and supplies on offer, she became certain that each operator was there for themselves. That's exactly who they would be prioritizing, whether that was the set of towering identical twins in the corner or the woman and her dog across the other side of the room.

She was jostled out of the way as they all descended on what had been laid out, Roshan slipping easily to the side as she moved in the opposite direction toward the blackboard. She leaned across the bar, grabbing the first scrap of parchment she could see and a pencil that was closer to a nub. Quickly, she recreated the map that had been drawn, taking up one whole side to do so.

The apprentice started wiping the board clean as soon as he noticed what she was doing. She flipped over the paper and scrawled the symbols as clearly and quickly as she could, making sure she got every dot, curve, and line was correct. When she glanced up, they were gone. Just a freshly wet blackboard remained.

"I'd destroy that if I were you," the apprentice said, voice low and dangerous as he took a step toward her. There was a deep growl and she looked down, surprised to see the black fur of the woman's dog glistening in the low light of the tavern. No, not a dog. She had underestimated the creature at a glance and it was very obviously something much more dangerous: a wolf. It was holding its ground and clearly communicating that if the apprentice moved any closer, there would be issues.

"Leave it," the stranger said, voice firm. The apprentice did so, clearly reluctant as he backed away. When he met his master, they conferred just out of earshot. There was one more glance thrown her way by the man who had spared her life in exchange for service. It was the last one he gave her before he slipped a hood over his head and the odd pair exited the tavern.

She was alone now. Actually, it was worse than that. Roshan was alone in a crowd of people the stranger had deemed as dangerous. She was well and truly cooked.

Chapter Six

The Road, 819

Bakhit had lied.

His last assistant hadn't "exploded" so much as been exploded. The past four, actually, had all died quite horrible deaths relative to the circumstances.

"I thought you said you were an inventor," Roshan asked almost immediately after he'd told her the fate of the last men to work with him.

"Yes, and what I have is the power to invent, and I can do either terrible or wonderful things, depending on how you look at it."

Bakhit had responded in the most natural way to him, which was simultaneously honest and complex. When he referred to a worker as once having had a "breakdown" she assumed it was of the mental variety.

"No, no," he'd corrected. "A breakdown of his structural makeup."

The job was no doubt dangerous, but there was something in the way he spoke about it – and the way he spoke about her doing it – that made Roshan believe it wouldn't be fatal for her. It would be different. After all, she could judge Bakhit on his words alone or she could judge him on his actions. He had been kind to her, not only with the constant supply of food and keeping her permanent residence in the House of Wisdom a secret, but with his encouragement of her learning. Yes, such shepherding had been to sculpt her into the kind of assistant he would need… but everything he had done meant something to her anyway, despite his plans. She trusted him.

Roshan had said yes. Bakhit had nodded happily, like that was exactly what he had expected her answer to be. After accepting the position, he informed her they would be leaving the city.

"Where to?" she had asked.

"The City of Silence," he replied, which sounded foreboding and terrifying to her. "Thatta."

Roshan had never heard of the place. Instead of using her remaining days exploring the Baghdad she'd never really known, she used that time to read up on the place which would become her new home. Having been almost precisely nowhere in her life, the journey looked like a long and perilous one to her inexperienced eyes.

"The Translation Movement is waning," Bakhit had explained. "I've made all the gold I can make from that and now there's a client in Thatta who will not only pay me handsomely but who will provide all the necessary comforts to get us there. His personal guards will be our security on the road. He's even letting us use one of his favorite carriages for traveling. And when we arrive? A beautiful home complete with every comfort."

It sounded like a fantasy. Roshan had little to pack since the House of Wisdom had provided much of what she needed. She couldn't take the books with her, the scrolls, the pencils, the manuscripts, even the beautiful paintings she had come to appreciate. Instead, what she could take with her was precisely three changes of clothes and five notebooks she had been rapidly filling with her own writing and practice.

The other thing that would be coming, too, was her newly gained knowledge. Not just the words she could now read and write to communicate her desires to others, but the possibility of *the world.* The hope of more. All the unknowable things and the sermons of great thinkers who dedicated their lives to unpacking them. The secret language numbers could provide and immeasurable ways they could be unpicked and reconstructed to tell new stories. The expanse of the world carefully hand painted on one of the many globes that sat in reading rooms throughout the building. Her finger would trace the shapes of places she never expected to visit but now, maybe, perhaps *could.*

She didn't sleep during her last night under that roof. Instead she paced the aisles, hands running over the shelves that had taught her so much. She sat in the back of the half-built observatory, curled up on one of the many thick cushions as she watched astronomers examine the stars and make intricate notes she would never have a hope of deciphering. She stole her last batch of dolmeh from the kitchen, only eating two and saving the rest for the journey ahead. She let the juice of a plum dribble down her chin as she watched water droplets splash from the courtyard fountain.

Roshan stared in awe at the scenes painted on the walls in rich red pigments and outlined with brushstrokes of glittering gold, each one telling stories of different prophets who came in search of the same thing through the doors of the Grand Library. Knowledge. Purpose. Power. She smiled at the secret joke between herself and this place. She had found all those things, absolutely. She had also found much more. It wasn't just that these walls had encased her safely at a time when she'd never been in more danger. They'd provided shelter and protection. Now they provided a way out.

When Bakhit collected her from the front steps the following morning, Roshan looked over her shoulder at the towering structure with mixed emotions. In part, because she didn't want to leave. Yet also because she wanted to, more than anything. She readjusted the headscarf, hiding all but her eyes from the outside world as she climbed into the back of Bakhit's carriage and nodded a greeting at the handful of guards accompanying them. Even though she was sheltered within, she would take no risks of being recognized until she was well and truly away from Baghdad. With her new employer consumed in his own thoughts and trawling through a freshly drawn diagram beside her, Roshan enjoyed being jostled about by the movement of the horses as they were directed through the winding labyrinth of streets. Her mind began to wander, old thoughts and memories emerging.

She watched the city she had never come to know pass by her window, Baghdad just as daunting to her as it had been when she'd first arrived, newly married. A child then, Roshan hadn't been full of hope and wonder. She'd had a fairly good idea of what her fate would be as she'd been packed into the back of a caravan with several others, none as young as she, but all seemingly just as wary. They had been right in their caution, yet that didn't spare them from the Harbor Master's cruelty, inflicting what he thought of as his rights onto "his slaves."

When she'd first arrived, the looming buildings of Baghdad had reminded her of the small village in the Zagros Mountains where she came from. The residents had built their homes right in the remnants of rock left behind from ancient volcanic eruptions. They looked like odd, tall beehives bursting right out of the ground. She missed the sight of being greeted by those uncanny silhouettes as she used to trudge up the steep slope to the center of town. It was far enough inland that she had no idea how the Harbor Master had found her village or why: the closest most of the people there had come to seeing the ocean was Lake Urmia. Yet she suspected her father had traded with him in the past, his loose lips telling the man of his three young daughters and the prospect of a pairing seeming logical after that.

She wondered what her parents had done when they heard the news. Her husband's death at her hands... surely someone would have been sent to her home on the off chance that Roshan would return there. Practically, it made sense. She could have carved her own home into the rocks and lived far away enough from town that no one would ever find her nestled into the hillside. When it was safe, probably at night, she could visit her parents and her sisters.

It could never be like it was before her marriage, but it could be something. It could be special.

Roshan let her delusions carry her over the borders of Baghdad and far, far away from anything she had ever known. The scenery changed from cramped and overly populated streets and slums to homes that became more spread out as they shifted to villages and then farms. There were long stretches when she saw no people at all, only fields shifting into lakes shifting into mountains. They made camp in the shadow of a mountain, Bakhit's primary guard telling him this would be safest as traveling further at night could be treacherous, not just for their vehicles.

"Bandits occupy the next leg of our journey," a man named Advi said. Everything about him was long, from his face to his perfectly symmetrical nose. He had long arms with an excellent reach, and when he ran his men through drills at the end of the day and the start of each morning, he did so using long sticks.

"Why would you use sticks when you have swords?" Roshan asked later, watching with fascination as they whirled through movements while backlit by the setting sun. Advi paused at the completion of the exercise, panting as he considered her question.

"Swords are dangerous," he replied.

"Yes, I imagine that's the point."

Bakhit chuckled behind her, intent on his work. Advi shrugged, as if the answer was obvious. "I teach them with sticks first so they can master the technique and the speed they need," he said. "When they're ready, we move on to swords."

"*You* don't," she countered. "Everyone else carries a sword except for you."

"As sharp as a blade," Bakhit mumbled in amusement. "That's why she's going to make a great assistant."

Advi waved at the other guards to continue, the sounds of rhythmic clacking quickly picking up again as wood met wood. He used his elbow to wipe the sweat from his face, sitting down next to her.

"Where I'm from, this was a fighting art," he explained. "Tahtib."

"Tahtib," Roshan repeated, trying to mirror his pronunciation.

"It's more of a performance tradition now, but it was taught to me by my mother–"

"Your mother?" she interrupted.

He beamed, as if knowing that piece of information would appeal to her sensibilities. "That's right. Anyone could learn it, and everyone had a right to."

There was a grunt of approval from Bakhit and she wondered how exactly the eccentric, old man had managed to find an employer with guards who viewed women as people, just like him.

"I don't carry swords because I do not want to kill, if I can avoid it," Advi continued. "Tahtib means I don't have to. I can keep my enemy at a distance but still inflict brutal force. Also, the principles are transferable. I can make anything a weapon if I want."

He reached across, picking up one of the long pencils Roshan had been using to take that day's dictation from Bakhit. He purposefully and expertly spun it in his fingers, the air making a small *whoosh* as it rotated in a rapid blur.

"I can teach you, if you like?" He smiled.

"She has no time," Bakhit suddenly snapped, all his amusement erased. "I need her to use that bright, young brain of hers. Not smash away her smarts with a stick."

Advi and Roshan exchanged a glance. The next morning, before Bakhit woke, she got up in time to see the red sunrise breaking over the hilled horizon. She stretched, waiting for the rest of the men, and then joined their group as Advi assembled them for morning training. He gave her a curious head tilt but said nothing as he ducked away and returned with another set of fighting sticks. He tossed them to her and she dropped one, caught the other. With a shrug, she figured everyone had to start somewhere.

By the time Bakhit emerged from the carriage with a big yawn and eyes already searching for the source of the sizzling sound that heralded breakfast, Roshan had bathed, changed, and completed her first training session. It became a pattern as they travelled.

The old man figured out what she was doing after a week, the blisters on her hands as she furiously scrawled a dead giveaway. Yet clearly he didn't mind, and soon Roshan joined the sunset sessions as well. If she thought she had grown strong and more physically capable during her year living in the House of Wisdom, that notion was hastily dispelled. It was *nothing* compared to where she needed to be just to keep up as the worst member of Advi's practice troop. Her forearms strained and her neck became pained and her back ached as she lay down at night, but her mind…

Always so busy and full, it cleared almost entirely as she fell into the rhythm of strikes. One one, two, one one, two, one one – parry – two, two – duck. She imagined it was close to what others sought during their daily prayers, the serenity and peace she saw on their faces mirrored on her own. By the time they arrived in Thatta after a month of travel, Roshan felt stronger and sharper. Her lean arms had become thicker, the flesh of her belly harder, the arch of her shoulders bulging.

Bakhit made a comment to her about no man wanting a wife with muscles bigger than theirs. Roshan swallowed a smile as she caught Advi's gaze over the engineer's shoulders, his eyes rolling in his head as he mocked the suggestion. He encouraged her in the same way Bakhit had, and she couldn't see the benefit for him except that Advi was teaching someone else about why tahtib was so sacred to him.

It was only once they arrived at Bakhit's new residence that Roshan understood. Advi and his men would continue working for Bakhit's employer, not Bakhit himself. She was pleased that her tahtib lessons could continue. It was a handsome, big home just on the outskirts of the city's main palace, with an enormous, domed roof that looked more like an extravagant cake dropped onto a residence than something that served a physical purpose.

"Our new benefactor has not one job for us but several over the coming months," Bakhit said as they were ushered inside. "I suspect that will stretch over a couple of years but this… this space will do nicely."

A mosaic of turquoise lined the walls of the entrance hallway, an intricate pattern repeating in a stunning display of someone's artistic talents. *What a gift,* Roshan thought. *To be able to create something so easily translatable.* You didn't need to read or write, to be able to fight or survive, it didn't matter what language you spoke. If you had eyes, you could admire the time and talent someone had put into creating something so beautiful.

"This will be your room here," Bakhit called, directing her toward a doorway nearby. "It's little more than a closet, but I need to save as much space as possible for the workshop."

Roshan had never had a room before. Ever. A closet to Bakhit was an *expanse* to her. She had shared with her sisters, then shared with the wives on an entire bottom deck, then shared with *thousands* in the House of Wisdom. She had never had anything close to her own space and now she had this: a bed, a window, a small desk, and a chest.

"Come on, we need to unpack!" Bakhit called.

Roshan took a deep breath before she dropped her things and followed the sound of his voice. Benches had already been assembled, along with crates of equipment brought in from Baghdad and wherever else Bakhit had based himself before that. They had traveled light, so there wasn't much for Advi and the others to bring in from the carriage. Instead, the bodyguard seemed more interested in the garden area out back, complete with grass, rose bushes, flowering night queens and vines creeping up over a crumbling brick wall. She joined him, trying to see what he saw as he scrutinized the space.

"This will make for a nice spot," Advi said, looking down at her. The edges of his eyes crinkled, the lines there stretching down his face and alluding to the years he had on her, even though he still appeared young in Roshan's eyes.

"For what?" she asked.

"Practice."

Roshan grinned, breaking away as Bakhit called out to her from inside while ushering everyone else out until it was just the two of them and a housekeeper so shy she seemed to jump at her own shadow. She held her hands behind her back in what Roshan thought was a respectful gesture at first, but realized it was to hide that she was missing her left arm below the elbow. It didn't slow the housekeeper for one moment as she joined them in setting up the workshop Bakhit insisted needed to be ready by morning. Pausing for a light dinner of spiced couscous and cold meats, they didn't finish until well after midnight.

Roshan went to bed exhausted, but still awoke at the time her body had decided was the natural order of things: sunrise. She groaned, stretching her calloused fingers, and considered going back to sleep. After all, it had been her first night in her first room…

Instead she got up. Her opportunities to know Baghdad might be gone, but if this place was to be her home for the foreseeable future, then she would know it.

She dressed and left the house, walking the sloping streets of Thatta in wider and wider circles until she began to understand the metropolis's layout. The sounds of Salat al Fajr told her when it was time to return home, and as she looked down at her hands, the morning light was so red it took her back to *that* night. Her worst night. She closed her eyes for a moment, remembering the feeling of the blood growing sticky on her flesh.

Someone brushed past her and her eyes flew open, evaluating her surroundings. No threat. No harm. No predators that she could easily identify. She was just a normal woman, in a normal marketplace, on a normal day. She marveled at every additional step she took home, appreciating the feel and texture of each stone beneath her feet. When she arrived, Bakhit was already eating breakfast and waiting for her. This was early for him.

"Ah, I knew you'd return," he said, swallowing a handful of prunes.

"Of course," Roshan replied. "We have an agreement."

"A woman of her word," Bakhit mused. "All right then, let's hold you to it."

As they got to work on his first assignment for the mystery benefactor, Roshan reassessed the relaxation she had felt earlier. Bakhit's past assistant – assistants, actually – had all died making his various inventions and for good reason. Depending on what he was asked to make and for whom, these objects could destroy a specific person, a specific thing, or a specific place. The outcome depended on his construction and that could be just as dangerous as the end result.

Bakhit was smart enough to have his assistants do the real dirty work, under his careful instruction of course. According to him, his assistants only died if they didn't listen. Her eyes had flicked to the housekeeper at one point, whose stare met hers and she knew without needing to hear it that this woman had been an assistant of his too once.

She'd been hurt and was of no use to him in the workshop now but continued to serve in the home.

And that's when she understood. *Quid pro quo.* It was a Latin phrase she had learned during one of her very first group lessons in the House of Wisdom and although her Latin had expanded significantly since then, that saying had really stayed with her. The twist in her gut made her understand why now. *Something for something,* she thought. Guiding her on a path to reading and writing was for Bakhit's own self-interest. The annotation of notes wasn't just to help accelerate her learning, but to groom her for the very specific qualities an assistant of Bakhit's would need.

Intelligence. An ability to take instruction. A genuine thirst for knowledge. Mobility. And – crucially – expendability. When they would inevitably reach their expiration date, there would be no family, no one close to mourn their loss, no one who could demand answers about why the flesh on their brother's face had been melted away. When he had offered her the job, she had asked him "where to?" when in truth, she should have asked him "why me?" Her bitterness stung.

Bakhit could not know it, but Roshan had an additional vital skill. Whether it was the smallest cog or the tiniest nut, she anticipated what needed to go where with her additional sense. It became apparent to her that Bakhit was a genius, yet much of his process was through trial and error. He trialed: the assistants dealt with the brunt of the error. Part of her should have felt betrayed by the hidden stakes of the bargain, but if she was honest, she had known it was coming.

There was always an invisible string, this one just proved easier to spot than some of the others. Roshan had to become comfortable with the tradeoff. One misplaced bolt and she was dead. Yet if she was careful, followed his instructions exactly, and exploited that intuition of hers, she could survive one day longer. She could get to see one more sunrise break over the curved rooftops of Thatta. She could feel the sweat dripping down her spine at the end of one more sunset practice with Advi. She could live one more day with the promise of a life that was as close to her own choosing as she could make it.

Chapter Seven

Fustat, 824

A fight broke out before she even realized it.

Roshan had been so focused on redrawing the map and the symbols, and studying the mysterious man and his apprentice, that she'd ignored the table of weapons. It became a free-for-all. Chaos descended on the supply that ranged from bows and arrows to what looked like a bronze sword with two blades splitting off from the same hilt. She wouldn't even know how to begin wielding something like that and considered it deadly, if difficult to use, rather than useful in battle. She noted that the redhead took the sword, elbowing several others out of the way to get to it. The blades reflected perfectly against her hair and she held it up to the light like she knew it.

"Her name's Mared," a voice said from behind. Roshan turned to find it belonged to the woman lingering in the shadows. She was the only other member of the group not engaging in the fight. She reminded Roshan of a raven, with sharp, angled features and black hair slicked back for convenience. A few loose strands escaped her ponytail and hung down in front of her face, seemingly unnoticed. The black wolf from earlier, the one who had stood bravely in front of her like a guard, was at the woman's side. The two of them looked like the oddest matching pair, both eyeing those assembled with interest like they were perfectly in sync.

"She's a warrior woman who thinks she's the next Boudica," the woman continued. "That's–"

"I know who Boudica is," Roshan cut in. The woman tilted her head with interest, her big, green eyes scanning the action while maintaining a conversation with Roshan.

"What's interesting is why she'd be so friendly with the former Roman soldier. That's Dias, the golden boy. He turned to a life of piracy after failing to defend his post on the island of Crete."

Roshan watched the two of them interact, Dias flipping a table to get at something he wanted. Their eyes made contact as they both fondled their weapons in a way that had gone far past flirting.

"It's hard to tell who's seducing who," she murmured.

The woman snorted in agreement. "The only thing Romans hate more than the Welsh are Persians, so I'll be staying out of his way."

Roshan turned her head with interest. "You're Persian?"

"Azadeh," she offered, reaching a hand forward for Roshan to shake. "From the coast. You?"

"Mountains," Roshan replied, introducing herself with a lie. "Isun."

An unreadable reaction passed over the woman's face before she had to duck an incoming projectile. A small crossbow bolt shuddered into the wall next to them. Roshan turned her gaze toward the shooters.

"The big boys are Geir and Gud," Azadeh said, identifying them. "Identical twins and highly sought after hired killers for any Viking ruler that can afford them."

The Northmen were identical in not just their enormous size, but the insidious energy projecting from both of them. One of them dropped the crossbow and they grunted in delighted unison as they each picked up axes that probably weighed as much as Roshan, strapping them onto their backs as if they were as light as a feather. She put them at six-foot-eight each and they were as ugly as they were tall.

"The old one is Wei." Azadeh subtly pointed. "Not sure specifically what he does, but he fled China because of some rebellion Emperor Xianzong was crushing in his province."

Dressed in subtle but expensive fabrics, Roshan watched as Wei parsed through the various items laid out, carefully lifting up implements and picking through various options as he avoided a dagger thrust there or a knee cocked here. He slipped in stealthily to grab a fire lance of some kind, extracting another that was much smaller and retreating to the edge of the room. Slipping a pouch out of a bag he was carrying, she watched with interest as he tinkered with each weapon like he knew exactly what he was doing. He tipped the first one upright, using the pouch to catch every grain of a sand-like substance that spilled from the rear of the barrel. No, not sand. Roshan had seen it before in Bakhit's workshop. In fact, he paid handsomely for the precious substance that was brought to him directly by clients not dissimilar to Wei.

"Explosives," Roshan said.

"Huh?"

She turned to face Azadeh. "That's gunpowder he's funneling. The Chinese invented it. If he had to flee a military campaign that was quashing an uprising, then I'd hazard a guess that he's very good at knowing how to use it."

There were only two left among the group, the angelic-looking child and his complete opposite: a woman with intricate tattoos that lined her fingers, hands, arms, and neck. She had just finished wrestling with Dias as she picked up a club from the weapons table that looked like it could only be made for her, with serrated teeth protruding from the edges as it hooked around. She smirked, clearly recognizing exactly what it was as she swung it rapidly through the air in a series of quick movements. It caught the attention of Geir and Gud, who did their best not to look threatened as they exchanged a wordless glance.

"Nafanua," Azadeh said. "Named after the Sāmoan warrior goddess, I heard her say."

"And the child?" Roshan prompted.

"Francis, a Christian prophet."

Roshan snorted. She couldn't help herself. "And what of you? What are your skills?"

"I'm good at gathering information, obviously," Azadeh replied, looking bashful. "And we're part of a package deal."

She gestured between her and the wolf, who seemed better trained than most humans Roshan had encountered. *That must have been the appeal,* she thought. Azadeh seemed too genuinely sweet and free with her tongue to face off against these other iterations of warriors. The wolf was the asset the mysterious man truly wanted and she controlled the wolf.

"What's his name?" she asked.

"Onyx," Azadeh replied, the wolf's head lifting up as it recognized its name from the voice of its master. "Obvious, I know. Yet there didn't seem to be anything that fit better. You can pat *her* if you like."

Roshan looked down at Onyx with caution. "No… thank you."

Her trepidation brought out a blinding smile from Azadeh. The woman couldn't have been much different to her in age, yet she had a lightness that Roshan envied.

"And why are you telling me all this, hmm?" she questioned. "Avoiding the fight to share details you could have kept to yourself as an advantage."

"Because I need an ally," Azadeh offered. "And I've decided you're it. We are supposed to work together, despite all of this." She waved her hand at the ruckus.

"You've decided?"

"Yes." Azadeh nodded, as if that settled that. "Onyx and I make for a great team, but two is better than one and three–"

"Is better than two," Roshan finished.

"I know why you're here then," she chuckled. "Intelligence. You're not foolish enough to get involved in all that."

She jerked her head in the direction of the infighting, which had settled down. Everyone had appeared to get a version of what they wanted and Roshan decided it was finally safe to take a closer look at what was left behind. She had nothing of use with her and she needed to inspect the remaining weapons. The heavy gaze of the others followed her as she did so. Nafanua wiped away a bloodied nose while Gud cracked his freshly torn knuckles. Whatever weapon she chose would tell them something about her they were desperate to know, much in the same way that each of the items they had selected gave away a little bit about who they were.

About the individuals, yes, but also about the information the stranger and his apprentice wielded. It wasn't just Roshan they knew everything about, but the others, too. She had seen the surprise on their various expressions as they had found – and fought – for tools specific to them. Her own shock emerged as she paused in front of what looked like a small club. Roshan's breath caught in her throat.

The stranger had said her villa had been ransacked and all elements of her life in Fustat destroyed when she was thrown into prison. Yet when she'd reached under her pillows in desperation as the soldiers kicked in her door, her fingertips had brushed the objects she risked keeping with her before she was yanked from her sheets and beaten. Roshan was sure they had been destroyed.

Yet, there they were. Well, at least one half of a beautiful, hand-carved set of matching clubs that had been a gift from what felt like a lifetime ago. She had never been given something so opulent and thoughtful in her life. Roshan had mourned their loss but pushed such sentimentality to the side.

All notions of being coy about choosing her weapons vanished as she snapped the remaining stick up. Who cared about what the others could read from this? This was hers. The soldiers would have recognized traditional tahtib sticks when they saw them in her villa, the art form being from this very region, and no doubt kept them for themselves. The surviving stick being placed here meant it had been obtained – probably through much difficulty – for her.

Roshan traced the flowers that had been carved and burned into the wood before polishing so they appeared glossy and perfect. There was a small circle, tinier than a coin, that when pressed would release the full length of the fighting stick in both directions. *Not now,* she thought, feeling sadness welling up in her chest. This was not the time to allow any kind of visible weakness. But as she looked up, Roshan realized it was too late.

They had all seen her go soft over something that made her vulnerable. A flash of triumph shone in Dias's eyes. Mared rolled hers out of boredom. Roshan saw a strange hunger in the expressions of both Geir and Gud. Wei looked away, as if ashamed for seeming so interested in her choice. Nafanua appeared sympathetic and Francis's wide eyes stared openly at her. Azadeh's gaze held only empathy and Roshan hated that the most, rapidly slipping the weapon into her belt loops.

She recognized two other items of hers on the table that were less special, but still significant. She added her old sword and trusty dagger to the sheaths at her hip and across her back respectively. Neither had been taken because, frankly, there were better swords and daggers that people had wanted or had some kind of sentimental value. Yet these were her tried and treasured tools. Also, there were notebooks, the kind that she preferred, along with several pencils that she took. On another table full of supplies, Roshan loaded herself up with what would be most useful: some dried meats, a goatskin flask, a container of water, roasted chickpeas and the barest of medical supplies. A sleeping sack was the only other thing she added, and she watched with interest as Mared overloaded herself while Nafanua took just a thick cloak and a set of leather gloves that covered most of her markings.

"We should set off," Francis said, his soft and feminine voice drawing everyone's attention. "If we don't leave soon a growing storm will set above us and make the journey most arduous."

"How do you know that, little boy?" Dias asked.

Francis looked above him, as if the storm was visible on the ceiling. "God has sent me a message."

Dias barked a laugh. "A message about how we should all begin the task we're indebted to complete? How vital."

"We *should* go," Nafanua urged. "The sooner we get there, the sooner this is done."

Roshan felt much the same way and appreciated her directness. That was all they needed to herald their exit, the group leaving scraps of weaponry and supplies behind as they headed out the way they had come.

"And horses," Francis continued. "We will ride on the Lord's stallions."

"He will be the first to die," Wei whispered in a dialect only Roshan understood. She hid her smirk as she stepped outside into the sun. It was just past midday and there were indeed horses waiting for them. Not stallions, however, but sleek Arabian mares bred for speed and efficiency.

"Could have just as easily been camels," Azadeh muttered as she passed her. "Ride together?"

Roshan wanted to say yes. She instinctively liked the woman, but Azadeh had also said she was Persian. If anyone could connect Roshan to her past, it was Azadeh. They might be allies now, but once this mission was over, hopefully in a matter of days, that would cease. Roshan couldn't allow anyone information that may lead back to her family. After all, she was still – and would always be – a wanted woman.

She shook her head politely and mounted a white mare of her own. There weren't enough horses for everyone, and Roshan suspected it was because the stranger was trying to force them to work together. Roshan tucked her feet into the stirrups, circling back and reaching her hand down to Wei. The older man eyed the horse suspiciously, as if he did not trust the creature and distrusted the idea of riding even more.

"Come now, old master," she said, watching the surprise emerge on his features as she spoke his own language back to him. "I am an excellent rider and gunpowder will only get you so far."

As she hauled him onto the horse behind her, he threw out his arm with a small yelp. Wei gripped her waist tightly as they trotted out of the city, his grip loosening when the horse didn't buck him off her back. Azadeh and Nafanua rode together, the wolf making the mare uneasy, necessitating they hang back until the animals grew more comfortable around each other. Geir and Gud had each taken their own horse, which would have annoyed Roshan except the Northmen were so big she wasn't sure the horses could take their combined weight. Mared, too, had a horse of her own, with Dias eventually grabbing Francis as their party increased in speed toward the border.

Roshan savored the silence during the ride, the wind whipping through her hair and the open road in front of them doubly welcoming. They continued even as the sun began to set, Dias soon leading the pack and pushing the distance so that they would be best placed come dawn. She might not like him, but he had a military manner. Clearly those years with the Romans at sea made him a natural leader for their purposes. When they finally set up camp it was just on the other side of dark.

There was no need to hunt due to their abundant supplies, but since some of them were perishable, Mared insisted on doing so. She returned to the camp with several hares, which she then skinned and cooked, long after the others had retreated to slumber. Roshan remained awake, uncertain about her traveling party and cautious about where and when she laid her head. Wei was happy enough to eat the hares and he settled down next to her, chewing in silence.

"It's good," he finally said, offering her some.

She shook her head. "Looks like it needs seasoning," she remarked.

He chuckled in agreement, setting down the remnants of his meal and pulling out a roll of canvas.

"What did you ask for?" Roshan questioned, curious as she watched him handle the package of fabric in front of him. It was too small for bedding. He unrolled it and she saw a series of tools tucked tidily away within various straps and pouches.

"Ask?" he replied.

"Everyone is being paid *something* for the completion of this task. You don't strike me as someone who covets riches…"

Humble was the word she wanted to use, but she wasn't sure that would translate to his dialect in a way that wasn't offensive.

"Neither do you," Wei replied. "Yet the craftsmanship that went into making those robes on your back requires wealth of a kind."

She examined the fabric of her garments; the texture and design which had been so interesting to her initially was even more so now that she had worn them for more than a day. True, it was advanced.

"Subtle way to change the subject," she countered, realizing that his conversational suggestion had distracted her exactly like it was meant to. Wei snickered acknowledgment, all the while never pausing as he continued to tinker amid their chatter.

"Were you blackmailed like Dias?" Roshan wanted an answer to her question.

His lip curled in disgust, as if the very thought of being associated with Dias was unfavorable. "Were you?" he asked.

Clever old man, she thought, her initial assessment of him being accurate.

"I owed a debt," Wei offered.

"It must have been a big one."

"The biggest," he murmured. "A blood debt."

"To… the hooded stranger?"

"To someone like him," Wei corrected. "He's not the

first man I've met like that, someone who belongs to the shadows but refuses to bend for them. A man like that came to my village once when I was a very young boy."

Wei retrieved the gunpowder from earlier and began to make a concoction she could only vaguely keep up with. Objects were her strength, not chemicals, and she was lost after her eyes tracked the retrieval of the first set of small tongs.

"His name was Li E and my people owed their future to him."

"How so?" Roshan pressed.

"Duling has two things: big, sweeping cliffs and immaculate flower farms. That was our primary trade, and my ancestors supplied the wealthy with the most exquisite blooms in the land. There was a yearly procession, the Flower Banquet, where various powers would compete. In order to secure the best produce, a man named Chancellor Yang Guozhong had dozens of farmers murdered."

She blinked, not quite fully understanding. "Over… over flowers?"

"*Exquisite* flowers," Wei corrected. "He massacred seventeen innocents so that his wagon would be the most stunning, the most eye-catching. My mother watched her parents die so that this man could win."

His long, thin fingers moved rapidly as he worked and Roshan remained captivated by both the actions and the horrifying tale.

"A man like that wouldn't have been punished usually, but he was," Wei continued. "He was murdered as brutally as the villagers, along with everyone he had enlisted to carry out his crimes. When the story reached Duling, no one quite believed them at first… until *he* showed up."

"He?"

"Tall, hooded, quiet, death," Wei stated. "An older man when I met him as a child, he

would visit the village every few years when he could. We were always to understand that the future we had, the possibilities for learning and expansion and safety and freedom, were because of him."

"When you were a boy…" Roshan mused. "The hooded stranger we met wouldn't have even been born then, respectfully."

Wei huffed a laugh. "He wasn't. But people like him, the people he works for – and who Li E aligned himself with – are eternal. When one showed up with a task, I was bound to complete it to the best of my ability. It's the duty for all from my village."

The older man was quiet for a while, Roshan having no more questions to pepper him with as she thought about all that he had said, and the ramifications. The thought of the hooded stranger she'd met being aligned with associates just as physically brutal was concerning. Yet there was a silver lining, this idea of what was *right*. She wanted to unpick that new thought, but Francis woke and wandered over to join them.

"What are you making?" he asked, leaning forward with curiosity.

"Bomb," Wei replied, keeping his answer simple and understandable, but its shortness caused Roshan to smirk, given how forthcoming he'd been with her. Wei switched back to his native language for Roshan. "I saw you copy that map. Do you have it?"

She nodded, pulling out the notebook and flipping to the page where she had tucked the scrap of parchment. As she unfolded it and held it up in front of him, Wei nodded.

"That is a narrow pass. If we can pull in front of the Martyrs, we can lay a trap they won't be able to escape. It will be easier than wasting time searching for their trail when, ultimately, they will have to cross through here."

"Close the pass," she mused, tapping at the end point. "It will be difficult with how far ahead they are."

"What are you saying?" Francis queried, his soft voice annoying her. Before she had a chance to reply, Wei grabbed the young boy by his arm and gave him a big grin, several teeth missing.

"Boooom," Wei said, mimicking the gesture with his other hand.

"Oh," Francis gasped, understanding now. He giggled, the response somewhat maniacal. "Lovely."

Why was he here? Roshan thought. *This alleged prophet from God?* The hooded stranger must have considered that he had some purpose. Everyone had their place, from the huge warriors like Mared and Nafanua, to the cunning ones like Dias and Azadeh, and the gifted Wei. Could Francis' prophetic abilities really be something that could help them? Wei tapped her on the shoulder, pulling her away from her thoughts.

"Rest," he said. She went to lay down and he added hastily, "We'll swap watches later. Now, I need to work."

"All right," she agreed, moving the lantern toward him so

Wei had additional light. He clicked his tongue in approval but said nothing else as he resumed his bomb making. Roshan settled somewhere not far from him, where he was still in her line of sight and she could keep a view over the whole camp. As she settled on a makeshift pillow, Wei's hunched position reminded her of another mad genius and the hours spent watching him work in that exact same position. *If it was Bakhit, he'd be humming some annoying tune by now*. The crackling of the firepit and gentle metallic clinks were the only sounds as she slept in the open field.

When sunrise broke, Roshan thought she was the only one awake to see it. She had swapped with Wei only a few hours ago, much longer than was fair, but the old man had let her rest. He had clearly needed the time to work, and she had been exhausted. A whole day and night's sleep uninterrupted would have really done the trick, but when she needed to, Roshan could force her body to operate on less. And right now, she needed to.

The horses started, alert that someone was nearby. More than likely Azadeh. No dramatic whining like yesterday, but several began breathing heavily, hooves pawing at the ground. Onyx settled on the damp grass nearby, tongue lolling out her mouth as she surveyed the coming sunrise. Roshan couldn't see any blood on her black snout, but she could see it clear enough against the wolf's white teeth.

"Onyx spent the night hunting," Azadeh said, taking an uninvited seat next to Roshan. The pair watched a figure emerge from one of two tents that had been erected, which were little more than fabric positioned over sticks. Dias had one tent, the twins had put up the other, and she could tell which was which by the Norse feet that protruded.

"Looks like she wasn't the only one," Roshan remarked, identifying Mared by the flash of her hair as she stumbled over to the fire from Dias's tent. Only embers remained, but the Welsh woman stoked it and then she served herself some of the leftover hare.

"Dare I say Onyx's meal was more appetizing?" Azadeh whispered.

They descended into a fit of quiet laughter, careful not to wake anyone else or alert Mared to their presence. The last thing either one wanted, it seemed, was to draw her into conversation. Azadeh took a steadying breath.

"What happened to you?" she asked, the smile fading from Roshan's face at the prospect of questions from this woman. "The cut above your eye, the bruising on your face… you move like someone who's hurt."

"I'm healing," Roshan corrected. "I just need more time."

"From what?"

She was careful about what she said. "I wasn't in a good place before this."

"Geographically?"

Roshan nodded but refused to say more.

"Ah, so that's how he did it," Azadeh remarked. "I wondered what he bought you with and freedom is the brightest prize of all."

Azadeh had said she was good at gathering information. The comment sparked Roshan's curiosity and she glanced away from the campsite, turning to the woman. "What about you? What was your price?"

"My father is sick," she replied, the information coming freely from her lips. "He's the future of my people. Kind. Compassionate. He loves and lives freely. All of my good traits come from him, and he does not deserve to suffer."

"The hooded stranger said there was a cure to what ails him?"

Azadeh shrugged. "That's what he said. He's taking it to my father as we speak, regardless of whether Onyx and I are successful. That was the deal. Father gets the treatment and Onyx and I will give everything until that item is back in his possession."

"If he ever had it to begin with," Roshan muttered. Azadeh cast her a curious look. "You're good. A good person, I mean. Wei, I believe, is good. I'm still not sure about Nafanua, Francis and Mared. Dias, Geir and Gud seem far more untrustworthy. It's clear they are compelled to complete a task because they are getting paid to do it. You're completing this task because it's the right thing to do. Your father is presumably safe. And yet you're still here, trusting him and working to return something that's been stolen."

"Huh," the woman said. "I hadn't thought of that."

Because you're a good person at your core, Roshan said to herself. *And that's why you probably won't survive this.* She glanced at the wolf, whose fur glinted in the early morning sun, alluding to the approaching heat of the day. Azadeh's best chance was her pet. Roshan got to her feet. Enough of the others had now started to wake that they would need to leave soon.

She offered Azadeh a hand, which she accepted, springing to her feet eagerly. Yesterday had been a long ride and there had been no opportunities to bathe, so Roshan knew she was likely ripe and growing riper. Somehow, Azadeh smelled like frankincense to her, as if she had a secret stash somewhere. She pushed it out of her mind, and the two women joined the others around the fire.

"Wei has a plan," young Francis said, his blue eyes bright in the morning light.

"Well then," Dias laughed, clapping his hands together sarcastically. "If the old kook who can't talk has a plan, then–"

"He can talk," Roshan cut in, voice hard. "Just with words you may not understand."

The soldier-turned-pirate flashed her a dangerous glare despite his unflinching smile. "By all means then," Dias purred. "Carry on, translator."

Roshan ignored the comment and grabbed a stick, using one end to draw a rough version of the map in the sand for everyone to see.

"According to the hooded stranger, they're crossing the Sinai border to join the Silk Road along the ranges," she said, checking with Wei who nodded. Whether he understood her or not, he understood the movements she was illustrating in the sand. "To do that, they must clear a hill pass. Wei's plan was that we make it there first, rig the cliffs with explosives and block the pass. That way they will be trapped when we attack and take the object."

There were murmurs of agreement as several sets of eyes studied the sand diagram. Only Dias was staring at her.

"Cute," he said. "It was said they'll be there by night, so if we want to make it ahead of them unseen, we need to leave now to arrive by early afternoon."

"Agreed," Azadeh chirped, cutting through the tension. "What are we waiting for?"

The troop broke apart quickly, with not much for Roshan to pack up on her end as she rolled up her bedroll and headed for the horse. She paused as she watched Dias circle around on his, offering Wei a hand and a ride for the day. The old man graciously shook his head, even offering a small bow that she thought was overkill. Regardless, Dias looked angry. He kicked up a cloud of dust as he rode off, setting a challenging pace for the others.

"With you," Wei said, and she helped him onto her mare, the two trailing at the end of the group. He needed to be at the pass first, so Roshan spent the rest of the day trying to pick their way forward rider by rider. They never did catch up to Dias. As the sun passed its highest point of the day, Wei tapped her on the back. She followed the direction he pointed, the arches and rises of the forthcoming hills indicating that they were close to where they needed to be.

Slowing down, she looked over the side of the horse to follow the tracks she could see in the dirt. Dias' path led them to the perfect spot and they dismounted, Wei's bag clinking and clacking as he all but skipped forward to examine the terrain.

"Ideally we'd do one on each side," he said, settling down on his knees as he began assembling the items. "But I don't trust anyone else to do this."

"What's he on about?" Dias asked.

"He's saying we need to leave him alone to work," she lied, beginning to turn away.

"Someone should stay up here with him," he rebuffed.

Roshan was annoyed because he actually had a point, but she didn't want that person to be Dias.

"We'll do it," Azadeh called, strutting forward with Onyx at her side.

"We?" Dias questioned. "We as in you and that wolf?"

"As a Roman, I thought you'd appreciate the Romulus and Remus of it all," she insisted, moving past him and in place behind Wei.

"We can't spare a soldier," Mared barked as she pulled her ridiculous sword free. "We need you, Dias."

Roshan was grateful for Mared's persuasion at that moment as she watched Dias's chest swell just a little. His shoulder pushed hers as he passed her, even though there was plenty of room, a swagger in his step.

"If I'm needed then…"

His voice trailed off as he joined the others in hiding the horses and all signs of their tracks. Roshan looked back at Azadeh with an uneasy feeling in her stomach. "Go," the woman mouthed at her, ushering her away with a gesture. Wei couldn't have cared less, his attention occupied by whatever he was rigging. Onyx let out the smallest of growls and she cast the wolf a look, as if understanding what was making her nervous.

There was nothing to do but leave them, the plan relying entirely on Wei's success up there so they could have success down below. Roshan joined the others, everyone spacing out into various positions on the left side of the pass so that when Wei's bomb went off, they wouldn't be crushed on the right. Francis was farthest away but still in sight. He'd been tasked with waving a piece of fabric when the caravan was close and then Wei would let off the explosives.

Then, everyone else would pounce once the Martyrs were trapped. The sun was setting rapidly and Roshan knew their arrival must be close. She crouched next to Nafanua behind a large outcrop of rock. Mared and Dias were visible across the way and the big, brute twins somehow found a method to make themselves invisible farther up front. She couldn't see Wei, Azadeh or Francis, but hoped that everyone would be ready.

Staying poised in silence, she heard the unmistakable grunt of a camel far off. They were mean animals, but they were fast and strong: ideal for tugging along a caravan. A few moments later, she felt the shudder of hooves as the ground rumbled beneath her feet. The Martyrs were close.

Her eyes caught on the frantic wave of fabric as Francis heralded their arrival. *Too soon,* she thought, given that the Martyrs weren't in clear view. *Too soon!*

Yet it was also too late, as Wei had now seen the signal.

There was one still, steady moment before an earsplitting crack rang out. Roshan's eyes widened as she watched half a cliff disappear and everything turn to chaos.

Chapter Eight

Thatta, 821

Roshan held her life in her hands. Quite literally, it turned out, with a bead of sweat trickling down her scalp as she held the iron tweezers. They were pinched on a piece of thread that she needed to connect to the end of a steel comb without touching the glass cylinder right next to it. If she did... well, she would go the way of the other assistants.

"Keep it steady," Bakhit cautioned.

That was easy for him to say. He was safely encased in a protective suit of his own making that – in the likely event of an explosion – would keep him relatively unharmed besides a few bruises and burns. The suit was restrictive, however, making easy movements difficult, so Roshan was the one who needed to connect and enable the latest device. Nearly there, nearly there...

Her vision flared and she moved her hand away incrementally. Her additional sense was showing her a path and she let that instinct pull her toward exactly where the connection needed to be made. There was a small sizzle as the pairing sealed and Roshan released her hand rapidly. Her breath came in short, measured gulps and she looked up at Bakhit. The old man grinned as he ripped off the protective helmet, hands clasped together as he inspected her work.

"My goodness," he sighed. "Very good. Very good. My hands might not have been steady enough."

"Mine nearly weren't," she mumbled, stepping back as he quickly added all the outer mechanisms to seal the chemical reaction inside. He shut the device. It looked like a music box with the deadly ingenuity hidden within, and could play the correct tune at the correct moment before activating.

"Now, now, don't be like that. You've outlived every other assistant I've had."

"Hoorah?" she said, sarcastic, as she left the workshop.

"By months!" he called after her. "That's impressive!"

Roshan was impressively annoyed as she stormed from the house, done for the day and done with Bakhit. She jogged, needing the release of energy as she took the steps two at a time and ascended to one of the highest points of the city right near a beautiful temple dedicated to a Hindu god of old, one that was no longer celebrated as the city's worshippers had dwindled over time. She darted past it, enjoying the burn in her legs, one that was matched by a more disagreeable burn in her chest.

She needed to do this more and more lately. The tension in the workshop felt like it bled into her pores, agitating her mind. Bakhit's wealthy benefactor – the one who funded both their lifestyles and had brought them to Thatta in the first place – was actually the city's grand ruler. His position had been won through much bloodshed, with his armies and allies significantly dwindled in equal measure. It had left him in charge but also in a tenuous position. It took time to rebuild an army. It took time to rebuild allies. What the prince did instead was pay for compliance by hook or by crook, which is where Bakhit had come in.

He never said where his inventions were going specifically. But what they did, Roshan could easily guess. They were used to remove adversaries of the political and personal kind. Anyone of note had poison tasters in their employ, so that method proved less effective than it once had. Objects, however, were much less suspicious. The music box she had been helping build that afternoon would survive anyone's strict scrutiny *if* they were looking for something suspicious, but of course... they had to be looking.

As it was, the objects themselves would come through trusted contacts or family friends, who might not even know what they were passing on in the first place. Although Bakhit was always secretive about the exact specifics of what the objects did, keeping his chemical concoctions and mechanical creations to himself, she could usually gauge their future impact via the makeup. Sometimes designed to target one person, maybe two, yet never more than that and never without the almost complete destruction of the object itself after it had been used.

As soon as a certain song finished playing on that music box, the handle cranked over and over, and the device would combust, taking out anyone in range. That was Bakhit's style, she learned: erasure. Like his objects which eliminated themselves almost completely once they had been used, Bakhit, too, would disappear after a time. He said the longest he had ever stayed in a city was five years, back in his native Sudan, when he had been the favorite of a once-beloved king. That ruler was dead now, overthrown by his younger brother, who was then subsequently killed by his eldest son, and the throne had been in turmoil ever since he'd fled.

Now, he stayed wherever there was money until the gold dried up, usually working on exclusive contracts. When that finished or he garnered too much unwanted attention, he would relocate. That was exactly why he needed assistants that were nobodies. If she was a daughter of no one, then *no one* would come looking when she mysteriously didn't show at the mosque for worship. In a way, Roshan was somewhat like Bakhit's own personal poison taster.

That was the deal she had made. And for the first three months, she had been so in awe and so enamored with everything that she didn't spare a thought for what she didn't have. The risks seemed worth the reward. Then each month that passed after that, the stresses and the labor and the weight had grown incrementally. There had been only one sure way to alleviate them, that being what she was currently doing: racing through Thatta. It was the first city she had ever come to truly know and therefore, the first city she had ever come to truly love.

She scaled the fence at the outer edge of a property to reach the second level. There was a front gate she could've used for an easier route, yet Roshan's strength had grown. Physical challenges that had once been impossible were now possible. She used the uneven surface of the wall to get her grip, the clay bricks providing the perfect footholds as she climbed. It was an eight foot wall and as she reached the top, she hunched low and sprinted across the narrow edge. It was all that was between her and the harsh drop on the other side.

She made it to the thick, sloping palm tree without raising the alarm and leapt. Suspended in the air for one perfect, poised moment, she landed on the trunk and slid down the length to the base. Roshan hit the ground with a gentle stumble, soundless, before taking a direct route to the small hut she was after. The windows had been left open to maximize the later afternoon breeze. *Bet they never have to worry about blowing off their face with one wrong move,* she thought. The moment the words rolled through her mind, she felt bad.

Entering the home, a purple curtain snagged one of the straps over her shoulder and she pulled at it, annoyed. This caused the bells of the wind chime to tinkle ever so slightly, and Roshan quietened them with a gentle touch. The hypnotic azure within the blue ring of the nazars hanging from the chime blinked back at her. Roshan wasn't quite sure how the evil eye worked, but she was certain staring at one for too long wasn't a great idea. She released the chime and as she turned around, she sensed movement too late. A huge shadow was on her in a flash, dagger at her chest and elbow pressed to her throat as she was slammed up against the wall so hard, the hut shook just a little.

"Unnff," she grunted as her head hit the surface.

"Isun?"

The narrowed eyes of Advi widened for a moment as he drank her in. Given his ruffled curls and bare feet, Roshan guessed he'd been sleeping. He withdrew his blade but not his position as he kept her pressed there, blinking away his slumber.

"I could have killed you," he whispered, trying to slow down his breathing.

"Oh no," she teased. "Not the threat of death. How would I ever bear it?"

Advi let out a soft, shuddering laugh as he removed the elbow holding her in place, replacing it with his hand as it rested gently at the base of her throat. He knew all about the nature of her work for Bakhit. He was one of the prince's bodyguards after all and his most trusted courier. He'd been the one tasked with picking up – and sometimes distributing –various inventions, always with odd instructions like "never tilt it to the side" or "if you hear a tapping sound, drop it and run." He knew what Roshan had to deal with every day, had been dealing with, and his growing discomfort with it had only increased hers.

"I was asleep," he said. "I got switched to night duty. I thought you were an intruder."

"I am," she countered.

The hard stone of his eyes melted into something softer. "You know that you're welcome to intrude anytime."

"Oh, I am?"

She pushed off the wall, stepping into him and closing whatever distance was left. He gulped, and she was intrigued by the reaction. She took him by surprise, using one of the fighting sticks he'd given her during that first practice session to sweep his feet from under him in a deft swirl. He landed on the ground with a thud and she pounced, pressing her knee to his chest and the length of the stick across his throat. A moment passed. He let out a booming laugh. Roshan grinned, leaping off him quickly as she sheathed the stick in the straps that crisscrossed over her back.

"So it's practice that you want?" Advi said, taking the hand she held out for him as he sprang to his feet. "It's practice that you'll get."

On the even numbered days, he either came to the house before his shift started or after it was ending. On the odd ones, she would come to him when his shift was ending or about to start. She'd caught him on his rare day off, so they went to the old, deserted temple and ran through drills until the sun was well and truly set. Even then, Roshan spared only a moment to use the sunflower oil she'd brought and illuminate the lanterns nearby so that they could continue.

She didn't want to go home. The wooden *click clack clicks* of the fighting sticks replaced the angry thoughts in her head, and Advi's jibes teased witty taunts from her lips. *It was the physical exertion,* she thought. She had to keep telling herself that as she lasted longer and longer in Bakhit's employ, unexploded.

As Advi and Roshan wound down the night, finally settling into resting positions on the weathered steps, Roshan felt at ease as she looked out on Thatta below. Haleji Lake glittered far off in the distance, and the homes of thousands twinkled as lit lanterns and candles glowed from within, the distinctive curved rooftops angling up toward the sky.

"You know," Advi began, taking a long sip of water before handing her the flask. "Tahtib is also used as a courtship ritual where I'm from."

She nearly choked on her mouthful before managing to regain her composure. "Liar."

"It's true!" He laughed.

"You said women used it as a type of performance art now rather than a fighting one," Roshan corrected.

"Yes, the performance of courtship. To seduce!"

"You can't just keep changing the backstory to suit your whims."

"And what are my whims?" he asked, leaning forward so that his elbows rested on his knees. Advi stared at her intently and Roshan was speechless, having to break his gaze.

"You're beautiful."

It came out so quiet, it was almost a whisper. Her head snapped back to look at him, to see if she had hallucinated the words. She had not. From the expression on his face, he had meant them. Sincerely.

"What? You look aghast! Is that such a foreign notion to you?"

Yes, Roshan wanted to say. Instead, all she could do was laugh. "Beautiful, sure," she scoffed. "With my hair plastered to my face with sweat. Covered in dirt. Sitting here with you, absolutely reeking."

"Exactly," he countered. "That's when you're the most beautiful."

He leaned nearer so that his face was dangerously close to hers. Roshan went to pull away, annoyed, but he caught her chin in his fingers.

"Tell me... you haven't once considered this?"

She was about to ask him what "this" was, but he answered that question with action. Advi moved slowly, pressing his lips to hers in a gentle, soft kiss. His whiskers brushed against her skin. This wasn't her. The thought of being touched by a man ever again had sickened Roshan during that first year off the boat. Those memories weren't long gone in her mind or on her skin, yet she'd been growing increasingly bold with Advi. Their sparring sessions were the only thing scratching the itch she felt deep within her being. The urge to fight, however. Not to love.

Carefully, she removed his hands from her face and pushed him away as gently as she could. Advi smirked, as if he could tell exactly what she was thinking, but he had to try despite his inner doubts. He took the rejection well, eyes running over her as he waited for her to say something. Anything.

She couldn't. All Roshan could think of was the Harbor Master, who the more she resisted the more brutal he became.

She shuddered at the echo of a different time, a different place, a different man.

No, not a man. A monster. As she blinked away the tears welling up in her eyes, she refocused on the person sitting in front of her. Advi. As far from the demon of her past as she could get. Tall, sweet, sarcastic Advi who worshiped the ground she walked on and spent his free time with her, sharing his culture, skills, and his story with her.

"I haven't once considered it," she said, before spinning on the spot and running away.

"Wait, please, I have to–"

She sprinted down to the steep streets of Thatta like a coward, as if she could outrun her problems if she just pumped her arms fast enough.

When she returned home, panting, it was to a mercifully quiet house. Bakhit usually worked through the night but with their latest invention finished, he'd taken the evening off. She stood in an empty house with nothing to occupy her time except the need for a bath and the worry that she had just ruined one of the only friendships she had in her life.

Disappearing under the warm water for a long moment, she emerged gasping for air. She'd soaked so long that the water had cooled. Yet she didn't want to get out. Roshan had yet to feel fatigued after the long and stressful day. Then she heard a knock at the front door.

Hastily, she slipped out of the tub and wrapped herself in a robe. No one should have been calling at this hour, so she wondered if perhaps Bakhit was returning home drunk… but he was usually louder. More disruptive. This knock was polite. She picked up the dagger she kept near her bedside, but part of her knew it would be Advi before she even opened the door and saw him standing there.

His eyes went from the dagger in her hand to her freshly cleaned face, a smirk on his lips as if he was proud that she would never answer the door unarmed.

"Advi…" she started, an apology on her lips. She sensed the want in him, but she shoved it aside. Ignored it. She had written it off as a standard male impulse rather than something specific to *her*. Yet now that she thought about it, in the almost year since they met, she had never known him to bed a woman.

She assumed he had, obviously. Men could not go without. Yet unlike the other soldiers she had trained with, she never heard talk of it. He'd never been seen courting anyone or even considering the idea of taking a wife. *Idiot,* she thought, cursing herself for not seeing it in its entirety. She had never been liked before, only desired, and those were two very different things.

"I'm not here about that," he said. "I respect your wishes and we never have to speak of it again."

She opened her mouth to say something, anything, to try and explain, but he cut her off.

"I'm here with a warning."

She felt her guard go up, stiffening for the killing blow that she expected to come on the tail end of every interaction with men. Eventually, today or tomorrow, there would be a price.

"I saw something yesterday," Advi continued. "Something that looked like Bakhit's work hanging around the neck of a sheikh I don't particularly trust."

Roshan tilted her head, confused.

"It looked like something he would make. Something you would make together."

"Oh?" It was all she had to say.

"The contract with the prince is exclusive, Bakhit knows that. The terms they negotiated were… strict. *If* he were to take on other clients in a freelance capacity, he would be in breach of that agreement."

"What would happen to him?" Roshan asked, feeling a

flash of fear for the old mentor, despite her growing mixed feelings about him.

"He would be imprisoned, no doubt indefinitely. Probably for the rest of his life. Skills like his are too rare to waste. It's his staff that would be executed, most likely in front of him so he can feel the full extent of the punishment."

She gulped, nodding her head. "Thank you. For… the warning."

Advi looked like he was about to turn away, but then instead stepped closer. For a fleeting moment, he looked down at her with compassion in his eyes. "Be careful," he whispered. He planted a kiss on her forehead before turning and disappearing into the night.

Roshan stood at the door in shock after he was gone, staring at the space he had occupied and feeling the exact spot where his lips had pressed into her skin. When she closed the front door finally, she retreated to her room in a daze, all kinds of warnings buzzing through her mind.

Chapter Nine

Sinai Border, 824

Rocks and debris exploded everywhere.

Roshan had thought she was far enough from the impact site but needed to duck to protect herself anyway. Stones and sand collided against her, Nafanua taking the brunt of it due to her more forward position. When the debris stopped raining down on them, Roshan's ears rang from the explosion. She couldn't hear anything at first, just the dull echoing through her skull. Then gradually, as that started to fade, she heard the shouts. She heard the clang of metal. She heard the roar. Pushing back onto her knees, she coughed as she shook off the dust.

She wasn't inhaling fresh air for long, however. As Nafanua got to her feet, she shook off the rocks, dust, and sand from her body like it was nothing, some flashes of red from bleeding scratches bright against the dirt covering her. She let out an annoyed grunt, eyes wide as she looked around and got her footing. When her gaze locked on Roshan, she thrust out a hand. In her other, Nafanua held the hooked club she'd taken from the tavern. No words needed to be exchanged.

Roshan threw up her hand, flinching at the pain in her shoulder as she was hauled to her feet. They rushed toward the action as quickly as they could. She did her best to take in the scene as she ran, blinking the dust and dirt out of her eyes. Either Francis had called it too early, or something had gone wrong with Wei's explosion. He'd blown up the pass, with the route completely and utterly blocked, but the trap hadn't fully worked because their targets had enough time to see what was happening and divert. In fact, the Martyrs had already almost turned around fully and were doing their best to flee in the opposite direction.

There was one large caravan being pulled by four huge camels who were being whipped in urgency by their two riders from the driver's position. Large wheels churned up dust as they rotated under a platform that extended out from the main structure. Guards were positioned along and around it as they traveled, presenting a visible defense designed to deter anyone attempting to do what Roshan and the others were planning. On top of the main structure was another, slightly smaller platform giving two or three additional personnel the perfect view to survey and target threats.

And they were dealing with several thanks to the quartet of Geir and Gud at the caravan's front, Dias and Mared at the back. Dias and Mared were outnumbered four to one, with there being almost a dozen guards surrounding the perimeter of the caravan. Roshan rapidly counted the number of Martyrs of Agaunum, who were easy to spot in dark, maroon robes glinting with a gold trim and their faces covered by a traditional ruband. There was a circular symbol in the same gold printed over their chests and she filed it away in her mind's eye, as it sparked some kind of recognition in her. Only their eyes were visible, narrowed and intense as they focused on fighting off the comparatively small number of assailants.

"What happened to six of them?" Nafanua barked, looking less annoyed about it than her words would suggest. She seemed positively *alive* in Roshan's eyes as the warrior sprinted at a boulder. She didn't slow as she leapt onto it, pounding up until she reached the top and launched herself off it. She sailed through the air, letting out a distinctive battle cry.

"Cheeeehoooooo!" she screamed, landing on the platform that extended out from the caravan with a definitive thud.

Nafanua swept through the men with her weapon. Dias utilized the distraction she created to leap onto the back, too. Mared pulled herself up and Roshan sprinted after the larger group.

There was a Martyr in prime position perched at the top of the small platform and he wielded an almost comically large bow. Roshan watched as the tip of his arrow pointed directly at his target: her. His elbow jerked back and gave her a fraction of a second warning before the projectile hurtled through the air. She dove to her left, feeling the air whistle as it flew past her and embedded in the ground with a hollow *thunk*. Roshan rolled until she could spring back up to her feet with a huff. Another arrow whistled over her shoulder, and she dodged, hoping someone would take them out soon. Assistance came from the most unlikely of places, the caravan swerving as Gud took out one of the main camel riders with a swing of his axe.

The animal made a horrible sound as its legs were swept out from under it. The rider threw themselves forward and in their final act, severed the leads that attached them to the caravan. It happened in barely a few seconds, yet Roshan watched it all unfold as if time had slowed down. The rider and the camel collapsed in a plume of dust, and she refocused back on the main objective.

Dias was clashing metal with metal as he exchanged sword blows with one of the guards, his blade running through the man hastily as he fought through the guards to get farther to the front and closer to the Martyrs. Mared was doing the same, but much more unsuccessfully. The Martyrs' companion-guards were wearing her down. Roshan hit the oval button on her fighting stick when she was close enough to the caravan, pulling up alongside it. Her thighs and her chest stung with exertion.

The stick's length sprang out and she braced her arms, hitting the dirt and using it to launch herself forward. She tossed her feet, using the momentum of her body like she had done this a thousand times before – because she had. She had just never attempted to land on a moving target. Roshan crashed onto the platform, her face scrunching up with pain. She retracted the stick as quickly as she could, getting it halfway down before a flash of silver came down on her head.

She blocked the blow. One of the companions tried to bear down on her as she lay on her back. They had the superior position, but she had the leverage and Roshan kicked both legs out and against their chest. She used all her strength to hurl them backward and they let out a cry as they flew off the side. Gripping the edge, she tried to regain her balance as the caravan rocked backward and forward even more unsteady than before. Four camels had been tugging it along evenly, but now with three, one side was unbalanced.

Geir landed at the front of the platform and his sheer weight alone did a lot to steady it. She lurched forward, about to scream at him to get off, but he was already swinging the axe that perfectly matched his brother's. It cut down a Martyr who had his back to him, the man letting out a pained yell as he fell to his knees. Satisfied, Geir turned away, so he didn't see what Roshan saw. The wounded Martyr paused, then sprang back up, seemingly unaffected.

She gawked in shock, able to do nothing but point as Geir almost thudded past her. His lip curled, as if she were an idiot for suggesting that the man he had attacked wasn't dead. But the two long daggers that plunged into Geir's shoulders quickly proved him wrong. He let out a loud roar, throwing his body back with a pained scream. As he spun, the Martyr went with him, the daggers providing the perfect grip. Gud – as if recognizing the sound of his brother – materialized at his side to provide aid.

The two Northmen were big enough brutes that they could handle themselves, and she began searching for a way into the caravan to find the case. Roshan slid one of the slatted, wooden windows back to reveal the interior. It was larger than she expected, and as she crammed her body through into the space, she was suddenly pulled backward.

"Ah!" she yelled, her hands scrambling as she tried and failed to get a grip on something. The last thing she saw as she was dragged out was one of the symbols, the shape glowing clear to her eyes.

The semi-masked face of a Martyr lunged at her as she spun around to face two hands extended toward her throat. They didn't get a chance to make contact. Just as their fingers were about to brush her flesh, a black blur darted forward. The Martyr yelled as Onyx bit into their hands, the wolf knocking them backward. Roshan got to her feet and rushed forward, looking for Azadeh who then nearly barreled right into her.

"Come on!" she panted. "We have to get off this thing, this is a disaster!"

Roshan didn't disagree. They linked arms for balance, struggling against each other as they made their way to the rear of the caravan where the others were fighting. A cluster of companions stood in their way and she opened her fighting stick, torso twisting and feet poised in the perfect position as she batted at them in a blur of movement. They weren't expecting such a weapon and Roshan swatted one of the companion's swords out of their hand, a second blow to their chest sending the companion backward. She stunned the other with a blow to the head, Azadeh seizing the moment with a spinning kick which sent another companion flying. Roshan watched as Dias's sword was knocked from his hand by two Martyrs he was battling at once.

"Mared, help!" he called.

Roshan saw Mared turn to answer Dias's call. She looked worse for wear, her eye swelling shut despite having a companion in a headlock. Mared released him, kicking his rear as she rushed to assist Dias. Pressed back to back, the two had better odds and pushed the Martyrs on them away. Mared flashed him a smile over her shoulder and Dias seemed about to return it when his grin faltered. Roshan guessed why and urged Azadeh to rush forward and further onto the back platform to help.

"Sorry, love," he told Mared. He lunged, spinning Mared around for a passionate kiss. The flame-haired beauty looked surprised, before returning the gesture as she wrapped her hands around his neck. A whistle sounded through the air as an arrow plunged right through her back. Dias pulled away just in time, avoiding the arrowhead nearly penetrating through her to him.

"Ack!" she cried, letting out a pained gasp. Five more arrows flew past, the archer desperate to get Dias as the Roman used Mared like a human shield. She coughed blood, clutching onto him desperately. There was a betrayal in her eyes that Roshan saw coming from a mile away. The question of who seduced who had now been answered in the most brutal way. Dias yanked her close and in her dying moments, said, just loud enough for Roshan to hear, "Love is pain."

One more arrow sealed her fate as Dias positioned her to take the brunt of the blow. He shoved her body forward and leapt off the back of the caravan. Roshan and Azadeh jumped, too, rolling in unison to soften the impact. Wei arrived and tugged them both to their feet, having struggled to keep up with the fight on the moving caravan. Francis was with him, hands on his knees, panting as he struggled to collect his breath.

Roshan shook off Wei's hand, stepping forward as their target charged on without them. The sun had almost entirely set now, with the shape just a lump against the dark purple sky, growing smaller and smaller by the second. Part of the caravan seemed to break off and vanish into the dust cloud, only to reappear a moment later. The shape split into two, revealing the unmistakable forms of Geir and Gud. Other figures dotted the ground, the bodies of all the companions they had killed.

She crouched down, pulling the face covering of one of the dead men free. No obvious distinguishing marks told her who he was or what was going on – and why he was dead, yet the Martyr Geir had killed still lived. She patted him down, but the search was fruitless. He could have been Punjabi, but he could have just as easily been any other ethnicity given how difficult it was to discern his facial features with his fatal head wound. There was a piercing whistle, and Azadeh stepped up with her fingers pressed tightly between her lips.

Azadeh's anxiety eased, the deep frown softening when the footfalls of Onyx came sprinting toward her. A smile broke across Azadeh's face, and she dropped to her knees, embracing the wolf. "Good girl," she whispered, the wolf licking her face as she cooed. "Good, good girl." Azadeh ran her hands through the creature's fur, scratching and petting her like she was little more than a puppy.

"Well, that was a shambles," Dias boomed, his voice light.

Rage ran through Roshan and she spun to confront him, but it was unnecessary. Nafanua loomed out of the shadows, blood streaking her face and the body of Mared dragging behind her. She dropped Mared at Dias's feet, glaring at him. "You killed her," she growled.

"I held the bow and arrow, did I? Fired those shots?"

Nafanua bared her teeth. "You used her as a human shield."

"And what do you care?" Dias countered. "You didn't even like the woman!"

She got right up in his face. They were evenly matched in height and almost standing nose to nose. "She. Was. One. Of. Us."

Roshan's gaze shifted to Geir and Gud, who had joined the group and positioned themselves on either side of Dias. The visual wasn't lost on her, especially with Azadeh and her standing at Nafanua's rear. The battle lines were drawn, with Francis and Wei fidgeting nervously on the sidelines. Roshan's eyes darted to Gud, whose fingers stretched as he gripped the handle of his axe. She cast Azadeh a look, with the woman tracking her eyeline back to the source of worry.

"Hey," Azadeh said, stepping forward as her wolf began to growl. "We're supposed to be fighting the Martyrs of Agaunum, not each other!" Azadeh then tugged Nafanua back, muttering something to her quietly. Wei and Francis found their place alongside them, the numbers now skewed in their favor five to three. Six, really, if you counted Onyx, which Roshan definitely did.

"That was a disaster!" Nafanua snapped, turning back to

the group, her anger redirected toward another problem. Yet from the dark glint in her eyes, Roshan could see that her fury was still there, particularly for Dias. "There were three times as many as we were expecting to fight."

"Hate to agree with the woman who looked ready to decapitate me," Dias said as Nafanua cut him a withering look. "But we were grossly outmanned. I don't think I even got near a Martyr."

Roshan had been wondering the same thing as she ran her hands over her face, pushing away the loose curls that had escaped her braid. "They knew we were coming," she said.

Dias snorted. "Dare I say Francis waving a blue sheet of fabric gave it away?"

"Before that," she said, closing her eyes as she thought about the footfalls she'd been listening to at the start. "They were slowing down even before they approached. They knew."

"Because they *saw* Francis," Dias repeated. His insistence made her suspicious, but it wasn't the only thing.

"I-it was the bomb," Francis stammered. "It wasn't me! The bomb went off too early and it gave them time to retreat."

"The child isn't right, he doesn't understand what he's saying," Wei told her, gripping on to Roshan's elbow with urgency. "It went off perfectly, it–"

"Translate him!" Gud grunted, the first proper words he'd spoken since they met. She actually hadn't known if he could speak before now. She had always assumed it was just snorts or guttural sounds. Geir joined in, shouting as well. Dias was yelling, Nafanua looking like she wanted to get back in his face, Onyx was barking, and Azadeh struggled to hold on to her silver collar.

"Stop!" Roshan cried, bringing the group to a halt. She closed her eyes with frustration, trying to focus her mind. "Just… everyone stop. For a moment."

"Let us pray," Francis offered.

She clicked her fingers at him. "Not. That."

Azadeh chuckled and they exchanged a glance. The woman had saved her skin more than once now. She wanted to believe she was an ally, but she couldn't… something wasn't right here, and everyone was under suspicion.

"We need to get back on their trail," Roshan said, pushing her hesitations aside. "We're not that far behind–"

"I brought the horses down," Wei said, gesturing behind him to where the mares were tied together.

"Then we pursue them while we still can. With the time that will take, we regroup. Come up with a better strategy. All right?"

There was a resounding silence from those gathered. She took that as a yes.

"Is anyone hurt?" she questioned. "Any serious injuries?"

She could see Geir bleeding from a deep cut above his clavicle, but he didn't raise his hand or even mention complications from being stabbed in the back. Nafanua limped slightly but stayed quiet as well.

"Fine," Roshan sighed, resigning herself to dealing with such children. "We move in five minutes."

She took that time to treat herself as best she could, ignoring the cuts and abrasions to wash as much dirt from her face as she could. Wei shuffled over to her as they each began to mount their horses, but Nafanua stepped in his way.

"He rides with me," she said, tone stern. "No disrespect, but I trust myself more in a fight to the death if it comes to it rather than... you."

Nafanua looked Roshan up and down in a way that made her feel small, which was fitting given how small she actually was compared to the Sāmoan soldier. Roshan glanced over at Geir and Gud, not liking the way either of them studied Wei in that moment. There was offense taken, but it wasn't intended. Nafanua wanted Wei to ride with her because she thought he was under threat from the others, plain and simple. Roshan nodded, heading toward her own horse. Azadeh had already mounted it and reached down a hand to help her up.

"If it makes you feel better," the younger woman said with a smile, "I'd bet on you in a fight with the idiot twins over Nafanua any day."

"I wouldn't," Roshan replied, smirking as she climbed onto the back of the mare.

They rode up front, with Azadeh proclaiming she was the best tracker. Roshan didn't doubt it. She had a powerful assistant in Onyx, whose sense of smell could lead them anywhere, even in the dark. However, it was Azadeh's gift at navigating through challenging terrain that proved vital given the conditions.

"We're not moving at speed," she said to Roshan. "You don't need to grip me that tightly."

"Sorry," Roshan mumbled. She was on edge after the brief and unsuccessful skirmish. Casting a glance over her shoulder, she searched for Nafanua and Wei in the dark.

They were on the white horse she had originally ridden and after several long moments, she spotted them in the low light. Roshan relaxed a little, even though the sight of Geir and Gud racing alongside them did little to quell her worries.

"Do you have a sword?" Azadeh asked, the question surprising her.

"Yes," she answered, having taken her own small but efficient one so it wouldn't weigh her down. "Why?"

"You don't use it."

"I prefer tahtib."

"The stick?"

Roshan nodded, before realizing Azadeh wouldn't be able to see her response and verbalized it instead. "Yes."

"You're good with it, but it won't save you against these enemies. Did you see them fight?"

Roshan frowned, considering her answer. "They're good, but they're not as good as you think."

"Are you joking?" Azadeh exclaimed. "I've never seen anyone better!"

Roshan had. Her mind went immediately to the hooded stranger, his abilities far exceeding not just the Martyrs but all of the greatest fighters she had seen in her life. Even Advi. She felt a pang in her chest and she pushed it aside, trying to concentrate on the present.

"They were expecting us," she countered. "Which always gives them the advantage. Then there was the additional layer of everyone they traveled with, the companions being capable enough in their own right. But that's not what made them formidable."

"They seemed pretty damn formidable to me, and I have a wolf on my side," Azadeh responded. "We barely made a dent."

Roshan did the math, calling out to each member of the group as they rode. Dias had dispatched three companions, Roshan had taken out two. Azadeh just the one, yet Onyx had gone after several and a Martyr. Nafanua remarked that she had three companions to match Dias, but when it got to Geir and Gud they were unsure.

"Two Martyrs," Geir said. "But…"

She watched the frown settle into his expression. He exchanged an annoyed look with his brother, who mirrored it.

"But what?" Azadeh prompted.

"They didn't stay down," Roshan said, voicing what she had seen and what worried her now.

"I saw that, too," Nafanua added, riding up alongside them. "I could have sworn I dealt a fatal blow, and *no one* survives the Tafesilafa'i."

She gestured to the weapon now strapped to her side, hands running down its arched shape lovingly.

"Yet the Martyrs got back up," Roshan finished. "Just like they did after Geir swept one of them aside."

She remembered him registering the fatality then turning away to keep killing, only for the Martyr to spring back after him, seemingly unaffected by something that would have annihilated anyone else.

"What are you saying?" Azadeh questioned, incredulous. "They're immortal? That's ridiculous!"

Everyone else joined in, scoffing at the idea.

"We just need to be better positioned next time," Wei said.

The twins proposed more weapons, bigger weapons. Given that they themselves were the biggest, breathing weapons Roshan had ever seen, she wasn't sure how much larger things could get. Dias wanted a cleaner strategy, something sneakier, and Azadeh surprisingly agreed.

Everyone else was in loud rejection of that while Roshan had fallen quiet, thinking deeply once again.

She had read about the story of the Martyrs of Agaunum years ago, the story staying with her in part because she found the idea of so many being aligned with the same cause, but also sacrificing themselves for such a cause, compelling. It repulsed and intrigued her simultaneously and she had wanted to understand the reasoning, never once considering that she might have the opportunity one day.

Roshan desperately needed to re-examine that text again or any account that mentioned them, as she felt like the answer was there. No, she wasn't saying they were immortal. Yet they were *something* and that something was the reason they could seemingly stand up to violent battery that should have proven fatal. It was the reason they were protecting the case instead of any other range of guards who would have been easier to hire… and weren't supposed to have died centuries ago. Roshan ignored the shiver that ran down her spine at the thought. She suspected this had a lot to do with why they had all been individually recruited for this mission, especially when the stranger should have been performing it himself after the physical prowess he had demonstrated.

She wasn't sure if the others knew about that, but she did. Roshan couldn't shake the feeling that she – and the rest of the team – were part of something larger, yet the logic was unclear at the moment. She was just one of the pieces being moved on a massive game board and she had no idea what the rules even were.

"Whoa," Azadeh cautioned, slowing the mare they rode at the head of their team. "Eassssy."

Onyx's glowing eyes were still visible in the dark. Roshan thought the yellow shine seemed to be some of the only remnants of light left now, the sun having fully set and all hopes of traveling safely gone.

"It's dark here," Francis said, voice cautious. "Different. Deeper. Like we're in the shadow of Satan himself."

"If by Satan you mean a mountain then, yes," Roshan replied. "That's exactly what we're in the shadow of."

She slid off the horse's back, patting it on the rump as she bent to study the terrain. They had been slowly ascending without realizing it, but the ground was growing too steep. With the large indents in the dirt, it was clear which direction the caravan had headed.

Striking a match, she used its fleeting light to examine the map she had drawn. She'd added her own small details as they'd traveled when she'd been able. What she'd seen far off in the distance during the day was now roughly where they stood. She double checked her assessment, squinting at the stars above and being grateful for yet another clear, cloudless evening.

"They're taking the mountain road," Roshan realized.

"Which will lead them… where?" Dias huffed, annoyed. "Across the Sinai Peninsula? What are we waiting for? Let's keep going – we can catch them."

"We can't *catch* them over ground like this," Azadeh snapped. "This is treacherous at the best of times, let alone at night. If we're to follow, we need to wait until sunrise at least."

"They're still going! We need to hurry up!" the Roman pushed.

"They have camels," Roshan countered. "And a caravan. Their moving power allows them to take the risk."

"We'll never catch up," Wei muttered, at first in his own language and then for the whole group to understand. "We'll *never* catch up."

He sounded deflated while, in contrast, Nafanua looked elated. "We could," she began. "There's another way. Close your eyes, breathe deeply."

Geir and Gud scoffed, refusing to do so. Francis did, however, but he opened his eyes with an even more confused expression.

"Do you smell it?" Nafanua questioned.

"Salt," Roshan answered, the tinge on her nostrils familiar. "Sea salt."

"The Red Sea is just on the other side of this summit." Nafanua nodded. "If we climb this instead of cutting around, we'll expend energy but save time. We can sail the rest of the way."

"Sail where?" Francis whined. "They'll still be in the mountains, and we'll be in the ocean."

"No, no, I like this idea," Dias mused, surprising everyone. "If the wind is right, we could shoot way ahead of them."

Roshan examined her drawn map, looking toward cities the Silk Road flirted with along the coast. Her fingertip traced a path, pausing on a familiar name.

"Karachi," she said. "We could dock there and cut back."

"They're expecting us to be coming at them from behind." Dias beamed. "They'll never see us coming from the front. Ha!"

His laugh was a booming beacon of elation, and he slapped Nafanua on the shoulders happily. "Begrudgingly, kills me to say this, but great idea," he told her. "The past is the past. Lead on!"

She nodded, a small smirk playing on her lips that dropped as soon as he turned away from her. *Good,* Roshan thought. She wouldn't trust him either.

There was only one way to proceed and that was up. Cautiously. Carefully. Come what may.

Chapter Ten

Thatta, 822

She had screwed up. In the same way that she hadn't been paying full attention to the situation with Advi, Roshan hadn't been paying full attention at home either. In critical ways, she had remained alive and unharmed in the workshop, which was a major win for all involved. Yet she had let other things slip, like the fact that despite the prince's position being quite secure in the city of Thatta now, their delivery demands hadn't decreased.

They should have.

She resigned herself to listening and learning about politics to understand the situation better, but once she grasped the clearer picture of what was happening, she discovered Advi was correct: Bakhit had been taking on other clients. More and more of them, in fact, of shady origins and questionable means who began to frequent their home. As the ruler's reign solidified, the demand for Bakhit's skills had lessened, but not the old man's desire to stay busy – or to stay compensated, greed being as big a part of it as anything.

Roshan paid attention to the visitors; many of them she had written off as suppliers over the past few months who had been bringing Bakhit ingredients and spare parts from exotic locations. That was still true, but she soon detected they also left with items of their own. She tried listening to the differences in the way they spoke, not just the words she couldn't understand but the accents, the subtleties in dress, the people they brought with them. All to understand more.

Her training sessions with Advi continued, too. She was grateful he never spoke of what had happened again. He treated her exactly as he had before, yet Roshan knew what could not be unknown. He cared for her. The fact that she could not return that affection didn't seem to matter to him, so long as they could still train and spend time together. Was that love? It seemed a terribly cruel curse that one could be satisfied with crumbs and remain forever unfed.

Love was something she would never risk, her own agency in this new life too valuable for her to dare lose it, especially when she had lived without it for so long.

When she had been trapped in that life, on that boat, unable to control anything about her future except, maybe, what the next minute held, and barely the one after that, there had been one thing Roshan was determined about. She would not give that man a child. She had been a child herself and the idea of rewarding that monster with something he desperately yearned for sickened her. She had turned to Talâyi for help.

"You will have to give him what he wants eventually," the older wife had said when handing her the herbs that would make sure nothing grew inside Roshan except hatred.

"I will never," she had replied, voice firm. Talâyi had gripped her hand then, squeezing it tightly as she made Roshan stare directly at her.

"This is what he took from me," she said, pointing at where her eye had once been. "For perceived *rebellion.* Imagine what he'll do if he finds out that–"

"He will never find out," Roshan had replied. "I would die before I let him learn it or *anything* about who helped me."

She had seen a tension ease from the older woman's shoulders then, understanding that this was part of her warning. Roshan had been new then, only a month since she had been taken from her home, and Talâyi needed to know Roshan could be trusted.

She could. Roshan would keep the secret of the herbs best consumed by tea and distributed amongst the other wives on a cyclical basis. Many resented it, but they understood their role: they couldn't hold out forever, but it could also be on their own terms.

"You know, all he wants is sons," Talâyi said. "When he knew that I was with child, he left me alone for eight long, glorious months."

"And then he never left you alone after that," Halima had piped up. "As soon as he knew you could carry to term, you were his prize. And where is he now, hmm? Where is your son?"

Roshan had thought it cruel to poke so clearly at Talâyi's wound. The woman may have been hopeless and reluctant to inspire hope in others, but Roshan understood that was only because she was realistic. She had seen many other girls just like them come and go. Talâyi was a survivor, but the cost had worn on her over time. Roshan had hissed at Halima to leave, not wanting the cut to go deeper as she looked at the sunken expression on the older woman's face.

"Think about it," Talâyi mumbled. "It could be worth the peace."

"And what if it's a girl?" Roshan said, voicing her greatest fear. If possible, Talâyi's look was even worse. Roshan had heard rumors about what happened when men as powerful as the Harbor Master and his brother were given an heir they didn't want. They'd proudly boast about having all boys, not a single female to weaken the bloodline. Yet in that moment, Roshan knew they weren't just rumors. It was true.

She took the tea and promised she would never stop taking it, no matter how much he beat her or called her a defect. Those days were dark, and they were gone, but the memories provided her with a warning about the burdens women were forced to shoulder and men were not.

Roshan's current life had many costs and one of them was the lack of female companionship, which she greatly missed. No sooner had she mourned it, however, than an unlikely solution presented itself.

There was a new client of Bakhit's, a woman from Damascus who – despite the age showing on her face – was still striking. She strutted with the confidence one acquired through lived experience, something that was imitated but rarely original.

This Damascene woman dressed in the finest silks yet

chose the most subtle of shades, her wealth hidden unless you knew what to look for. Roshan had watched her during her first consultation with Bakhit, the lady regarding her with interest in stolen glances between the many notes the old inventor took.

"I'll be back in seven days to see if you're successful," she had told him, placing an object on the table before making her departure. She paused at the doorway, considering Roshan with a pointed glance from head to toe. "Are you the assistant?"

"Yes, ma'am," she'd replied.

"Bakhit has mentioned his pride about you and your abilities. You must be able to read."

"I can, yes."

"And write?"

"Yes," Roshan confirmed, before adding: "And count, not just basic equations but complex ones as well."

She wasn't sure why she had felt the need to impress this lady, but she was compelled to do so.

"In the name of Atargatis," she said, stepping forward with smooth precision. "My name is Maryam and if you ever need a change of career, you look for these."

She handed Roshan a small piece of green fabric, the shape of the white flower from which the older woman took her name drawn there in some kind of dye. Roshan's head snapped up, examining the woman and wondering if the offer was legitimate.

"You will not be poaching my best worker today, you clever vixen," Bakhit boomed, ushering her toward the door. "Out you go, out."

Said clever vixen cast him an indulgent look before giving Roshan a wink, which said that she wouldn't give up so easily. Closing the door behind Maryam, Roshan tucked the floral design into her pocket and hid it from her master. She followed Bakhit back to his workshop where he was examining something under the light from the sun that was magnified by mirrors he had angled from a skylight in the roof. It created an almost perfect, intense beam and Roshan leaned in to see what the woman had left behind.

"Is that a piece of copper?" she asked, noting the color and qualities of the metal.

"It is," he mused, eyes narrowed at the tiny shape.

"And… what is it supposed to do?"

"Prevent pregnancy."

"Excuse me?" Roshan spluttered.

"Don't be coy, I know you've read the texts. You know the way of the world."

"I… it's… uh…" Her words failed her. "How?"

"The properties of the copper, Maryam says, bound with silkworm guts. It sounds like an old wives' tale to me."

"Old wives know a lot," she countered, feeling defensive. He examined her over the object, mouth open as he scrutinized Roshan in a way that made her feel like he was analyzing her more than she'd like him to.

"That they do," he relented. "And if we can prove the theory, we'll have an order of two dozen to deliver by the end of the week and a long-time return customer."

"What on earth would you need–" Roshan cut herself off, realizing the answer.

"Ah, there's the clever girl," Bakhit chuckled. "The oldest

trade in the world, my dear. Let's see if we can modernize it just a touch."

Roshan's blood ran cold at the mention of five terrifying words.

"I have something for you."

She stayed still, pretending she hadn't heard them spill from Advi's mouth as he lay beside her, the two having stretched out side by side at the old temple as they finished that evening's training session.

"Isun," he pressed.

It was the name she had been going by for as long as she'd known him, and she was tempted in the moment – just that moment – to tell him her real name. She couldn't, though. She knew it would doom her. Choosing a pseudonym because of the moon's glow she'd basked in on her first night of freedom was as close to the truth as Roshan would be able to get.

"What for?" she said, her tone softer than her sharp question.

"You deserve it, firstly." Advi grinned. "And you've been working so hard at the sword and dagger, even though I know you hate it."

"I don't *hate* it," she pouted. "I just don't like having to start over again."

He laughed. "Being bad at something is humbling. It motivates you to improve."

Advi had introduced the new implements to her a few months ago, offering her a lighter blade of curved metal favored by soldiers in the prince's guard. Her fingers had tightened around the hilt, unsure with how she felt about it. Advi had handed her another weapon, a small but thick dagger.

It hadn't felt natural to her the way stick fighting did, the wood like an extension of her own body as she leapt and swirled and thrust with the implement. The sword and dagger were harder simply because they were new, but she told herself she would master it. Everything just took time. Now, she watched as Advi retrieved a long, rectangular box that he had managed to keep out of sight during that night's session. There was nothing special or decorative about it, as if he knew that anything extravagant would scare Roshan and send her running. He would have been correct. Even so, she sat up and took the box suspiciously, feeling its weight in her hands. He laughed, and she narrowed her eyes at his amusement.

"You're handling that like it contains a cobra," Advi said, laying back as he placed his hands behind his head. "Open your present."

This took her by surprise. "Present?"

"What did you think it was?"

Roshan shrugged. "I genuinely thought it might have been a cobra."

"Now I'm rethinking the gift–"

"No, no," she snapped, cutting him off. "I want it. It's mine. I've just… never had one before."

Roshan suspected Advi might be in love with her, but she didn't truly know that to be true until she opened the box. Pushing aside the fabric which protected the contents, she gasped as she looked inside. Two fighting clubs lay side by side. Her fingers traced the shapes and the intricate design of flowers and stars which had been carved into the wood. She lifted one out of the box, feeling the weight as she studied the details more carefully. Set inside the center of a star was a small sphere that stood out because it protruded from the surface of the weapon.

"Press it," Advi said. She cast him a glance, seeing the pleasure in his expression at her obvious delight with the gift. "Go on, press it. Just angle it… this way."

He leaned forward, twisting her wrist slightly. Confused but intrigued, Roshan did so and let out an exclamation of delight as the wooden length extended from each end in a blur of movement.

"Oh," she breathed. "*My.*"

"You only use one in combat, but they're supposed to be gifted as a pair."

They were proper fighting sticks now, full length and all her own. Lifting her arm so she had more range, she spun it expertly in a complete sphere and relished in the *whoosh* of air she felt move past her face. They were perfect. Perfectly weighted. Even the intricate carving was only at the center of the tahtib sticks, providing additional grip that she usually had to create for herself by carving a grid pattern with her own dagger blade. This was *much* better. It was the perfect present. She pressed the button, watching with glee as the length retracted back on both sides until it looked like nothing more than an ornamental club.

"Bakhit," Roshan whispered. "I'd recognize his handiwork anywhere. He made these?"

"I wasn't sure how you'd feel about that," Advi admitted. "But you already had your own set of fighting sticks. I wanted these to be special."

"I love them," Roshan said, meaning it but immediately regretting the words.

Hope flashed in his eyes, like she was about to say she loved him next. She couldn't do that. She wouldn't. Instead, she leaned forward and hugged him. It was the best she could do to mirror his thoughtfulness, but the truth was Roshan couldn't say those words because she didn't feel it.

She didn't love him. She doubted that she'd ever have the capacity to love. She loved the way he made her feel, and she admired the way he so freely shared his knowledge with her, giving Roshan the weapons she needed to defend herself and move through the world with more protection than she'd ever had before. He also never pried, never pushed her for answers about her family or her life before.

Advi knew about her deal with Bakhit, of course, but never asked why someone would enter into such a brutal, fatalistic bargain. He didn't ask about the scars on her back, the ones that ran from her shoulder down to the start of her tailbone and were glimpsed during training.

Advi had a unique gift for knowing where the quicksand was and being able to skirt around it so that Roshan never felt cornered. She was secretive for a reason, and she guessed part of him knew that. She suspected it was more likely that he hoped she would become more open with him over time. Maybe that was true. Maybe she would. Until then, all she could do was give him her time, which felt safer.

And she needed safe.

When she returned home that evening, Bahkit wasn't there. He'd been spending more and more evenings with the brothel madame honing the design she'd brought him. Unlike the other pleasure houses in the city, Maryam's was mobile. It was a smart choice because it meant any greedy soldiers wanting a cut of her business couldn't find her easily. You had to know where the women were and to know that information, you had to know a trusted customer. Break that trust and you couldn't frequent their establishment again, which was a devastating loss for those who relied on their services. Roshan had tried to pass on Advi's warning to Bakhit about his other clients and while the old man had listened at the time, he had not slowed that business down one bit.

"I'll be careful," he told her before addressing the heavy exhale she let out. "*More* careful."

"Or you could stop altogether?" she offered.

He laughed like Roshan had suggested something utterly ridiculous. "Do you know what it took for you to learn to read? To write?"

She opened her mouth to reply, but he cut her off.

"To master tahtib?"

"I don't think I have mastered it," she said.

"Dedication and patience," he said, ignoring her. "Those qualities are required to master anything. It has taken me a lot of dedication and patience to get here. So yes, I will be more careful. I'll disguise the items better, select my clients with more consideration, but I will not stop."

Roshan hoped this was true. She felt he said this to placate her, but what could she do? Bakhit's two true masters were knowledge and money. He got one by utilizing the other, so it was a vicious cycle they were trapped in. Instead she put her head down. She worked. She concentrated. She alleviated the stress of knowing each day could be her last if she didn't commit fully to what she was doing with her hands and her mind. She continued her own quest for knowledge, starting to pick up more of the languages spoken by the rotating roster of Bakhit's clients.

With her skills now far beyond what she could ever have imagined when she first examined scraps in the Grand Library, she was able to refine her own reading and writing. She dreamed in the languages she learned, her subconscious sorting the words and the meanings. Advi kept her busy, too, her tahtib practices now shifting to an evenly matched duel and her swordplay started to improve as well.

They had been in Thatta for a few years, the passing of months marked by Bakhit constantly telling her how much longer she had survived compared to his other assistants. Three times longer now, he'd said. Roshan had met the gaze of the housekeeper, unable to stop her eyes traveling down to the limb she had lost while working in this very same role once. She had been lucky. If things went badly for Roshan, well, Bakhit already had help in the home. She'd have to take Advi's recent pleas of running away seriously, the two fleeing the city for a new life they could make entirely their own.

"Whatever we wanted," he murmured once while they trained. "With your brain, I don't think there's anything that could stop us. An oyster, this world..."

Yet they never got the chance.

It was late in the evening when she heard the crash of the vase near her window. She jerked upright in time to watch the flowers smash to the ground. Roshan knew it was Advi climbing through the window immediately, but through the fog of sleep she belatedly realized how peculiar it was for him to sneak into the house when he freely used the front door.

"What are–"

Her words fell away as she caught a better glimpse of his face, streaked with sweat and his panic clear.

"You have to run!" he said, the words gushing out in a desperate puff of air.

"Advi, what–"

"They're coming! The prince knows, he's sending guards here as we speak. I could barely make it ahead of them to warn you."

She was still trying to understand while Advi flew around her room in a blur. He grabbed clothes, notebooks, her fighting sticks, and threw them into a bag.

"To arrest Bakhit," she murmured, understanding now. "To execute the rest of the household."

"Hurry! You need to move, waste no time."

Roshan's adrenaline spiked in response to his fear. She sprang out of bed, donning her most versatile and nondescript robes that could stand up to most conditions and climates. She whipped her hair back into a tight bun at the base of her neck as she grabbed the satchel from him and swung it around her body. Advi took her hand, pulling her to the window. She paused, yanking back, and he threw her an annoyed glance.

"The others," she said. "I have to warn them."

"No you don't!" he snapped, grabbing her hand. "There's no time!

Roshan shook her head stubbornly. She thought of the

housekeeper, her expression grave every time she watched Roshan walk into that workshop. She feared for her, just like she had probably feared for herself and all the others. She didn't deserve this. Even at the thought of Bakhit she felt a pang, which was conflicting to say the least.

"I'll meet you out the back," she said, pulling her hand free. "I'll wake them and be gone, it will only take moments."

He looked like he wanted to argue, but there was no time. "Hurry."

He climbed back out the window. Roshan spun and raced through the house, banging on bedroom doors. She heard Bakhit's annoyed grumbles as he woke and she was just about to run into the housekeeper's room when she heard the thud against the front door as it echoed through the whole house.

She didn't linger a moment longer, telling herself she had done all she could as she sprinted through the house. She heard the soldiers burst in just as she flew out into the courtyard, the decorative pavers hard under her shoes as she extended her stride and bolted. Yells came from the bedrooms, Bakhit's voice clear amongst all the others.

Roshan leapt upward, clinging on to the thick branches of the tree that grew up the length of the house's back wall. She had done this a hundred times, at first to challenge herself and then as a means to slip from the house without detection. Her feet and hands moved instinctively and she mounted the top of the wall in less than a few seconds. Throwing one leg over the side, she straddled the edge and spared her first glance back.

Bakhit was on his knees, hands held behind him as he

continued to demand the reason they had barged into his home. It wasn't really his home, a soldier reminded him. It was the prince's and he was a resident of Thatta due to his majesty's good graces – graces that had evidently shifted. She watched the old man's face drop as the housekeeper emerged from her bedroom, wrapping a shawl tightly around her shoulders. Her eyes focused on Roshan's room as soldiers tossed it, coming out empty handed. Roshan felt a sense of defeat spread through her like a toxin. Bakhit was one thing, but this woman… she hadn't been able to save her. She didn't deserve what was coming.

"Pssst."

She looked down to see Advi waiting for her, hands extended to break her fall. She dropped and he caught her, lowering Roshan down to street level. Hand linked in hers, they ran. He led the way, setting the pace as they navigated through Thatta's many back alleys. They were just about to turn down a central street when a figure barreled into Advi. The impact broke their hold on each other and he went flying.

Roshan was still partially hidden from view by the barrier of the alley and her path forward was blocked by the bodies of other soldiers. They sped past in a blur, yet she recognized many of their faces. These were some of the men Advi oversaw, the young soldiers he had trained. The ones he had laughed and joked with as they traveled. The ones he had protected from reprimand when they screwed up, trying to find another way to teach them instead. He was pinned in a heartbeat, their mass holding him down as another soldier screamed at him.

"You warned her! Didn't you, Advi? Tell us where she is!"

She hovered in the shadow of the alley, unseen by their number and hesitating about whether to step forward or not. She was prepared to give herself up if it meant they would spare him. Yet when she inched forward, Advi's gaze connected with hers as he was brought to his knees. His eyes widened and he shook his head in a tiny, incremental gesture that only she saw. A dagger was brought to his throat, exactly like the one he had trained her with.

"We're coming for all his customers and what the old man doesn't know, she will. Tell us!"

Advi's lips sealed into a hard, solid line. He looked up at the man pressing the blade to his skin, eyes defiant as he said without uttering a single word that he would never tell him. He would never tell any of them.

The flash of the dagger was so swift Roshan barely saw it. She slapped a hand over her mouth as blood spurted from Advi's throat. Their gazes connected for the last time, and Roshan bit into her fist to stay quiet, watching Advi's lifeless body slump onto the street beneath him. A few of the soldiers had the grace to hang their heads in regret and she felt anger surge through her. She wanted to attack them, to kill them, to punish each and every one of them with her bare hands.

Yet Advi had always valued her brain and she implored herself to use it now. There were ten of them. One of her. She had her fighting sticks, one dagger, and a lightweight sword strapped to her back. It would not be enough. And she wouldn't waste his sacrifice for stupidity. She pulled away from the scene, backing down the alley reluctantly.

When she finally spun, hot tears streaked down her face as she sprinted along the alley.

All those hours she had spent exploring Thatta and relishing her freedom paid off now. She skirted around the search parties, avoiding the areas where she could hear the heavy footfalls of soldiers and the sound of metallic armor clinking as they searched for her.

Not just me, she thought. *All of his customers.*

Bakhit's gifts might mean that he remained physically unharmed and imprisoned, just like Advi had warned all those months ago. The prince would make an example out of everyone else, though. Not just those in Bakhit's employ, but those who had bought his products in clear defiance of the agreement Bakhit had made.

Her mind sparked an idea and Roshan changed direction, heading toward the busiest part of the city. Near the now closed market and the heart of business, she kept her face hidden beneath a hood as she searched every surface, every inch of brick and wall. The first hint she found was near the entrance for a tavern and she nearly passed it, stepping back and pausing. Her finger gently touched the shape of the maryam flower, its hunched petals drawn on the wall in white chalk.

She discovered the next sign half a block away. Roshan used the flowers as markers to lead her toward hope and away from carnage. She prayed that she would make it to the brothel first, that she would beat the soldiers inevitably looking for Maryam and her transient pleasure house. She hoped that on the list of clients they would come searching for, the madame's name would be last.

Roshan uncovered the first caravan parked near the entrance to an alley, the last flower over a block away. A man who looked like he could kill someone with a single punch sat on a stool at the entrance, keeping guard. Given the relaxed nature of his posture, he hadn't yet heard about what was happening. The second he saw her, his silhouette shifted. She must have looked ragged, sweat and tears dripping from her as she stumbled forward.

"Please," she said, watching his eyes widen. "Get Maryam. Tell her… tell her she must run. *Now.*"

Chapter Eleven

Sinai Peninsula, 824

An hour to rest and recuperate was all they could spare before a rope was passed around among the group. Azadeh muttered something to Onyx, pointing off into the distance and throwing her arm wide twice. The wolf seemed to understand what she meant and when Azadeh caught Roshan staring, she simply whispered, "She'll meet us on the other side."

A far more preferable thought than having to strap the creature to one of their backs and lug her up the ascent, as Roshan suspected the wolf weighed probably more than Francis.

"Let Wei go first," Azadeh said, as Roshan surveyed the mountain in front of them with trepidation. "He seems the most confident. You go in the middle, and I'll anchor us at the rear. If you slip or fall, the weight of both of us will be enough to hold you in place until you get your balance again."

Roshan appreciated the reassurance because she needed it. Geir and Gud exchanged a glance as if they were nervous, too.

"Everyone, try to and stick close together," Dias called, overhearing their conversation. "That way, if anyone gets in trouble, someone won't be far away to help."

They began their ascent and would reach the steepest part of the mountaintop near dawn, meaning they would tackle the most dangerous portions in full daylight instead of foreboding darkness. The only good thing about climbing during the night, however, was it disguised how high up they really were. Roshan didn't feel one way or the other about heights, but she wasn't too enthused about being maimed beyond recognition. The concept of plunging down a crevasse to her death wasn't particularly appealing either, but the only thing worse would be actually surviving. Laying there in great pain, hopeless and waiting for death to come in the form of a wolf or eventual blood loss seemed quite grave to her.

The pain in her hands kept her focused on the immediate task rather than on her fears, however. The skin on her palms blistered against the rope as they continued to climb, each of them tied to each other in groups for safety. Her fingers cramped as she clung to each outcropping, searching for a better grip as she continued up higher. She was freezing as she pressed herself against rock so cold it felt like ice, but Roshan was desperate to try to keep herself as close to the mountain as possible, so she wasn't swept off the side in one of the powerful gusts of wind that rushed by every few minutes.

Sunrise broke over the horizon just as they neared the top, the light bloodthirsty as it cast a piercing red glow over their party. Roshan was at the front of the group, tied to Azadeh and Wei. Nafanua, Dias, and Francis were linked in another trio, with Geir and Gud making up their own duo. The three clusters moved slowly but steadily at a good pace. Initially, she'd been worried about Wei, but the old man was much more capable than she gave him credit for. He was lean but also speedy and strong as he moved from ledge to ledge.

"In my village, we used to lower each other over the edge of the cliffs to collect ibisbill eggs," he told her, inching up to a spot higher with seemingly little effort. "It was dangerous work, but it was delicious."

She let out what should have been a laugh but was closer to a nervous puff. She was struggling herself, conscious of the fact she was the weakest link compared to her two companions.

Francis wasn't much better, given he had shorter limbs than everyone else, so his reach was limited as he fought to find safe footfalls and grab positions. Thankfully, he was tied to two of the strongest in their group, with Nafanua and Dias trying not to drag him along. Geir and Gud were fast approaching Roshan's higher up position and mercifully, they all made it to the summit intact. Everyone took a moment to collect their breath before beginning the descent, which was just as perilous. Steeper in some parts, with a massive drop leading to deadly slabs of rock, indicating there would be no surviving if one of them fell.

The rock surfaces were slick, the morning dew making them slippery and adding an extra degree of difficulty. The rock, too, seemed even colder somehow despite the sunrise, and Roshan shook her hands as she felt her fingers cramp painfully. Her pause held up the line, and a small shower of pebbles rained down on her as Azadeh looked down to see why she had stopped.

"Are you okay?" she called.

"Fine," Roshan shouted in response. "Just give me a moment."

"Blow on them," Wei added from below.

"What?" she questioned.

"The warm air from your mouth will loosen the joints."

She did so, surprised at the immediate difference she felt. She gave the old man a pleased look and he smiled up at her, his own hands moving to a lower position as he continued their descent. Her victory was short-lived, however, as with the next reach Roshan felt her foot slipping mere seconds before she fell. She let out a panicked yelp, her hands scrambling to get a more secure hold as she slid several feet down the mountain face. The plunge took Azadeh with her. Roshan heard Azadeh cry out, too, as they almost landed entirely on Wei's head.

"Hang on!" Nafanua called, but Geir and Gud were closest. It was a disconcerting sight, the two mountainous men skittering sideways across an actual mountain as they rushed toward them. Their trio was bunched together, Gud bending down to remove Wei from their path and Geir lifting Roshan ever so slightly to the side where she'd have better options to grip.

"Thank you," she said, breathless. Had she misjudged them? Geir grunted in response, beginning to move away and up toward Azadeh. His brother went to do the same, but as he did so his foot flung a series of rocks downward. Roshan only heard the crack they made against the cliff surface. It wasn't until she heard Wei scream that she spun back just in time to see one the size of her fist hit Wei in the side of the head.

His neck snapped forward and she could tell the impact was significant even before blood gushed from a wound at his temple. He lost consciousness momentarily, his eyes fluttering shut as he slid downward. Even fading from the injury, he had the presence of mind to push himself hard against the rock so that he didn't free fall.

"Wei!" she screamed, horrified, as he slid down farther than he should have. He'd come loose, breaking free of the rope and the safety that the three of them had by being tied together. Her cry must have startled him back to consciousness and his eyes snapped open at the last moment, his hands immediately clawing to grip something – anything – in front of him. She saw him straining as he tried to hang on. She could also see his eyelids fluttering, Wei blinking to keep the blood out of his eyes from the wound on his head as well as to keep conscious.

Roshan began dropping down as quickly as she could, desperate to get to him but also not able to move as fast because she and Azadeh were still looped together. She felt the tug of the rope pulling against her and she grunted with frustration. Her gaze focused on the figure of the woman above, urging her to hurry as she looked at the struggling old man.

"Hang on Wei," she told him. "Hang on, I'm almost there."

He nodded, the gesture calm but his face contorted in pain. She felt the line slacken

a fraction and she hustled down and across, almost able to reach him.

"Just a little farther," Roshan pleaded, not sure who she was speaking to. Wei's lip trembled as he bit down, his hands shaking with the strength required to stay still. She couldn't stop looking at his fingernails as she reached out, extending her arm as her fingertips brushed against his skin.

The quick around his nails was bleeding and he let out a gasp of pain as one of his nails snapped right off. His hand pawed at the rock, and Roshan threw herself out even farther, hearing Azadeh yell above her. It was useless. The blood on Wei's hands slicked the stone and Wei fell backward and away from the mountain. He seemed frozen in position at first, eyes locked on hers as he plummeted away from them.

"No!" Roshan screamed, her hand still reaching out for him as he became a small speck. The old man never once cried out or screamed as he fell to his death. She closed her eyes at the impact, unable to watch, but the sound underlined the fatality. There was a scuffling sound next to her and she felt pressure against her shoulder, the comforting presence of another person.

"We have to keep moving," Azadeh said, her voice trembling.

Roshan didn't reply. She just hung on exactly where she was.

"We can't stay here, come on. The sooner we get down, the sooner we can see him."

That's what did it. Roshan opened her eyes to see Azadeh's face firm and determined.

"All right?" she prompted.

"All right," Roshan replied.

Her hand movement mirrored Azadeh's and that was how she continued to descend, her mind blank and her stomach gutted as she copied exactly what the other woman did. She couldn't stop seeing him, Wei's body perfectly still as he disappeared off the side of the mountain, the threads of broken rope flailing behind him. Those tendrils told her something and by the time she made it to the steep, sloping ground where they could walk rather than climb, she was quite certain she knew what that deep dread inside her was.

Francis was hysterical, sobbing and pawing at his face. Nafanua's expression was grim, Roshan knowing how the woman felt because she had the same emotions swirling through her. She had tried to protect the old man and she had failed. They both had.

"How far was that?" Francis wheezed. "Did he fall fifty feet? In the name of the Lord…"

"It was a hard climb," Dias said, hand slapping Francis on the shoulder as he tried to comfort him. "It was a hard climb for everyone, but he was very old, right?"

He turned to the twins to back him up. They remained voiceless and expressionless. Eventually, Gud shrugged. "He was weak," he grunted. "Only the strong can survive."

"In the name of the Father–"

"Look, there's the harbor!" Dias exclaimed. "Let's stay focused on the mission and keep moving. I can steal us a boat and we'll be setting sail in no time."

Roshan stomped off in the opposite direction.

"Hey!" Dias called. "Where are you going, girl?"

"She's going to find the body," Azadeh snapped.

"We don't have time for that," Geir mumbled.

"Not as a group, no," she replied. "But you all go on, gather what we need and find the boat. I'll grab her and catch up, okay? Give her a moment."

Hearing someone else placate the others annoyed her deeply and she increased her pace, angrily marching in the direction where she thought Wei's corpse might be. They'd had to leave the horses on the other side of the mountain, stripping them of what they needed and setting them free, but she could have done with a mare now. The foot of the mountain was thick with fog, making it difficult to see far ahead.

"Wait," Azadeh called, her footsteps pounding after her.

Roshan ignored her, stumbling on the uneven surface of the damp, black rocks as she fought her way forward.

"Isun, I'm trying to follow you – wait! Please."

The footfalls increased as Azadeh jogged to catch up with her, and then Roshan was spun around as Azadeh grabbed her shoulder.

"Hey–"

"It wasn't his age!" she yelled.

Azadeh took a step back at her sudden outburst. "What?"

"It wasn't his age, what they said back there. They killed him!"

Azadeh's gaze softened, her tone sympathetic. "Isun, he was *very* old. And he was losing a lot of blood from his head wound. You not getting there in time isn't a failing on your part. You tried, harder than anyone. Dias was right about something: that was a tough climb. We nearly fell ourselves. It's a miracle we lost just Wei."

"Just Wei," she echoed, shaking her head with frustration. Roshan pulled away, continuing her march forward.

"Let's just find his body, you do what you need to do, and then we have to catch up to the others," Azadeh said. "If we don't they'll leave us behind and the freedom you bargained for will be all be for nothing."

"He could climb," she argued. "He used to cliff climb in his village. He knew what he was doing. You saw him. He was faster and better at it than any of us."

"Is that what he said?" Azadeh questioned, falling in step beside her. "You're the only one who spoke his language. No one else knew what he was saying."

"Exactly. They killed him and made it look like an accident, not knowing that he wouldn't accidentally fall to his death because of his past. I was the only one to hear that, so when they call him *weak* and *old,* they're just underlining their guilt."

She fell silent, not because she was done explaining her fury, but because a dark could be seen through the fog. Roshan came to an abrupt halt, pausing as the mangled frame came into view. Onyx was already there, waiting patiently next to Wei's body like she knew they would come. The wolf looked the way Roshan felt, exhausted and panting. Clearly even the wolf's route had been arduous. The sight was horrific. Not much of the man she'd briefly known remained recognizable amongst the tangle of blood and broken bones.

Roshan dropped down to her knees, reaching out a shaking hand to pull the rope that was still wrapped around his waist loose. Roshan examined the frayed ends, comparing it to the length that had been tied to her. Holding the two pieces in her hands, she analyzed what she saw and closed her eyes, thinking about the events as they had unfolded.

"I thought they were so eager to help us," she whispered, blinking everything back into focus.

"Who?" Azadeh asked.

"Geir and Gud. Two men who have shown nothing but contempt for everyone else in this party, who suddenly flew across the rock when we fell."

"They know we stand a better chance against the Martyrs the more of us there are, so–"

"Do we?" Roshan questioned. "You said they fight for money, right? Whoever has the funds to hire them acquires their services. Maybe that fee is dependent on who's left to split it with."

"Fine," Azadeh huffed. "Say you're right. Why take out Wei? You and I are much more of a threat and were in a more perilous position. Why not sabotage us?"

"Maybe they tried," she offered. "Maybe that was part of the plan. While they were making it look like they were helping us, they severed his rope. Gud pretended to slip, Wei was hit by the rocks and fell to his death. If we hadn't gone after him to help, everyone would have been distracted by his struggle and not been paying much attention as Geir yanked one of us free."

Or maybe the others would have seen, shrugged and carried

on, she thought. After all, that would be three fewer obstacles standing in the way of whatever they had been promised in exchange for their service.

"I think," Azadeh said, her voice careful, "that you saw what I saw back during the battle: Dias using Mared to block a stream of arrows destined for him. You saw that blatant disregard for the life of someone else on this team and that feeling has turned what was an unfortunate accident into a secret murder plot."

Roshan looked up at her from the crouched position on the ground. It seemed crystal clear to her, so how could Azadeh not see what she saw? Her problem was that she quite liked the unusual woman and her wolf, which perhaps blinded her to the truth. Maybe she did believe Roshan. What if she had seen and understood everything that happened because she had been a part of it? Just because she seemed diametrically opposed to the twins, that didn't mean she was. Roshan had thought of Francis and Wei as in conflict, yet the young man had been shocked and horrified by the elder's death.

"I'm sorry." Azadeh shrugged. "I just don't see it. And we need to get to the harbor before they leave us behind."

Roshan looked away from her and stood up to indicate that they were indeed about to move. *I'm not paranoid,* she thought to herself. *I just might not be paranoid enough.* Azadeh turned to head to the water, Onyx whining just slightly before loping off after her master. Roshan lingered, sorry for the old man she had barely known but whose loss she felt immensely. She wished she had been able to do better by him, yet the twins had been right about one thing.

Life was cruel particularly to the weak, the kind, the sweet, the compassionate, the good. It shouldn't be that way and she would do anything to have the power in her hands to change that.

Instead, all she could do was reach down to the dead. She liberated the sack that had contained his gunpowder only to find it empty. He'd used it all. She frowned as she felt another weight within, reaching inside to retrieve what looked like a small, jade trinket. There was something carved there that she couldn't read because of the blood. She wiped it clean, recognizing an intricately carved rendering of a peony, and pocketed it for later. Duling, Wei had said. Roshan would find a way to get it back to his village and the people who cared about him. She jogged away from his corpse, her mind and her body so exhausted she felt like she begged her limbs to move. The exercise did little to dissipate her anger, but did plenty to allow her to compose herself.

She'd been a fool to think of Azadeh as a friend: she was little more than a colleague of convenience at best. At worst, she was someone who was actively working to pick off each of the companions on the team one by one. Either way, she couldn't be trusted. Roshan mentally kicked herself for being so forthright, for sharing her theory with her in a moment when her emotions were at their highest. If Azadeh was involved, her guard would be up. And if she wasn't working alone, she would want to communicate to her associates as soon as possible that Roshan was suspicious.

There was barely a town at the foot of the mountain. A cluster of buildings and a few weatherworn sheds greeted her as she slowed to a steady walk. Azadeh's back and Onyx's wagging tail were up ahead as they all marched down a wooden jetty. At the end of it, Dias was on board the stolen but swift looking dhow. It wasn't exactly the one Roshan would have picked, the dhow being less likely to stand up to bad weather if they got unlucky and a tad cramped for all of them on board. Yet they needed to cover the maximum amount of distance in the minimum amount of time and make land ahead of the Martyrs. This was a trading vessel with a long, thin hull designed for transport and speed.

It would do the job, yet she felt an uncomfortable prickle under her skin. The hairs at the back of her neck stood up and she rubbed a hand along her nape, trying to calm herself. She'd been on boats since Baghdad, obviously, small vessels designed to transport a handful of people. This was by far the biggest and therefore the closest to the one she had been imprisoned on. Even just the taste of salt on her tongue started to invoke horrible recollections of the Harbor Master and she swallowed the bile building in her throat. *That is not a weakness,* she told herself. *That time on board is a strength now, it gives you the advantage.*

She watched Geir and Gud shake their heads, muttering about there being no supplies. The fact they were alone on that jetty also spoke volumes to her. Any fisherman worth his salt would have either been just returning to shore or just leaving. The emptiness said this town was dying as fast as its industry.

"That's fine," Nafanua remarked, hands crossed over her chest. "The moana will provide us everything we need."

"What does that mean?" Francis squeaked, his face still looking pallid.

"Fish for dinner," the woman remarked, leaping onto the boat. "Fish for breakfast. Fish for lunch."

"I hate seafood..." he mumbled, looking sad and pathetic. He also looked weak. She considered that Wei – although not posing an immediate threat to the twins – had been selected to go first because he was easy to kill. Why struggle with a harder target when there's a more accessible one right there? Going by that logic, Francis would be next on the mysterious murderer's list.

"Here," Azadeh said, reaching out a hand for Roshan to take as she climbed on board. She ignored the gesture, using her own battered and bruised hands to grip the side and hurl herself up. Hurt crossed Azadeh's features, but she quickly tried to hide it as if she didn't want Roshan to see that she had been offended. The message had been received, however, and as they set sail, Onyx and Azadeh stayed as far away from her as possible.

How nice, Roshan thought sarcastically. *Giving me space.* Her advantage was that Roshan had experience on the water, not just as someone who had been imprisoned in a boat, but as someone who had that prison move with the tides and the currents. If the Harbor Master ever had to journey outside of Bagdad's harbor, three of the wives would be selected to travel with him and she had often been an unlucky recipient of his "kindness." Talâyi had theorized that it was Roshan's rebellious streak, but Roshan had always thought it more likely that he was just waiting for the right moment to throw her overboard. None of the other people knew that about her and she would keep it that way. Let them think she was green at sea.

Let them think her guard was lowered. Dias was clearly the most comfortable as he scurried from one end of the dhow to the other. He adjusted the settee sails so they would catch the perfect angle of the wind, which was mild right now but would become stronger as soon as they cleared the protection of the mountain ranges wrapping around the coast. She could already see the effects of the wind in the bend of the trees up ahead, their leaves shaking and their trunks bent.

It was going to be a rough ride, but that was all right if it came at the cost of being a fast one. She was not relaxed on this boat. She was not calm among these people. She didn't like the idea of so much space being between her and land when every other occupant of the boat could be an enemy. There was no honor among thieves and these people were worse than that. Out of the corner of her eye she kept track of Francis. It wasn't hard as his hair was so blond it was almost white, so he stood out.

Part of her should have felt guilty about keeping him in the dark about her assumptions. Then again, if her theory was correct, he'd be the next to go. All she had to do was watch and wait. It was frustrating. She needed to be more concerned with their next confrontation with the Martyrs… especially given how poorly their first skirmish had gone. She had been unsettled by what she'd seen of them in battle, thinking that the Martyrs' unnatural durability was the biggest threat of this quest. Instead, she remained focused on the greater danger lurking amongst them on this boat.

No sooner had she thought that than there was a horrible scream…

Chapter Twelve

The Silk Road, 822

The brothel madame had never heard of an idle threat in her life and when Maryam extracted the whole story from Roshan as quickly as Roshan could tell it, they fled Thatta that night. Men were kicked out of the caravans mid coitus, her girls bundled up and springing into action like they had done this dozens of times before. They probably had, Roshan realized.

Roshan traded the warning for safe transport, joining Maryam's entourage and climbing into the smallest carriage at the front that belonged to the madame. The older woman barked orders at the four burly men who worked for her.

"They're my lovers," Maryam said, watching Roshan's interest in them and misinterpreting it.

"Can they fight?" she asked in response. "Because the prince doesn't have soldiers that look like them, but he does have more than four."

Sympathy softened Maryam's face. She reached out, taking Roshan's hand and squeezing it. It was such a small, gentle gesture but it affected Roshan immensely. She wanted to sob, to scream, to wail. But she had done that in the past once, and all it brought her was more pain. Instead, tears streaked from the corners of her eyes, and she pulled her hand away, angrily wiping them off her face.

"You don't need to do that with me," Maryam said, voice gentle. "We don't let men see us cry. They interpret it as a sign of weakness and not one of strength."

The older lady leaned forward, using the sleeve of her beautiful silk dress to wipe at the wetness on Roshan's face like a caring mother.

"Yet amongst us, we let it out. We women are a safe space, do you understand? Oftentimes the *only* safe space."

She sniffed, nodding slightly. They were silent for a long while, Roshan exhausted but unable to sleep as she sat next to Maryam and the caravan traveled farther and farther from the city. The rocking back and forth of the carriage was strangely comforting as she peered out of the slatted windows, the structure not much different from the caravan Bakhit had used once. This was bigger and better designed, with expensive flourishes like shelving and sections that folded out into beds with the simple pull of a handle.

She watched as Maryam made up her own, the madame encouraging her to doze while she could. Roshan shook her head, not wanting to close her eyes and be greeted with the last image she had of Advi. The older women slept, the men drove the camels on, swapping out to rest when they were relieved by the women. Roshan studied them, some younger than her, but many older, ranging in every height and size and physical type you could imagine.

"It's important to have variety."

She was startled at the sound of Maryam's voice, turning to find the woman awake but still laying comfortable in her cot-like bed.

"Everyone has a preference, so you want to make sure you cater to that," she continued. "While also finding women who have that something… extra."

Roshan both did and didn't know what she meant, curious as she watched a plump woman with rosy cheeks expertly ride a camel down the length of their traveling procession. The woman was confident on that huge, smelly beast when many other riders – even experienced ones – would have been nervous handling a creature so massive. There was a freedom in the way she laughed, shouting out to a woman she called her sister.

"You have that something extra," Maryam said.

Roshan was firm but respectful. "I could not do this job."

Maryam tilted her head. "Why not? You'd have money, freedom, sisterhood, power."

"Power?"

"Is it not a powerful thing to be desired?"

"In my experience such a trait has proved dangerous," Roshan said, earning a knowing chuckle from her companion.

"What do you plan to do then, hmm? If Bakhit's not dead, he's imprisoned and not able to help you."

"I don't need his help," she mumbled.

"What do you need?" Maryam asked.

Roshan had some money, she had a few weapons, she had her notebooks, and – mercifully – she had her life. "Where are we going?" she wondered.

Maryam smiled, her gaze sharp. "China. We'll put as much distance between us and Thatta as possible. We can work our way along the route there, but as soon as we cross the Indian border the prince won't pursue us further."

"Is he in pursuit of us now?"

"Not that I'm aware of. Thanks to you, his soldiers are probably still looking for us in the city."

Roshan considered the path in front of her. For all intents and purposes, she had what she had always wanted: freedom. Not the idea of it or the future prospect of it: actual, real, tangible freedom in her midst. She had fallen into it, yet something about it didn't feel liberating at all. She had freedom without direction.

"I need a purpose," she said, finally. "To answer your earlier question."

Maryam looked at her thoughtfully, pondering her answer. "I don't know if I can give you that, but I can give you a purpose here."

"I told you, I can't do that job–"

"Not with the men, good heavens, girl. You have the personality of an ox. You'd scare off customers. We need to seduce them, not reduce them."

Roshan blinked at the harsh but fair assessment.

"You can count, yes? You're good with numbers and words?" Maryam pushed.

"I am," she replied, not ashamed to admit it.

"Good. That I can use. My books are a mess. I have

been doing it myself for the past few years but a proper bookkeeper… that would be invaluable. In exchange I can offer you board and meals. Here, with us. And a fee, of course, but I can't promise it will be much: our earnings are variable depending on… the climate."

The scenario Maryam described was close to ideal. If Roshan stayed with the madame, it meant she could put even more distance between herself and Thatta, Baghdad, and all the places she needed to avoid for a while. And within the brothel, she wouldn't stand out in the same way a woman traveling alone would. She'd be disguised amongst their number but not actually have to trade in flesh.

"Bakhit used to complain about the *click clack clacking* he'd hear with you and that tall soldier, what's his name?"

"Advi," Roshan replied, the mere sound causing a lump in her throat. "His name was Advi."

Maryam paused, considering what was displayed on Roshan's face. Roshan thought that the hollowness in her eyes and the gray pallor of her face might make sense to the other woman.

"I'm sorry," the older woman said quietly.

Roshan couldn't even say anything, just bit her lip instead lest she start crying again. Her friend was dead. Mourning for him was painful and wouldn't change that one bit.

"I'm sorry," Maryam repeated, firmer now. "If what Bakhit said was true about your training, and if those callouses on your hands are anything to go by, we can always use someone with your physical prowess, too."

"I can fight," Roshan confirmed.

"Well?"

"Well."

"Excellent. Every woman who works for me can defend themselves because they've had to. Even then, even with my lovers and our combined cunning, another fighter will not go astray when we need it. The roads between cities can be rough even when you take the safest route."

And that was how it came to be: Roshan, the new bookkeeper and off-and-on bodyguard for Maryam's mobile brothel. This new life she had stumbled into didn't have all the creature comforts of her past one, like her own bedroom. She was assigned a space which jostled with the impact of the rough terrain in what was partially a lounging area where the girls would entertain customers and engage them in idle chatter before they slinked off to engage them in other things at the rear of the caravan.

There were five separate structures to their procession, including riding quarters at the front and guard quarters at the rear. Each one had a purpose, like living areas and sleeping compartments for the women. Then there were the two business caravans dedicated solely to pleasures of the flesh, with the fourth caravan split between the kitchen and the lounging area. Maryam and her lovers had the fifth space all to themselves, which was her right as the woman who had earned it.

The biggest perk of the job was the reduced likelihood of Roshan's death arriving as a result of a fatal explosion. Not that there weren't plenty of other dangers, however, but Roshan was amused that she was in less danger than ever before. Maryam hadn't undersold the threats that came with this way of life, however. Bandits, raiders and rapists populated every travel route but were especially an issue when you were transporting a fleet of beautiful women and their income.

Roshan's first fight arrived when the caravan descended a tricky hillside. The uneasy grunts of the camels alerted her to the presence of others. She was riding up front with Maryam's lovers, enjoying the fresh air and change of scenery when they were suddenly attacked.

Fighting stick in hand, she leapt from the caravan with careless abandon as she slashed and swept her way through half a dozen men before they retreated. Maryam's lovers had done away with a handful of their own, but when the story was told over breakfast that day it was Roshan's ferocity that sent the bandits running.

She wasn't sure that was true and thought it more than likely the ruffians ran as soon as they realized they had bitten off more than they could chew. Yet she didn't deny that the sight of several unconscious bodies on the road behind them was comforting.

Lately, she had no solace in sleep, often waking from nightmares where the Harbor Master's face hovered over her. His sick, smelly breath clogged her nostrils, the scent so viscerally disgusting it immediately pulled her back to *that* place and *that* night. As she reached for the dagger she had hidden under her pillow and plunged it into his neck, the face shifted.

It became Advi's, spluttering and gasping as he bled out on top of her. She would panic, trying to stem the blood flow with her hands but the blood wouldn't stop, only becoming worse and worse until she began to drown in it.

Roshan would wake up screaming on a nightly basis. She slept in the bunks with the other women, who she thought would hate her for the disruption. Instead, they were kind. They were compassionate. They would coax her back to sleep, reminding her of where she was and that whatever she thought was happening wasn't true.

The way the women worked together, the way they cared for each other despite everything, reminded her so much of the other wives on the boat. The wives probably would have looked down on Roshan's new companions, but in reality, these women had more opportunities than the wives ever had.

They had meals every day, the quality shifting depending on the cook and their specialty. They had their own money which they could spend as they liked. They were seeing the world, the sights shifting from small towns to bustling seaside cities. They had adventure, but mostly importantly, they had love. Some in the romantic way, all in the physical sense, yet also the kind of enduring love amongst them all as they lived and worked together as a unit.

A sisterhood. That's what Maryam had called it. Roshan had never seen a more accurate representation of the idea. After a month on the road, her nightly terrors started occurring less frequently, soon dropping to the odd occasion. She needed the rest as sorting Maryam's books required all of her mental energy.

Roshan had been given a small office space between where meals and drinks were prepared and the entertaining lounge. It was a tiny area with just enough room for her and perhaps one other person to fit on a bench seat that was stacked with cushions for maximum comfort as she spent her hours there.

On one side, she had an open window which kept a steady supply of fresh air flowing through the tiny space as she worked. It gave her a visual distraction when she needed to pull her eyes away from the numbers and rest her mind for a moment. Maryam was cunning, street smart, and surprisingly compassionate. A multifaceted human and savvy businesswoman? Absolutely. Yet she was objectively terrible when it came to records documenting the business.

According to the papers, she had been running the mobile brothel for twelve years, deciding to strike out on her own after watching the limited options for her peers once they aged out of the work. Maryam was careful with her funds, tucking her money away and slowly building meaningful connections with clients who could help her acquire what she needed to make her idea a reality. Those wealthy benefactors had made up the difference between what she had and what she didn't financially, which became especially helpful when she became her own boss.

Maryam had paid them all back, she insisted, all except for one, who she kept involved as a silent partner for the political passage he granted her. His finger in the pie guaranteed a certain level of protection for Maryam and a consistent investment that regularly paid out for him. Roshan learned all of this from the books. This mystery man was listed simply as Xex – a pseudonym – and his personal records were kept by Maryam herself.

That first month, Roshan had blanched when the first overflowing box of scrolls was dumped on her desk, the information organized in no particular order and prioritized at random. She began picking her way through the information and had started at the beginning, flattening each scroll and sorting them into a chronology that made sense. Then she began transferring the information to notebooks, drawing up columns and adding annotations so the entire history of Maryam's business could be tracked with the simple flick of a page. She had sections for incoming transactions and outgoing payments – not just to those whose loans Maryam had been paying off but vendors like Bakhit had been as well.

It had taken months and as much as it was frustrating, it was also satisfying work. Soon she could see the progress emerging in front of her, with the scrolls reorganized and sorted for storage. All of the legible information was now accessible in a series of notepads Roshan stacked in shelving built into her workspace. She had quills of every variety one could want, along with pencils, wax seals, stamps, and an array of supplies that she looked on as a different kind of weapon but just as vital and dangerous.

Her workspace was separated from the main part by a curtain, which kept her shielded from the eyes of customers, but still meant she heard everything. She preferred it that way, as Roshan was sometimes unable to work in silence. The hustle and bustle of the business was a soothing background noise, yet it also did a lot to help improve her ear. The breadth of languages she learned had increased exponentially since she joined the women, in part because many of them could speak three to four different dialects each and had a passing grasp of another dozen to satisfy various customers.

"You need to soften your tongue," one of the women had instructed Roshan as she practiced her Russian. "You're speaking too much with the front of your throat."

She demonstrated the sound, Roshan nodding as she tried again and mimicked the sound. It wasn't exact, but it was significantly better. That was the thing about this kind of learning: she had always been better at writing and reading the different languages than speaking them. Yet that was purely because she didn't get enough practice. She thought about all the times she had heard the Harbor Master degrading such women as little more than "mindless and worthless," exploiting men to pay for nights that were their birthright. But that oaf could barely read or write! He could barely speak his own language succinctly, whereas these same women he'd loathed could navigate whole nations with their tongues.

When she arrived in those cities she had only read about or heard of in hushed whispers, she could move through them with confidence. If business was booming, their operation was nocturnal, and everyone slept during the day. Roshan, however, would wake early, getting started on cataloging the funds that had come in from the night before, checking and rechecking what needed to be put aside for overheads and then determining what was profit. That took a few hours and once it was done she had time to explore before returning in the early hours of the morning just before sunrise.

She walked the streets of Chang'an that had been organized like a grid, every turn and corner making logical sense. She listened as gongs were beaten three hundred times each morning heralding the start of business for the east marketplaces. She'd join the crush of hundreds, sometimes thousands of customers, bodies pressed against each other as she'd watch street dealers conduct complex schemes with shell and cup games designed to empty pockets. Roshan marveled at the market magicians, gasping and clapping in delight with other spectators as they created fire in the air with little more than powder hidden up their sleeves. She was desperate to understand how it worked, while also not wanting to ruin the illusion for herself.

She spent hours at the Giant Wild Goose Pagoda, her neck stretched upward as she gawked at the towering feat of engineering. When winter arrived, level after level was dusted by a light snowfall, making the place of worship look like one of the cakes displayed in the bakery windows nearby. Roshan watched as lines of monks dressed in bright orange robes and handwoven sandals shuffled to their destination. With kind smiles on their faces and gentle nods as they passed, she wondered about the differences between their lives and hers.

She wandered through the remnants of An Lushan's garden when it opened to the public, wrapped in a fur-lined coat with gloves protecting her extremities from the cold. She examined the plants that seemed trapped in time as ice and snow preserved them in stasis, the city's many canals freezing alongside them. Roshan visited the location of a famous assassination that had occurred just a few years earlier, a chancellor named Wu Yuanheng who was slain by assassins while leaving his home, the killers eventually fleeing with his head. It had been gruesome and bloody, yet she couldn't deny the morbid curiosity she'd felt while learning about the event. She frequented a Persian bazaar in the west marketplace, comforted by the smells and sounds of home, if only for a brief moment.

Maryam and the women joined her for an evening, watching as the stars gained company in the form of thousands of homemade lanterns that were illuminated and set free to float high up into the sky for a festival. She smiled as children played a game with a rolling ball in a mountain village, the women cheering for the opposing sides and Roshan being surprised by the sound of her own laughter.

She danced, Maryam doing her best to teach her the rhythms of her people when they returned to her homeland, a song strummed on the oud, a ney accompanying the tune and percussion kept with the beating of the darbouka.

She watched tahtib performed in the city of its birth, her heart panging at the thought of Advi and what he would think if he could see her now. Yet he couldn't. He was dead, his own life sacrificed for hers. The best she could do was make the most of the gift he had given her.

Roshan passed through parts of the world she had only read about in stories. She walked through cities that she had only ever seen recreated through art. She relished the possibilities that had become her reality.

Chapter Thirteen

Red Sea, 824

Roshan sprang to her feet, racing after the sound of the scream down the starboard side of the boat. Azadeh was shouting, asking after everyone, but Roshan ignored her. She heard the sound of a splash and as her eyes searched the faces of those on deck, looking for who was missing, something hard slammed into her. She grunted in pain and was whacked overboard, briefly seeing what she assumed to be the swinging boom that must have smacked her from behind. Roshan hit the water hard, the sea choppy enough that it marginally softened her fall.

Her lips parted in surprise, and she inhaled a mouthful of seawater, immediately spitting it out as she fought to get to the surface. The churn of the current and the chop of the boat spun her around and pulled her under, Roshan kicking her legs furiously as she tried to get her bearings. She was a good swimmer – she had hours trapped on the Harbor

Master's boat to thank for that – so she wasn't afraid of drowning. Yet the sword that was strapped to her back, the fabric on her body, even the weight of her shoes all added to the force pulling her down and making it even more difficult for Roshan to reach the surface and save herself.

Suddenly, there was a tug at her shoulder. She almost fought against it, thinking it was the mysterious someone who had aided her unexpected plunge into the water in the first place. Yet the determined force yanked Roshan upward. She broke the surface with a gasp, coughing and spluttering seawater as she tried to fill her lungs with fresh air instead. She needed to breathe before she could fight off whoever had her.

"Stop that," came an annoyed voice, a hand batting hers away.

Roshan was still so shocked by her rapid redeployment from the boat to the sea that she didn't quite comprehend who spoke at first. It wasn't until she looked up, her eyes tracking the tattoo markings that spanned the arm holding her up to the surface, that she realized it was Nafanua. The woman had one arm hooked through the loops of a fishing net trailing behind the boat, half of her body submerged as she stayed limp. Water shredded around her in small waves, and her other hand held on to one of the straps looped across Roshan's chest.

She made such acts look like they required no effort whatsoever; her muscles flexed as the seawater dripped off them. Yet Roshan knew that even though she was small in comparison, she was still heavy, especially when soaking wet. Spluttering, she copied what the other woman had done, reaching out and grabbing on to the net as they both climbed up into a better position. They floated behind the boat, the few inches gained to reach the net a real effort as Roshan fought against the force of the water moving against them.

The others hadn't seen them yet, since part of the net was obscured by the dhow's lone sail. She watched as the long, wooden length of the boom remained steady, only moving when Azadeh pushed it out of the way to get to the stern. She leaned over the railing, her eyes searching the water desperately as she shouted and pointed. *Is she that good an actress?* Roshan wondered. She didn't think so, her eyes shifting to the others.

Dias was doing a good job of theatrically looking panicked, whereas the twins shuffled about doing what he instructed and grabbing ropes from wherever he pointed. She could barely make out the top of Francis's head, only spotting him when his white hair caught the light. Roshan's eyes flicked back to the boom, its positioning and its girth. She was sure that's what had sent her flying, yet it didn't move on its own. It had to be shoved. It required weight behind it, but the movement could be disguised as a simple repositioning of the sails.

"Do you know how hard it is to drown me?" Nafanua snarled. "My ancestors were the original wayfinders. We navigated the world using merely the stars."

Roshan turned her head to the side, resting on her wet arm as she looked at the woman. She didn't think there was anything "mere" about the stars, yet she knew that was the last thing to mention as she observed the dark clouds that settled over Nafanua's expression. She looked like she was ready to deal death, her jaw clenched tight and her eyes narrowed as she stared up ahead at the people on board.

"You cannot drown *me*," she growled, as if the very thought was ridiculous and offensive. Roshan was angry, too, but the primary feeling in that moment was exhaustion.

"Who sent you overboard?" she asked.

Nafanua shook her head, the fury almost seeping out of her pores. "I didn't see."

She turned her head, her sharp stare piercing Roshan's as her eyes asked the same question.

"Me neither."

"There is a traitor on that boat," Nafanua muttered.

"We're all traitors. Isn't that why we're here?"

The woman beside her looked flabbergasted for a moment. "No. Some of us are here for honor."

Roshan's myriad of questions had to be put to one side at the sound of Azadeh's yell as she spotted them tangled amongst the net. Onyx began to bark.

"There! Hang on!" Azadeh called. "We'll send rope out."

Roshan watched the flurry of movement as the young woman began coming up with a way to safely get them both on board, shouting directions and wrangling others as she demanded action. Nafanua and Roshan exchanged a look as the looped end of a rope was thrown out to them. The dilemma was clear: stay here and safely away from whoever had wanted to drown them in the first place. Or get back on board, dry off, and try to be comfortable for the remaining journey, but in the proximity of that threat.

"I don't want to stay wet for another day and night,"

Roshan said quietly. The water was warm, even as they passed through various currents. It wouldn't stay that way, however, as soon as they cleared the coast and entered the Gulf of Aden. The longer they stayed half submerged, the colder they'd get. They'd get even more so when the sun set, not to mention other threats of various sea creatures who might find the prospect of two human-sized meals dangling overboard too enticing to pass up.

"You first then," Nafanua remarked. Roshan nodded, taking a moment to get unwoven from the net and secure Azadeh's flung rope around her waist. As the others pulled her up, she glanced back at the woman left behind. Nafanua looked poised, as if the moment she saw something she didn't like, she'd be gone or remain exactly where she was – out of reach.

Roshan was the experiment. Feeling hands under her armpits as she was hauled back on board, she knew that if the flash of a knife was suddenly visible and against her throat, Nafanua would refuse the rescue rope and release herself from the net altogether. Swimming to safety had better odds than facing those on deck.

"Are you okay?" Azadeh exclaimed. "What happened? Francis said you dove overboard to save Nafanua."

"Heroic," the alleged witness said, his head bobbing up and down solemnly. "A true savior."

Roshan studied his seriousness, his tone, trying to discern whether he actually believed that or had seen something else. If it was the latter, was he trying to cover for someone or just pretending to be a harmless bystander who couldn't reveal the truth?

"Let me help," Roshan said by way of answer, taking the end of the rope and throwing it back. It flitted through the water at first, hanging in the churn and whitewash as Nafanua eyed it like it was a snake revealing its poisonous fangs.

"Take it," Roshan called, hinting that it was all right. It wasn't, but Roshan selfishly wanted Nafanua on board. If she had been thrown overboard first, that meant Nafanua was the one person she could be certain hadn't tried to take her out. That meant she could trust Nafanua. That was more than she could say for anyone else, although she felt like her suspicions about Azadeh had been misplaced now that she watched her behavior.

There was a slight release of tension in her chest once they were both back on deck, Nafanua shoving through the group as she made her way to the front of the boat. Roshan followed in her wake, her side satchel heavy and an annoying reminder that much of what was in there was now lost. Glancing inside, her notebook was soaked, the pages almost see-through as the ink bled, making all her notations useless. The symbols on the case were nothing but smudges now, lost to the ocean like her map. Just like she was meant to be. There was no point even trying to air dry them out so she tossed the satchel and notebook to the side in a wet pile.

The Sāmoan warrior was dressed more lightly than she was, but the few layers she wore were stripped as Nafanua squeezed every last drop of seawater out and hung them to dry.

Roshan left her clothes on, not wanting to expose the secrets of her skin to a boat full of enemies. Besides, the unusual makeup of the garments the hooded stranger had acquired for her came in handy. Her cloak was almost completely dry in moments, along with the trousers and blouse, while her undergarments retained the most water. She stripped off her top layer, using it as a self-made canopy to shade her from the hot rays of the sun. The salt from the ocean dried on her like a prickly crust as the two of them sat there. Neither of them spoke, Roshan watching as Nafanua hung over the side of the dhow for a quick moment before returning with a live fish caught in her bare hands.

She quickly killed it by whacking it against the deck, then used a tiny knife to descale it in front of Roshan's very eyes. She didn't bother to cook it, instead slicing away chunks of edible meat. Nafanua handed a pink morsel to Roshan and she accepted, offering some of her soggy chickpeas in return. They went back and forth like this until the food was gone, washing it down with the last of Roshan's wine. The others left them alone, seemingly understanding when not to poke an angry bear: specifically, so soon after you had tried to drown said bear.

"What did you mean before?" Roshan asked, voice low enough that their conversation stayed just between them. "When you said you were here for honor?"

"Exactly what I said," Nafanua replied.

"You weren't paid?" She wondered if perhaps Nafanua owed a blood debt to the hooded stranger like Wei.

Nafanua shook her head. "My brother Toa and I were both going to come, but he's the chief of my village and needs to stay as war rages between the east and west of Savai'i."

Roshan mused on the response, unsure what that had to

do with honor. She opened her mouth to ask when Nafanua cut her off.

"In my culture, everywhere those symbols appear, great evil follows," she explained, nodding her head to the wet pile of Roshan's ruined notebooks and map. "Whole tribes suddenly in conflict with each other, islands wiped out in eruptions overnight, treacherous whispers spoken by someone adorned with a symbol just like the ones on the case."

"So, when the stranger came to ask for your help, you and your brother were willing to freely give it? No questions asked?"

"What kind of questions could there be?" Nafanua replied, Roshan noting the genuine confusion on her face. "Evil doesn't have a motive. It just is or it isn't. And fighting it? You either do or you don't. Regardless of the outcome, there's an honor in that." Nafanua tapped her chest right above where her heart was to emphasize the point.

Roshan dropped the subject, blind faith never being something she had an abundance of, especially when it came to matters of life and death. She and Nafanua clearly approached this mission very differently and they slipped easily back into a calm silence.

From then on, Roshan didn't offer to help the others in sailing or navigating the boat, even though she could have. She had no generosity of spirit left, only enough energy to remain perfectly still and watch the sun set as they hit the open waters of the Arabian Sea. She dozed for a few hours, Nafanua insisting that she do so and that she would keep watch. It was an uneasy, unsatisfying sleep, full of dreams where Roshan plunged down mountains only to drown in a swirling sea of black, thick water that was closer to oil. It was pungent in her mouth as she swallowed it; her screams turned to gags as she gasped for air once more.

She jolted upright with a start. For a moment, consciousness brought no relief as it seemed an endless black expanse pressed down on her. Then, slowly, she realized the black expanse was the night sky reflected in surface of the ocean. It wasn't until part of that blackness shifted that she understood Onyx was next to her, the wolf awake and alert which was fortunate as Nafanua was sound asleep. *So much for the back-up,* she thought, even though she knew how exhausted the woman must have been.

"I told her to rest," Azadeh said, voice barely more than a whisper. Her presence forced Roshan to straighten up out of alarm, pausing before she clocked the hunched figure sitting near the bow, elbows resting on her knees.

"She should have woken me," she mumbled, rubbing her face as if the physical friction would stir her to alertness quicker. She pulled her fingers away from her skin, feeling the flakiness of the salt there now that it had solidified like sand.

"The saltwater will be good for your cuts," Azadeh told her. "It will help the healing."

"Remind me to thank the person who threw me overboard then," she replied.

There was an uncomfortable moment between them that lasted several minutes, the silence stretching as endlessly as the sea that stood between them and their goal.

"I'm sorry," Azadeh remarked. Fatigue made Roshan

think that she was apologizing for being said person and Roshan took a moment to think how odd such a confession was.

"I'm sorry I didn't believe you about Wei," Azadeh clarified.

"Oh," was all Roshan could say. She didn't want to give Azadeh a free pass that easily.

"I didn't see who did it," she continued. "But Geir and Gud–"

"Does it matter?" she countered. "It was probably more than one person."

Onyx let out a big yawn, the wolf's white teeth like bright flashes in the dark. She eyed the creature nervously, wondering if Onyx was hungry and whether that was another problem she needed to worry about. The wolf eyed her as well, perhaps sizing up whether she was the kind of prey that would make for a satisfying snack. The answer seemed to be no as she bent her head and began chewing at the bone wedged between her paws. The way the wolf threw her head back and forth sparked a memory for Roshan as she watched Onyx attempt to get the best leverage on the snack.

"You know, my youngest sister used to get the fits."

"The fits?" Azadeh asked.

"Mmm," Roshan mused, surprised to be telling this story. "My mother believed that

onyx stone was the best way to treat it. She'd trade with travelers all the time in our village to try to accumulate more. Think she had about five scattered around the house at various points, just in case."

Azadeh looked thoughtful as she cast her a sideways glance. "Did it work in the long-term?"

"I don't know," she admitted. "I never got to see."

There was comfort in the recollection as much as there was sadness. She pushed those thoughts to the side, needing her wits about her as the hours of night melted away into morning and the sea grew rougher. It had been choppy when they left, now it was verging on chaotic as a gray dawn broke. The sound of Francis vomiting mixed with the sloshing of the waves, and Roshan was left with no choice but to help as she wrangled the settee sail to steer them in a precise direction.

By observing the position of the sun, she determined it was just past lunchtime when she first spotted land, the visual of the coastline flirting with Roshan as she squinted. Yet the mirage solidified and soon other boats could be seen dotting the waters as they rode the northeasterly winds at speed. Karachi's silhouette was unlike any other, the spikes of the city and the huge mounds of the many religious monuments building on top of each other as they drew closer. This wasn't her first time here, but she had never seen the metropolis from this angle. She itched to make land.

She hated to admit it, but Dias was an excellent sailor even in the challenging conditions. He steered them in and around the busiest sections of traffic so that they eventually slowed in a section of the harbor that was quieter than the others. It was still bustling – in a city like this, every spot on the docks was precious – but the workers surrounding them were poorer, their clothes worn, and their faces weathered.

They would ask fewer questions about a new boat full of strangers offloading in the city than if they had veered into the more convenient positions next to merchants and foreign traders.

"In the name of the Father and by the power of the Holy Spirit," Frances muttered, dropping to his knees when there was solid ground beneath him. "I worship thee and praise thee, Lord, for the safe passage granted to us."

"Praise me," Dias remarked, strutting past him as he made the sign of the cross. "I'm your god of the sea."

"The god of something," Nafanua muttered quiet enough for Roshan to hear. She smirked, throwing her a look of acknowledgment.

"We need to find an inn," Dias pressed on. "Somewhere we can recuperate for a day, gather what we need, and get a detailed map if we're to track backward. No offense."

He directed that last part at Roshan. Had he already planned for this? Her map would have indeed been useless if it was attached to her would-be corpse as intended.

"I know where to get a new map," Roshan said, earning a surprised look from Azadeh.

"You've been here before?"

Roshan ignored her question. "I can get one, I just need a few hours."

"All right." Dias nodded. "I can look at camels once I get some sleep."

"Horses would be faster," Gud remarked. Having rarely spoken his preferences until now, Roshan wondered if the big, scary man was opposed to camels because anyone who had dealt with them knew they could be extremely fast when they wanted to be. And smelly. And mean. And suspiciously precise when they spat at you.

Nafanua led the way, her attitude doing as much to carve a path through people as her size. The hooked club she held made it seem like she was ready to use it at a moment's notice and no one should test her. There was always a reliable selection of inns near the harbor in any city and Karachi was no different, their troop having to pool coins in exchange for board at one of the more popular ones.

The busy nature of the place was a benefit, with the constant turnover of people from every kind of land imaginable buying them all a form of anonymity. They were able to get one room, but it was large enough for the remaining seven members of their party to fit. Azadeh did a convincing job of passing off Onyx as a dog by slicing a piece of fabric from a woman's sari as she passed by and tying it around the wolf's neck like a bow. It wouldn't have fooled Roshan, but she wasn't the harried innkeeper dealing with an influx of people bumping in and bumping out.

There were nine of us once, she thought as she observed the space everyone was assembling into. Dias fell face down into a hammock. Gud took one of the few beds, and Geir stayed at the window as he looked down at the lane below and kept guard. The streets of Karachi were anything but safe, but they would be safer than remaining with this nest of vipers. Roshan made to leave only to find Azadeh blocking her path.

"You're going?" she asked.

"That's what acquiring a new map means."

Azadeh blinked at Roshan's harsh response, and Roshan felt regretful for a moment, but it was just that: a moment.

She needed to be free of Azadeh so she could do what she needed to do and obtain a map, yet she was also concerned.

She had expected Francis as the next likely target for the twins, Dias, *whoever.* Not Nafanua, one of the strongest and most challenging marks. Roshan had been an additional target of convenience. The choice to attack Nafanua simply didn't make sense and she needed some time to think it over. Alone. She left, Azadeh following her out of the inn and remaining on her heels until she hit the street.

"Please," she begged, spinning Roshan around by the shoulder. "I'm sorry! I said I'm so sorry. I should have listened when you..."

She paused, tears almost spilling from her eyes as she struggled to find the words. This girl was smart, but she was also sweet. Roshan felt a pang in her heart as she thought about the way this world devoured sweetness like it was precious honey from her home village. Her mind flashed through the faces of all the sweet people she had known and the terrible things that had happened to them. She felt an unreasonable desire to protect this one and she couldn't quite explain why. She stepped forward, pressing her hand to Azadeh's cheek.

"You already apologized," Roshan said. "And I accept that apology graciously, friend."

Azadeh blinked, fat tears plopping onto the skin of Roshan's hand.

"Right now, though, I need to acquire not just a new map but information," she continued.

"Information about what?" Azadeh questioned.

"You need to watch your back. You need to watch

Nafanua's and she'll watch yours in return. You two need to stick together until I return because there's something rotten here, but there's also something rotten out there."

She pulled her hand away, gesturing around them to underline her point.

"We still need to reach the Martyrs – again – and fight them in battle – again. It can't go the way it did last time, with fatal blows seemingly having no effect and them knowing where we are and what we're doing before we do."

"Immortals," she whispered.

"They are *not*," Roshan said, refusing to believe such ridiculousness. "There's something else going on and I'm going to find out what it is."

"How?" Azadeh questioned.

"By going to the library." She shrugged, as if it was the simplest solution in the world.

Because it was. She pulled the stiff hood of her robe up, giving a curt nod of finality as she went to leave. She watched as Azadeh went back inside, and only then did Roshan set off for Karachi's answer to Bagdad's House of Wisdom. She had only been there a handful of times, but she knew she would find what she was looking for there.

Karachi had been her home once and she found the twisting laneways and towering archways of the city comforting. Everything else about this task so far had been distinctly uncomfortable, so she'd take the streets she could recognize by scent and sight ever so gladly. There was a bazaar enroute, and Roshan made a slight detour as she searched for the stall belonging to one of the best cartographers in the business, Rishki. She told him what she needed and paid handsomely for it, buying two maps: the one everyone knew including routes that were frequently used and one that documented secret shortcuts that could get them there even quicker.

Rolling the maps up tightly and slotting them into their distressed leather packaging for safekeeping, she vowed to review them as soon as she was able to sit down in the library and study the details. She'd have to be quick, as she worried about leaving the group unobserved for more than two hours. Horrible visions of her returning to a room dripping in blood, everybody needlessly alienated and Geir and Gud triumphant, filled her mind. No sooner had she thought that than Roshan caught a glimpse of one of the twins. She pushed the thought aside at first, discounting it as her mind projecting the fear into reality.

Yet there was another figure – just as big and just as broad – stalking down the side of a laneway running parallel. Roshan paused, using the reflection of an ornamental shield at one of the market stands to examine what was behind her. Sure enough, when she stopped, the figures stopped. It was undoubtedly the twins, and as much as they were trying to stay out of sight, they consumed any eyeball unfortunate enough to land on them.

She felt the skin on her neck prickle as she moved on, trying not to run or alert them to the fact she was aware they were following her. But it was tough fighting her instincts to sprint until she got to better terrain. Her feet quickened subconsciously, her pulse matching as she bumped up against shoppers, rushed past families, ducked under drying racks of meat. Sparing a glance behind her, she thought she had lost them for a hopeful moment, and she started to crack a smile.

The gesture dropped from her face rapidly as she turned the next corner and saw Geir blocking the route forward. She came to a dead stop, pivoting back only to find that path guarded by Gud. The twins had herded her into the perfect spot, letting her think she was the fox when all along she'd been the hare. She was isolated now. They were enormous.

And there was no mistaking what was on their face: deadly intent.

Chapter Fourteen

Tabriz, 823

There wasn't any safe or sane reason Roshan was back in Kandovan.

The only explanation she could offer was that she couldn't resist. Maryam's caravan had been traveling toward Armenia and she had suggested Tabriz as a potential stop. It was a smaller city, but a city nonetheless. Their wares were so greatly appreciated, it bought Roshan time. She hired a horse from a local stable and had ridden over on their first evening there, unable to resist the temptation. It was dangerous to do so, that trail full of predators of both the animal and human variety.

Yet she had to return to her childhood home. Her eyes hadn't gazed upon the village in nearly a decade, and since then she had committed the most serious of crimes. It would condemn her family if it was thought they were in communication with her, if she was spotted or found. So she had stayed away, put her sisters and her parents in a box deep within her heart and never spoke of them in the hope of protecting them. She had been the daughter of no one. Now, for just a moment, just one night, she wanted to remember where she'd come from.

Hood pulled down and tight around her head, cloak billowing behind her as she rode, Roshan realized with a start that she wasn't that young girl anymore. The horrors she'd been through made her grow up too fast and there was no going back. The child she'd been had never left the landscape she was now reacquainting herself with as the sun set over the crest of the many mountains that defined this place. They were like huge, jagged teeth that formed a mouth jutting up and trying to swallow the sky. As the light got even lower, those same peaks loomed over her like huge, ominous figures.

She wasn't scared however. She was returning to her home a woman. Yes, a woman who was a murderer. But also a woman who had money, her *own*. A woman who controlled where she went and who she went there with. A woman who could read and speak the tongues of lands she could never have fathomed existed when she was a child – let alone ones that she had dreamed she might visit in person. A woman who knew the ways of the world through the stories told by the stars, who knew of the possibilities held within the mind of every individual. A woman who had seen the kindness in others, as well as the absolute depravity. A woman who could defend herself if she had to.

She didn't have to be proud of the things she'd done to be proud of the person she had become. So Roshan felt almost buoyant as she pulled on the reins, slowing the horse as she mounted the final crest toward the village. And there they were, the beehive homes she associated with the happiest times of her life. Or at least the purest. Even at night they still looked bizarre after all she'd seen of the world, with lights from inside the towering cones illuminating them from within. There were a few villagers far ahead returning from their day of work in the fields, others from the meticulous task of harvesting honey from the nearby, carefully cultivated hives. There were a few lingering traders too and she took a wide berth around them, steering the horse off the main trail.

The traders dropped down onto a lower route and Roshan looped around the far side of the village, eventually dismounting in the safety of thick shrubbery. She patted down the horse, her eyes scanning the normal life bubbling away in the place she'd grown up. Many people were heading in for the evening, while others still pottered about as they continued their business. She looped the reins securely around a tree, the horse's nostrils flaring as it caught a whiff of the treat she had squirreled away for this precise moment.

"Yes, yes, you've earned it," she murmured, presenting the apple which was gobbled up in an instant. She smirked, leaving the horse and her eager sounds of crunching behind as she made the rest of the way on foot. If she'd ridden straight to her home it would have been worse than heralding her arrival with the blast of a ceremonial horn. She needed to be careful, unseen. So she circled, taking a larger loop as she wove her way through the outer homes.

Her footsteps were soundless as she ascended a small rise that marked her parents' residence from those around it, her father having told her that it once belonged to his elders and would belong to her one day as the oldest. That door was shut to her now and bolted.

But that's as it should be, she told herself. *That's how it had to be.* Lights were on inside, a burst of warm yellow visible through the windows carved into the sides. She froze as she heard her mother's voice, specifically the sound of her mother cursing under her breath as she hastened to save a flame flickering in the evening breeze. For all her bravado, Roshan felt like a child momentarily. She pressed a hand to her lips, afraid of the small gasp that might escape and give her away.

It was shock. She was *shocked* and euphoric and devastated to hear the voice of the woman who had raised her. It was a sound she had never expected to hear again. She also hadn't anticipated the tears that flowed, wiping them away as quickly as they formed. *This will not do,* she scolded herself. She hadn't been sure what she would find when she came here, but life carrying on as normal wasn't it. She moved around the outside of the house to where she and her sisters had all slept in the same room together. Her sisters weren't there.

As she inched closer to the window and peered in, it was clear neither of them had been there for a while. Married and moved away? It made sense. They would have been grown women now with lives and families and homes of their own.

She hoped they had made better matches than she had.

She hoped that the bargain she'd been sold into had been enough to secure them brighter futures. She leaned against the small house for a moment, soaking in the figures of her mother and father moving around the kitchen as they now prepared dinner. They looked older and yet somehow… not. They were a little hunched, a little slower, but still carried on exactly as they had while she had been there, except now all of their girls were gone. She smiled as her mother batted at the hand of her father, who had been trying to sneak a not insignificant chunk of her mother's delicious honey cake into his mouth.

"Roshan?"

She froze, ice in her veins as the name she never spoke freely was suddenly said out loud. The voice had been quiet, barely above a whisper, and she turned to face the speaker.

It was her sister, the middle child and the prettiest of the three of them, Bolour. So much about her was completely transformed, from the plump puff of her cheeks to the swelling belly that she ran her hands over nervously. But her eyes… Roshan would have recognized that stare even if it was coming from a different face, a different body, a different time or place. She would recognize her sister anywhere. Bolour's eyes were doing the same to her, darting over every detail of Roshan as she stood in the dark like she was stuck in place. Because she was. She felt Bolour glance at her wrist, where she still wore the bracelet made for her by her sisters ahead of a wedding they'd been forbidden from attending. The colored glass beads were faded now, scratched in some places. Like her.

"You can't be here," Bolour whispered, breaking the

silence. "There are people watching the village, waiting to see if you come back. Even after all this time."

"I know," Roshan said, although she hadn't seen anyone. "I was careful, I snuck in after dark, I just… I needed to see them. You. To check everyone is alive and well one last time."

Bolour sighed with relief, the tension visibly releasing from her body the moment Roshan said she wasn't planning on staying.

"We're all right," she replied.

"Mother and father?"

"Happy. Healthy. They worry about you a lot. What happened, where you went…"

"If there's a way to safely tell them I'm alive and well, please do."

Bolour nodded, Roshan noticed the small containers of honey that were sitting in a basket perched against her hip.

"And you?" she asked. "You're pregnant?"

The first genuine smile flashed over her sister's features. "I am. A boy, I think. That's what I've been praying to Allah for."

"Your first?"

"Fifth."

Roshan blanched at the thought. "Five!"

"Only three are still with us," Bolour noted, sadness dripping from her tone. "But Amon and I are blessed with a fruitful family."

"Amon… the lanky boy from the next village over? The one who was always taunting the goats?"

"He's a very respectable honey farmer now," she said in a huff. "And my husband."

"Of course, of course..." Roshan murmured, unable to shake the picture of Amon the boy from her mind and imagine Amon the man. "And you're... happy? You love him?"

"Absolutely," Bolour replied, her words underlined by the truth that glowed from her cheeks. She beamed with love.

"And he treats you well? He respects you? He doesn't beat you? He–"

"No!" Bolour gasped. "Nothing like that, ever. Not all of us made your choices."

The last comment surprised her, and Roshan blinked like she had been physically slapped. "There was no choice," she said, voice cold. "If you'll remember, father had agreed to selling his daughters and the Harbor Master's preference was you. The only choice made was me offering to go in your place."

Bolour shifted, looking over Roshan's shoulders like she was uncomfortable with the direction this conversation had taken.

"And I'm glad I did," Roshan continued. "You would not have survived a month with him, let alone the years. Masha would have fared even worse."

A flash of something at the mention of their other sister, just a fleeting reaction, passed across Bolour's face but Roshan didn't miss it.

"How is Masha?" she asked.

"Oh, you know, she's well." Bolour looked away.

Bolour was lying. She had always been terrible at it in her youth and now as an adult, she had somehow grown even worse.

"Save the mistruths. Is it the fits?"

There must have been something in her tone that caused her sister's gaze to snap back up to hers. She had been avoiding eye contact, but Roshan's firmness demanded attention.

"I'm not..." she sighed heavily. "No, she hasn't had a seizure in years. She grew out of them with puberty, I think, but... I don't know if she's all right. Her husband won't let me see her. She's not even allowed to visit our mother and father anymore."

Roshan felt the tension in her jaw as she ground her teeth. "Who is her husband?"

"Bogd, he's a Mongolian merchant. He already had two older wives, but Masha didn't have many prospects after I married for love and you... well. She had to take the first offer that came."

Roshan bit her lip, hating the thought of their youngest and softest sibling being locked away with someone cruel. "Where do they live?"

"Tabriz," Bolour replied, her eyes once again downcast as if there was shame in knowing this information, that she knew what Masha was going through but couldn't do anything about it. Roshan knew exactly what her sister was thinking. She had her life and her family. That was enough, she guessed. It had to be. Women like them were powerless when it came to dealing with men like *him*.

Roshan nodded, taking her leave as she began to slowly walk away. She paused as she passed her sister's shoulder, squeezing gently. Bolour was never one to enjoy a hug, even more so now, given the years and the time and the history that had passed between them.

"It was good to see you," she said. As she made her way through the darkness and out of the village, she heard her sister's voice call out behind her.

"He's dangerous, Roshan."

Roshan paused, not bothering to look back as she let Bolour's words settle into her very core.

"So am I," she replied.

Roshan rode back to the city with a renewed sense of purpose. She returned to the caravan during the busiest period of the night for the women working there, a thoroughfare of men coming and going as business was conducted. Her mind buzzed with the possibilities, simmering with the thrill of having seen her parents, at having heard them, let alone getting to speak with Bolour despite how stilted and strange and awkward that conversation had been. More than anything, she was desperate to find Masha. She wanted to see what kind of life her sister led and if there was any way she could help her.

There was one person who was particularly adept at gathering this kind of information and could point her in the right direction. He wasn't a customer of Maryam's per se, but he was a regular. Traveling seemingly almost as much as they did, he usually linked up with the caravan once they arrived in one of the cities or larger towns. His name was Dervis, and he wasn't much older than Roshan. In fact, she couldn't quite work out exactly how old he was as he had one of those faces that seemed both young and old at the same time.

"He's not just a skilled thief," Maryam had explained to

her. "He's not just good at acquiring any kind of trinket or object your heart could desire. He's also great at stealing information as well."

Every few months he would show up at the caravan and he and Maryam would make a transaction of sorts. She was unsurprised to see him there when she returned that night, dismounting her horse and returning the mare to the stable owner nearby. When she arrived at the caravan, Dervis was sitting on the steps that led up to Maryam's carriage, legs crossed and elbows propped against the wood like he was extremely comfortable. As he conversed with Maryam, she chuckled at something the Turk said and he smirked. He was always smirking, there being a permanent smugness attached to him. When he smiled, he appeared momentarily younger than the twenty-something years she placed him at. Roshan nodded at them as she passed before backtracking and lingering for a moment, trying to figure out how to voice what she needed.

"It's nice to see you," he said coolly as she pulled up a chair.

He had taken an immediate interest in her, the one woman constantly traveling with them as a companion who didn't take part in the same business practices that the other women did. When he learned that she was their bookkeeper, Dervis had grown even more intrigued. She had enjoyed his visits to the caravan because he was linguistically gifted as well. Roshan was now able to hone her own language skills with multiple sources as she bounced between the different women and guards. Plus, Dervis always seemed to return with some new dialect on his tongue from some faraway land he'd just visited.

"You look worried, young scholar," he said. He was always calling her that, partially a joke, but also partially done in seriousness. He clearly valued her intelligence, and she was almost fluent in his native Turkish thanks to his tutelage.

"I *am* worried," she replied. "I need information on someone, and I know you can get it."

"Information is one of my most popular products," Dervis remarked.

Maryam tilted her head with interest, intrigued. Roshan so rarely asked for anything, let alone asked something of Dervis.

"How does it work exactly?" she questioned. "I tell you what I need, and you give me a price?"

"You tell me what you need," he began. "I get it and then I give you a price."

She narrowed her eyes, understanding the trickiness within the fluidity of that bargain.

"Come on," he teased, observing her trepidation. "I know you're good for it. You never spend money on anything. Whenever I visit the caravan, the girls always have requests for me, always have something they want or something they need liquidated. But never you."

"Liquidated?" she echoed. "What does that mean exactly?"

"It's hard to travel with so many valuables," Maryam supplied. "It's dangerous, too. Dervis is the person I use to convert various payments into smaller, more manageable sums, like precious stones."

Ah. Roshan now understood that what had seemed like

marbles clinking together in a pouch as Maryam and Dervis exchanged hands was actually a transaction. Roshan had observed it dozens of times, knowing the precise numerical value as she annotated it in the records that she kept, but never realizing exactly what it was.

"Precious stones are good," Dervis agreed. "Scrolls, tapestries, art, fine silks all work just as well."

"And these are stolen items?" she questioned, interested.

"Sometimes," he replied. "Sometimes they're obtained through legitimate measures. You know, if you ever want to learn more about what I do, I'm always looking for new sta–"

He never had a chance to finish that sentence before Maryam whacked him forcefully on the chest. He let out a puff of surprised air.

"No poaching!" she said.

"Now, now," he replied, a slight ache to his voice. "Isn't that how she came to be in your employ in the first place? You poached *her*."

"I said no such thing," Maryam huffed, neglecting to mention that was exactly how Roshan had come to work for her.

"Just the information," she said. "I'll pay for it, but *only* if that information is valuable and *only* if you come through."

"You have a deal," he replied, extending his hand. Reluctantly, she shook it. "Do you want to speak it or..." He glanced at Maryam.

"I'll write down what I need. Burn it when you're done."

"Absolutely," he agreed. "But keep the details simple. My reading journey is a gradual one."

She nodded, retreating to her office where she began

catching up on the day's books. When she finished, she retrieved a piece of parchment for Dervis and was about to write her sister's name but paused, considering. After a moment, instead she wrote the name of the man considered to be her brother-in-law and everything Bolour had told her about him. She added what she wanted to know and a note about the treatment of his wives. That put distance between her and Masha. After all, Masha would be just one of three wives Roshan potentially had a connection to *if* Dervis assumed she was doing her due diligence for a potential match for a friend or another connection.

She handed off the note to him a few hours later, the Turk asking for clarification on a few words before he set off. One of the women had told her that he had a network of thieves willing to work for him in each city, mostly children. The rumor went that Dervis had once been a child thief himself, and as he grew up, he had hustled his way up the chain of command. Although his operation was relatively small, she could see the ambition in his eyes. She knew he wouldn't fail her.

It was another two nights before he circled back to the caravan. Roshan was taking her dinner outside with several others when he returned, his eyes scanning the faces present until they settled on hers. He jerked his head and she set down her bowl of ab doogh khiar, gesturing at him to follow her to the small space that was her sanctuary.

"This is cramped," he said, ducking down low as he folded his body onto one of the cushions in front of her desk. "This is where you work? There's so much paper, this place is a fire hazard."

"What did you learn?" she asked, eager.

"Nothing good," he sighed. "The man comes from wealthy parents, which should have set him up for life, except he has become known for squandering his wealth. Notorious for it, actually. The way I hear it, he's in deep. He owes *a lot* to *a lot* of very, very dangerous people."

"That's good," she mused. Upon seeing the confusion in his eyes, Roshan explained. "Loan sharks would kill him, wouldn't they?"

Dervis snorted. "What's the point in that? They'd never get their money back. These types of people are more likely to take something of equivalent value."

"Like what?"

"That answers your next question: the wives. Particularly his most recent one. Pretty, delicate little thing."

She frowned, not quite connecting the pieces. Dervis could see her confusion outlined clearly enough.

"Sharks don't have just one revenue stream. They have several – usually spread out – which is how they can guarantee that if one source wanes, another will come through. For example, do you know how Maryam was able to get the capital to kickstart this little operation of hers?"

"Yes," she responded. "She invested everything she'd saved from years in the business, took out some loans, then had the assistance of... a wealthy benefactor."

Those had been Maryam's words and Roshan hadn't found them odd at the time. The way Maryam had positioned her explanation made it sound like a rich and regular client of hers who was just as invested in her business idea as she was, and that she would pay him back when the time was right. She felt like a naïve, juvenile idiot in the moment.

"She's in with the sharks," she mumbled.

"Swimming with them," Dervis replied as he slid a parchment across the table. "I didn't much understand this, but I recognized a few names so thought you could take a look. You can't keep it. I need to return it by morning before someone notices it's missing."

Roshan unrolled it, her eyes widening as she scanned the figures there. Maryam wasn't the only one who kept good books apparently. So did the people who kept the debtors' accounting in order. The figure was staggering, even at a glance. Maryam had paid off her smaller loans like she said, but her silent partner was quite loud. She focused in on the name Xex, it having popped up in those early books as the source of Maryam's major loan. Although much of that was paid off, too, the interest was astronomical. It meant that what Maryam had borrowed had multiplied almost every year she'd been in operation which was – Roshan calculated – almost fourteen years. It was a devil's bargain with truly no way for Maryam to ever be in the clear going by these finances. She was trapped.

"Does she know?" Roshan asked.

"She must," Dervis replied. "Whispers tell me there's about to be a hostile takeover. The sharks will start running this caravan themselves, and Maryam will be either out of a job or on her back again. More girls will be cycled in, including one or two of the newly acquired wives taken as payment."

Roshan leaned back, listening to this information with a sick feeling in her stomach.

"You should get out," Dervis suggested. "Now. While you still can. These kinds of people… they see only one use for women and it's not as bookkeepers."

"And go where?" she questioned, allowing herself to spiral, desperation rising. "And do what?"

"My job offer still stands."

She analyzed his expression to see if he was telling the truth, if he really meant it. She was surprised to see that he did.

"I've stolen out of desperation before," she told him. "Clothes and food and books–"

He laughed. "Of course, books would be a necessity for you."

"I cannot do what you do. I do not think I'm equipped."

"I have other people for that," he said, batting a hand. "I have myself for that. This, however, I can't do." He gestured at the stacks of paper around them, where she had compiled years of data into manageable documentation.

"You've seen all kinds of paperwork from all around the world," Dervis continued. "You could mimic it, recreate it. You can read and write across languages. You'd be the perfect fence."

"Excuse me?"

"I meant no offense." He grinned, amused by her reaction. "Me and mine acquire the goods. A fence is the person who helps us re-home them. You'd track where the objects came from and where they needed to go, creating the paperwork needed to make any transactions seem legitimate. Smooth. If it was needed, that is."

Ah, now *that* she could do. There was a hint of victory

on his face as he read her interested reaction, understanding that this task appealed to her.

"I leave for Karachi next week," he said. "I could meet you when my business is concluded."

"And what of the girls here?" Roshan questioned. "I just leave them to new management?"

"I didn't say that..."

He trailed off, but his stare was firm. He meant for her to tell the women. Warn them. Maryam had told herself that many of the women she worked with had chosen this life and valued both the freedom and funds it brought them. However, they were about to have that freedom taken away and she knew without even having to ask Dervis for a second opinion that Maryam would not communicate the coming threat until it was too late. The caravan only had value if it had women willing to work it. She would need everybody to remain and would probably still be required to offer her own body as well.

"I'll come and work for you on one condition," she said, finally having the opportunity to create a bargain of her own. To his credit, Dervis didn't reply with "anything." He seemed desperate for her services, but if he communicated that to her, it would put Roshan in a better position and him in a weaker one.

"Name it," he said.

"Negotiate an exchange for me. If I can clear Bogd's debts, he releases the youngest wife. She's free to go, no shame or stigma to her name. Her honor intact."

Dervis let out a long breath. "I can approach him with that offer, but I don't know if he'll take it."

"I saw the numbers. He's losing all his wives, not one or two. This way he loses one, keeps two, and is out from under the weight of his debts. Xex will not make him a better offer."

"Indeed, he won't," Dervis mused, leaning back as he stroked the hairs at his chin that were barely thick enough to form a goatee. "Do you have enough?"

"Yes."

She had been slowly building her fortune since Thatta, and although it wouldn't be considered immense by the standards of the richest men in this city, it was still significant. Erasing Bogd's debts would take almost everything Roshan had. She would be back to owning only the clothes on her back. But for Masha, it would be worth it.

"All right." He nodded. "You have a deal but if I may, I'd suggest making the payment in garnets."

"Garnets? Why?"

"Because compared to other – how would Maryam put it? – precious stones, it's

difficult to tell fake garnets from the real thing. And Tabriz has some of the most gifted forgers I've ever come across in my short life."

He gave her a wink and without another word, he left. She sat with the information, understanding washing over her at what he'd just suggested. There was little time to waste.

She didn't sleep that night. Everything of value to her was in that office and it didn't take much to pack what she needed and prepare to leave the caravan. Next, she slipped a street urchin more than she should have so that he'd take her to the city's best forgers once daylight broke. They sold both real and imitation garnets, she learned, with the ruse working best when they were combined together.

She soon learned that Dervis had made the bargain successfully, and he would make the trade-off that night, Masha's freedom active as soon as the debt payment was done. Roshan only had half a day with the caravan left before she was gone, and she waited until Maryam exited for her daily spa, accompanied by her lovers. Then Roshan acted quickly, moving from woman to woman as she shared Dervis's information. They trusted her, they'd spent over a year together now, and their belief in Roshan was what would save them. Some of the girls started packing immediately, while others gave a nonchalant shrug.

"What else would I do? Where would I go?"

These were very similar questions to the ones Roshan had asked Dervis the night before.

"One boss is as good as another."

She embraced the women she was closest with, good wishes whispered and kisses pressed into cheeks before she slung her pack over her back and began to make her own way. *Would it always be like this?* she wondered. *Forever building a community only to abandon it every few years?* She longed for permanence.

As she waited outside the spa, she paid the same street urchin as before to send word to Bolour and the urchin took off at a rapid pace. When Maryam exited not long after, freshly bathed, her relaxed expression dropped at the sight of Roshan.

"No," she said. "You're leaving?"

"I am," Roshan replied. "I know about the loan and

whatever Xex told you, don't believe him. They will trap you and take from you until there's nothing left."

Maryam's face tightened. "You told the others, didn't you?"

Roshan's heart dropped just a little at Maryam's question. Clearly Maryam knew what was coming. She had always been smart.

"Yes," she responded. She had liked and lived and learned from this woman. Roshan wouldn't lie to her. Maryam stepped forward, cupping a hand to her face. A thumb stroked the skin under her eyes in a tender gesture.

Then suddenly, it was over.

She turned from Roshan and sashayed off into the market, hips swinging dangerously and lovers in tow.

"I walk toward my fate," she called, waving a hand above her.

And so, Roshan would walk toward hers. She crouched on a nearby rooftop, waiting as midnight crept closer, fighting stick in one hand and fingers resting on the hilt of her sheathed sword. She did not want violence. She wasn't particularly fond of it. Yet money, sex, power, and violence were the four critical languages men like this understood. She could be fluent in all of them if she had to.

Her back stiffened as she watched Dervis walk out onto the street below and for a moment, she thought he was alone. He had played her! His hands were empty, so clearly the payment was gone but... then out walked her sister.

Masha was limping and Roshan let out a small whimper as she saw how frail she looked. Not just thin, but skeletal. Her eyes appeared haunted, and Roshan wanted to kill this husband of hers. She wanted to watch him bleed just like the Harbor Master had, come what may.

Her rage subsided as she heard Bolour's voice, her other sister running toward their sibling and crushing her in an all-encompassing hug. Masha broke down in tears, sobbing into Bolour's shoulder on the street. Dervis looked uncomfortable at the sight of weeping women and, after a moment, excused himself, his task complete. He disappeared into a nearby laneway and Roshan's gaze flicked back to her siblings. It was like watching a scene from a beautiful painting play out, the perfect moment frozen in front of her, one she was unable to ever partake in. Witnessing it would have to be enough. Bolour's husband was there as well, and Roshan had a newfound respect for Amon as she observed the way the beekeeper shepherded the two sisters down the street.

A child ran up to them, tugging on Bolour's robes as Masha continued to bury her head into her sister's shoulder. The street urchin handed them a small pouch, and Amon gasped as he took it from Bolour and peered inside. It would be a fortune to them, that collection of garnets. Real ones, of course. It was the very last of what Roshan had, the rest going to the street urchin who'd been as useful as he'd promised. Bolour's head snapped up, her neck swiveling around as if she was searching for something, searching for Roshan.

Roshan couldn't be sure, but as she stood up, she felt like their eyes connected for a moment. She wanted to offer a wave, offer something, take responsibility for bringing Masha's freedom about, but she'd done all she could.

Roshan turned away from her sisters, setting off toward Karachi to start again without a single coin to her name but feeling richer than she ever had in her life.

Chapter Fifteen

Karachi, 824

Gud lunged at her first, Roshan throwing herself backward as she tried to roll and unsheathe her sword at the same time. There wasn't enough space for her to retract her fighting stick, which was a shame because the only way she was going to survive this was by keeping enough distance between herself and the twins. If they got hold of her, trapped her between their arms, they were so big in comparison she wouldn't put it past them to crush her to death or snap her neck.

Geir reached out in a rapid grasp, trying to grab her hood. He made contact and she was yanked toward him as he latched on to the fabric. She spun her now bare blade as best she could, not able to make a clear cut, but slicing at his wrist. Blood sprayed down like artful dots of red paint.

"Gah!" he yelled.

She wished she'd taken his whole hand off, but wounded

would have to do. Roshan had to get out of there. But where? Her two exits were blocked by the twins, so running out of the alley was definitely not an option. Pain suddenly ignited through her scalp, stopping all escape calculations, and Roshan screamed as she felt herself jerked by her long plait. Geir's brother had capitalized on the lure of her exposed hair and she flew backward, landing on the hard ground with an *oomph* that took the breath out of her.

Time slowed in the moment, her focus narrowing to the sliver of blue sky she could see between the uneven slices of roofing above her and wooden beams jutting out from unfinished construction. This was the exit she hadn't realized was there the whole time. Her body was pulled through the dirt by her hair, Gud drawing her toward him like a snake twisting around a stunned desert mouse. *Let him think that,* she thought, rotating in his grip and pushing the pain aside.

He had learned the lesson from his brother and saw the slash of her blade a moment early, jerking his hands back to stay clear of her range. That was what she needed as she sliced down on her plait, severing the strands and the hold he had on her. She used the point of her blade to help leverage herself up on her feet, sparing a moment to sheathe her sword as she ran at the wall. She used a cluster of crates discarded as trash to launch herself up and off, flying through the air until her hands connected with one of the wooden beams. Splinters cut into her palms and she ignored the tiny pricks, straining as she used her upper arm strength to pull herself up.

She felt the hands of one of the twins brushing her feet, desperately trying to grab her ankles and stop her ascent.

She kicked free as she swung up and balanced on the narrow wooden surface, feeling the weak beam begin to buckle under her weight. She leapt for the next one above her just as it fell away in a spray of clay and plaster. Roshan swung her feet, gaining momentum, leaping from one to the other, pausing to grab an additional grip on windowsills as she kept racing upward.

She hit the first rooftop with a grunt, stabbing through the weathered materials with her dagger so she didn't slide back into the metaphorical lion's den. She quickly glanced down, watching as Geir and Gud struggled against each other to follow her path upward. They might have succeeded if they'd managed to work together, but they were so desperate to go after her they were bashing against one another and falling, even going so far as to use the same beams she had which couldn't handle their body mass.

Good, she thought. That's what she had hoped for. Bracing her knee under her body, she found her footing and climbed higher onto the rooftop. She could hear the twins shouting below, desperate to see where she was going so they could follow. She assessed the distance between two rooftops and leapt, suspended in the air for a few seconds. She hit the opposite roof with a *bang* and rolled, springing up swiftly as she began running as fast as she could. It was challenging to get an even tread going with the dips and depressions in the rooftop surfaces.

The important thing was she was free of the brothers and making good ground as she put distance between them and her. Roshan risked another glance down through the laneways below, clocking their bulk as they attempted to follow her on foot. They were struggling to keep track of her, and she felt a spark of victory at being able to escape a fight she could never have won hand-to-hand.

Her joy was short-lived, however, and she slowed to a stop. Balanced on the edge of the roof she was just about to leap from, Roshan spun her hands to steady herself and came to a complete halt.

And then what? she thought. Escape this skirmish, then return to the group at the inn? Geir and Gud pretend it never happened? And neither does she? No, there was no way. They would kill her the second she returned, find another way to eliminate her, or she would have to plan a way to kill them first. The last option seemed impossible, so where did that leave her? Roshan needed to get rid of them, but how?

Her hair was so short now it bobbed just below her chin, the light brown strands blowing in her face as she stared at the Karachi cityscape from above. She assumed she knew this place better than the twins did. That would be her advantage. She might not be able to beat them in direct combat, but she was clever and stealthy enough that she could challenge them in other ways. Roshan retraced her steps, shuffling to the edge of another building so that her silhouette was visible from below instead of hidden as she ran in the center of the rooftops like she had done previously. She needed the twins to see her, so she used her foot to kick a tile free, watching as it fell to the ground, smashing into pieces right in front of a newly emerged Gud.

The Northman skidded to a stop as he looked up. Roshan turned around just in time, hoping that he saw only the barest hint of her. She heard him yell to his brother and a shout in response echoed back. She slowed her pace so they could follow, Roshan leading them away from the market and closer toward Karachi's residential areas which sat just on the outskirts of some of the most opulent palaces she had ever seen. Her line of sight was fixed on the tops of pristine, white pillars that stood out from the increasingly wealthy array of buildings.

The easiest entrance was around the north side and she veered in that direction, checking that the twins were still following. She smiled when she saw that they were.

The final distance she would need to cross was a span greater than she could jump. She lowered her head and sprinted, trying to generate the greatest amount of speed as she lifted off her side satchel, throwing it over one of the many outcropping laundry lines that extended from one building to the next. She threw the straps over the middle, gripped the new loop on the other side, and threw herself forward hoping she'd created enough momentum as she flew across the street below.

She landed ungracefully on a lower balcony, its interior shielded from outside street view by white shutters just as immaculate as every other part of this grand building. She peered over the railing, watching as Geir and Gud crashed into the courtyard below like water buffalos at a feeding hole. There were gardeners attending to both the landscaped hedges and a variety of fruit plants that required more water than it took to hydrate a human. All of the workers turned around at the commotion. One immediately dropped his tools and ran, a reaction Roshan guessed the twins were probably used to, based on their huge appearance and massive axes. What they wouldn't expect was for that gardener to return moments later with three heavily armed guards in tow.

There was a flurry of excited giggles on the other side of the balcony she had landed on, and Roshan rapidly pivoted away and crouched low. The balcony door was flung open, shielding her from view as women poured out from inside. As their hands gripped the railing to observe the chaos down below, she observed intricate henna patterns painted on their hands, the floral shapes and dots wrapping around individual fingers. Their nails were perfect, their skin luscious and glowing with oils and lotions that had no doubt been acquired at great expense to preserve their beauty.

This was the harem of the second richest man in the city, and these women were his most beloved gems. And like all treasures, he protected them fearlessly. Roshan had only come to this property a few times while living in Karachi, but never to this entrance. Yet like most places that made Roshan wary, she had assessed the various entries and exits in case she had needed them. Thankfully, she hadn't then. Now, however, that knowledge proved critical.

The guards here wore the best armor money could buy, their entrance to the courtyard heralded by the metallic *clank clank clank* of body plates. Through a sliver in the shutters and the balcony's edge, Roshan peered down to watch as Geir and Gud were surrounded. The guards shouted at the twins in a language neither could understand, and the two men looked like the most threatening incursions to the sanctuary that one could imagine.

The head guard yelled at them to raise their hands. They glanced blankly at each other. The guard's intent was made clear as he thrust a spear forward, forcing their limbs upward. Gud let out an annoyed snarl that could have come from Onyx, whereas Geir – perhaps the marginally smarter of the two – pivoted around to assess their exit.

That path closed in front of their eyes when the last of the guards encircled them and extended their spears outward. More orders were shouted and more orders were ignored.

What couldn't be misunderstood, however, was body language. As a young soldier became overly zealous with the tip of his weapon, he prodded Gud. The Northman's wrist still dripped blood from her earlier slash, and he let out a pained and annoyed sound, grabbing the end of the spear and yanking it – and the soldier – forward. The young man looked barely eighteen and clearly he wasn't used to such an aggressive offense from someone so outnumbered. He tripped forward and straight into the Northman's arms. It looked like a hug which turned fatal rather rapidly. She flinched at the sound of his snapping neck, watching as the soldier's dead body dropped to the ground.

There was the briefest of reprieves as the air around them seemed to hang still for a moment. Then, chaos. The rest of the soldiers drove forward in unison, and Gud let out a piercing cry as a spear was struck right through his shoulder. He flailed wildly, taking several guards down with him as the soldiers attacked and the two brothers fought back. They behaved exactly how Roshan had hoped they would, their shady natures accurately making the soldiers assess them as a threat and respond in kind.

Roshan used that moment to take her leave, risking being seen. She stretched her body upward, careful not to jostle the door and shove any of the women packed onto the balcony. Balancing on the railing, she slowly and strenuously pulled herself back up on to the roof using the edge of the gutter rim for leverage. Her last glance back was toward a massacre of not just Geir and Gud, but every guard the twins destroyed with them – quite a significant number. The twins looked like butchered meats sold at the market, their bodies stabbed through with stiff rods.

She turned away, all her concentration focused on a path forward. Geir and Gud wouldn't be a problem anymore, but if she took a misplaced step and plummeted to the harsh surface of the street below, then all would be for nothing. The commotion had drawn the interest of everyone within radius to the harem and as she scaled rooftop after rooftop, she was inadvertently pushing toward the quieter pockets of the city. She still needed to head back toward the library, but as she shimmied down the side of a building and dropped onto the stairwell of a residential block, Roshan realized she was filthy.

She was covered in dirt and dust and all manner of grime, not to mention all the blood: not just theirs, but her own that had been drawn in the skirmish. She looked like a criminal and exactly the kind of woman who would never be let through the library doors. With a grimace of frustration, she knew her next order of business would be to find somewhere she could bathe and change. But change into what? She had no idea. Her side satchel was still hooked tightly around her body, the maps she'd earlier acquired safe, yet there was no change of clothes inside that could help her. She'd have to steal something and so maintained a steady and straightforward pace.

She kept her eyes focused up ahead as she wove through the labyrinth of Karachi laneways, windows opening up into each other and giving residents a view of the interior of neighboring homes. Every so often, she'd pull something free from a strung clothesline. A pair of pants here, a loose shirt with wooden buttons from over there, a simple cloak to throw over everything, a headscarf, some undergarments that would get the job done. Her vision was momentarily blocked as she ducked under a billowing sheet and when she had a clear view, she froze.

At the end of the laneway was either a huge, black dog or what she hoped more accurately to be a wolf. Onyx sat at attention, pink tongue lolling out of its mouth like Roshan was exactly the person she expected to materialize on the other side of a canopy of laundry. Roshan let out a small exhale and relaxed slightly. Onyx made several sharp, quick barks and Roshan frowned, wondering what that was supposed to communicate to her. A few seconds later, she foolishly realized the message wasn't meant for her as Azadeh jogged around the corner. She had a small sword gripped in her hand that Roshan doubted the woman knew how to use properly, but she benched that bitter thought as she saw the relief overcoming Azadeh's face.

"They left!" she said, running toward Roshan. "By the time I went back inside, the twins were gone. I tried not to panic, hoping they might have just left to get food but–"

"It's okay."

"–they're following you, I'm sure of it!"

"I know."

"You… you do?" She blinked, coming to an abrupt halt in front of Roshan. For the first time, Azadeh seemed to fully assess Roshan's appearance. "They found you."

"They did."

She watched as the woman's eyes nervously flicked past Roshan's shoulders, as if she expected those huge twins to come thudding down the laneway at any moment.

"I need to find a bathhouse," Roshan said, taking the other woman by the elbow. "I'm too noticeable like this. I'll explain on the way."

"I just passed one," Azadeh replied. "A few lanes over. Let's go."

It was closer than she expected, Roshan handing over coins so Azadeh could secure a private bath, and when their attendant vacated, they slipped inside together with Onyx trotting along. She spoke as she undressed, her recounting of the twins' ambush and their eventual demise paused at intervals as Roshan had to wince or hiss in pain as she pulled her clothes loose. The dried saltwater and blood made for a sticky combination, not to mention the other wounds she could feel. It wasn't until she slipped under the surface of the warm, fragrant water that she started to feel better.

There was a collection of oils and soaps and scrubs in small dishes at the water's edge and she let herself have the luxury of using them to wash herself clean. Azadeh was already clean, looking like she had barely a hair or robe out of place as she sat with her feet trailing in the water. Her face was like the changing seasons as she listened, Roshan recounting the trap she'd fallen into and then the trap she'd set for Geir and Gud as she plucked splinters from the softened skin of her palm.

"That's it then? They're dead?" Azadeh asked, the hope audible in her voice.

"I don't see any way they could have survived," Roshan replied, moving on to wash her clothes next and wring them dry. "Not with those injuries. At least if you're here and they're there, Nafanua is a little safer, too. She just has to keep an eye on Dias, but I think she could take him. The twins were clearly our main threat. Either way, they're not our problem for the rest of this mission."

"Mission…"

The other woman's words trailed off and Roshan realized why. Her eyes gave her away as they'd been staring at the curve of her shoulder, stuck like a fly in honey. Part of Roshan was ready to feel self-conscious, this being the exact reason why she kept so much of herself covered. Not out of shame, but because it made her memorable. Recognizable.

"What happened?" Azadeh whispered. "Those scars on your back…"

"I used to know a man."

"A Persian man?" She tilted her head with interest, the question not verbalized. "You're careful about what you say, especially around me," Azadeh explained further. "Which made me think you might be Persian, too."

Roshan smirked. "This Persian man had many wives. He used to call us his slaves and he treated us that way. If you misbehaved, you were punished. With a whip."

"And you misbehaved a lot?"

Roshan didn't linger on those memories often, even though she wore them in the twists and knots of her once-torn flesh. Halima had always been the best when it came to healing, having taught Roshan everything she knew from the trick with ants in lieu of sutures to using a homemade concoction with honey and rose hip oil. She would soak rags with it, a physically and emotionally exhausted Roshan laying on her stomach while the fabric was placed along the tattered skin.

Roshan let herself disappear under the surface of the water, scrunching up her face in the private sanctuary it created. Too many recollections weren't helpful right now. She re-emerged, getting a temporary shock as she swept her hands back over her hair. The ends were so short and jagged it startled her.

"I forgot," she murmured, fingertips brushing against the tips.

"It suits you," Azadeh replied.

"It looks like a man's," she countered, examining her reflection in the water's surface. "Which is handy, actually."

Roshan erased the image looking back at her with an idle splash, stepping out of the water one stair at a time. Azadeh sprang up, throwing a towel around Roshan's shoulders.

She gave her a smile of thanks.

"Can you read?" Roshan asked.

"No."

"Write?"

Azadeh shook her head, like she was embarrassed. Roshan remembered how that felt once, how limiting, how angry she was about the restrictions forced on her by those desperate to keep her in her place. Or worse, those who never spared a thought about her at all.

"I can teach you," she said, pulling on the clothes she'd stolen, wanting Azadeh to have that same power Roshan had always wished for her sisters, too. "Until then, I need your help."

"With the maps?"

"I got those. We're going to the library."

"But..." Azadeh looked uncertain.

"You have eyes, you can recognize symbols, you're smart. That's what I need."

Azadeh had nothing to say to the compliment, her eyebrows shooting up in mild surprise.

Roshan packed up her still damp and stolen backup attire and they left the bathhouse together in step. Both women wrapped their faces as they neared the looming pillars that marked their target. The benefit of this library compared to, say, the House of Wisdom were the dozens of stairs leading up to entrances on all sides. Everything in Karachi seemed to be built with some sort of battle to ascend or descend in mind. On a day like today, when the weather was warm and the air humid, the steps resembled a thoroughfare as the city's scholars and visiting geniuses made their way in and out constantly.

Clusters of scholars sat on the steps, some chatting excitedly with each other and gesturing wildly, others hunched over with their heads down as they furiously scrawled on pieces of parchment. Azadeh whistled and pointed at a spot out of sight for Onyx to wait, but that was the last flash of confidence Roshan saw in her for a while.

Azadeh kept glancing around, her body language nervous and her eyes wide through the sliver of fabric that exposed them.

"Relax," Roshan told her, seeing a touch of herself in the woman. "Anyone can come here."

"I only see men."

"It's mostly men," she conceded. "There are some women."

She didn't add the "less and less" part out loud, or how the few women who did visit here now were often maligned or made to feel unsafe unless they were accompanied by a male guardian. Both she and Azadeh were dressed neutrally, their gender not obvious at a cursory glance, but if one really paid attention, it could be spotted easily. So they slipped around the side, Roshan leading the way as they took one of the first staircases up to the higher levels and toward the archived volumes.

"What are we looking for?" Azadeh asked, just as Roshan paused when she spotted the destination. It was illuminated in front of her, that special instinct she'd always had telling her exactly where she needed to go as she set off toward an aisle that brightened incrementally. That couldn't be the explanation to her friend, of course: that sometimes she just *knew* where things were meant to go.

"Egypt," she offered instead, pointing up at the symbol at the end of the aisle. "Specifically, the late third century..."

She trailed off, eyes tracking through the years as they were marked, her fingers touching the shelving which housed hundreds of old scrolls and preserved parchments.

"That story you told about the Martyrs," her companion muttered, realizing their purpose.

"It was just from memory. I want to check what accounts they have. See what I missed."

Roshan stopped, relieved to see the thick spines of a few books that covered the period amongst parchment on Christian saints. She took the ones that appeared brightest to her and pulled a few others loose that she deemed relevant. They retreated to a table tucked in a corner she assumed would have few visitors due to its poor positioning amongst the shadows of the library and away from any natural light. Azadeh retrieved a nearby candle, a pencil and some scraps of paper that were free to use while Roshan got started, leaning back as a plume of dust erupted from the first volume. She slid the other over to the opposite side of the table, earning a startled look from Azadeh.

"I can't–"

"This is how we start," Roshan said, cutting her off. She quickly jotted down the key things she wanted Azadeh to look for and then handed her the paper. "This first word – 'Martyrs' – and the next – 'Agaunum'. Just look for letters that resemble these and follow this order, as well as the number six and anything with a variation of this symbol."

She tried to sketch it as best she could, the shape looking like a numeral overlapping six times until it was a contorted star of sorts. Her pencil froze as she looked at what she'd drawn, realizing that it wasn't dissimilar to the hieroglyphs that had been etched into the walls of the prison.

"Duat, home of the Gods," the hooded stranger had said. "Also known as the underworld. Hell."

His words echoed through her mind and she scribbled them out, along with the drawing, feeling uneasy at the similarities. What she'd seen on the Martyrs' robes was slightly different, but only slightly. She gave the paper to Azadeh and watched as the woman's eyes narrowed in concentration, fingers touching what Roshan had written and her stare flicking back to the page.

"It looks like a six-pointed cross," Azadeh remarked. The comment proved insightful to Roshan. She'd been coloring its meaning with her recent experience in hell, when really she should have been contextualizing it through the Christian men who wore it.

It was slow going at first, and Roshan felt the constraints of time, wondering what the maximum amount of time they could spend away from the inn was before something drastic happened. Dias could leave without them, except she had the maps and local knowledge that meant she was vital. Nafanua would wait for them... if she thought they were alive. If word of the two huge men who'd been caught trying to infiltrate the harem got back to her, she'd make the connection. And she might think that Roshan and Azadeh had been slaughtered, too.

That was a pressing concern, but the current one was in front of her as she skimmed through the hagiography of one Saint Maurice. An Egyptian military leader, he was said to have led the Theban Legion of Rome in the third century... also sometimes known as the Martyrs of Agaunum. It was his account she was most familiar with, having read it several times due to it being a key text a scholar had been trying to translate back in Baghdad. As the scholar had picked through it at the House of Wisdom, she'd read over his work day by day, getting the story in fragments. It reconfirmed what she had remembered: six thousand, six hundred and sixty-six men who converted to Christianity and were martyred together in 286, their deaths making the land they died upon hallowed.

"Here," Azadeh said, shoving new material over. "What does that say?"

"'The holy Martyrs who have made Agaunum illustrious with their blood,'" she recited from the text, which was more of the same really. "It's the letter of Eucherius. He's talking about how Agaunum is a 'sacred place' because of those who died there by the sword for Christ."

"I didn't know it was a real place."

"Mmm… wait."

Azadeh was just about to take the text back when Roshan's eye caught on something. It was a series of illustrations supposed to recreate memorials erected in the Martyrs' honor, some dedicated to specific saints like Maurice, but there were many from the Legion who had been canonized. The exact markings she had copied – it felt like years ago – from the chalkboard were lost now, but they were odd enough that they remained seared into Roshan's mind. The shapes were… distinct. And there they were, drawn on the graves of dead men almost six hundred years after they would be marked on the case her group had been hired to retrieve. She closed her eyes for a moment, the shapes on the parchment flashing in her mind's eye as she compared them with what she had glimpsed being transported inside the guarded caravan. She was certain they were the same, which begged the question… what did they mean? And where did they come from? Because part of the reason they stood out was that they did *not* match the surrounding Christian iconography.

"I do not understand it," Azadeh said, as if plucking the very thought from Roshan's mind.

"What part?" she questioned.

"Christianity. Or any religion really."

"You worship no god?"

"I feel like I may find one, but I'm quite certain it won't be the kind that values the needless suicide of six thousand men. What could Francis possibly find there?"

"Not much," Roshan noted. "He's quite small."

Azadeh flashed her a look of surprise. Her face cracked into a smile and they both attempted to stifle a series of giggles.

"Anyway," Roshan began, trying to get them back on track. "The number was said to be symbolic rather than factually accurate."

"Here's another from the sixth century, I think. Is that the right number?"

Roshan glanced at where Azadeh was pointing and nodded. "Late sixth century, yes. The account of Gregory of Tours."

She was quiet as she read, her mood still elevated from the brief burst of levity they'd just had. It quickly dropped as she kept going, and Azadeh noted the shift.

"What is it? You look gray."

"He became convinced that the Theban Legion had miraculous powers of healing," she said.

"While they were alive?" Azadeh asked.

Roshan shook her head. "Following their death. During

a pilgrimage, he discovered a cult dedicated to them who used the dust from the soldiers' graves to perform rituals of healing."

"Healing of... the immortal kind?" Azadeh questioned.

"Guess what this cult was called?"

Her new ally didn't need to reply, both of their faces grim as the answers Roshan sought were presented on the page right in front of her. She didn't want to accept them. She wasn't even sure if she believed them. But she had seen warriors who seemingly couldn't be killed, six warriors who aligned themselves with Christian soldiers long dead, and whose resting place held all the clues whether she wanted to connect them or not.

"The Martyrs of Agaunum," Azadeh whispered.

"We need to get back to the others," Roshan replied. "As quickly as possible."

Chapter Sixteen

Karachi, 823

Roshan couldn't quite believe what she was looking at. The mechanism was cogged, using old metal parts that had been beaten with tools and heat until they were wielded into submission. The flexibility came from reeds, with the plant life having been treated and preserved until it was leathery. It was sturdy. Durable. It made the whole thing work together rather seamlessly… which might have been enough to convince her.

Yet, as she positioned the device under a shard of golden light she'd amplified with a reflective plate of bronze so she could analyze the detail up close, it was the threading that gave everything away. She used a tiny set of pliers to lift the copper wiring. It practically sparkled under the direct rays, a beam of sunshine running along its length.

He was always someone who learned, someone who evolved and improved his technique rather than ever getting stuck in his ways like so many of his peers. After Maryam had first brought them the devices back in Thatta, he started to incorporate the metal in all kinds of work after finding all kinds of uses for it. In the months that had followed, copper had become his signature. And here it was, the key component of the timepiece she was about to re-home.

Bakhit was alive.

She guessed he had been, at least for a while, but Roshan had always assumed that the already old man would find imprisoned life too stifling. It would eventually take its toll on his mind and creativity, then his body. It wasn't until she had taken on this work for Dervis that she was in a position to cross paths with him – via his inventions – once more. And here it was, definitive proof. Bakhit was alive, and he was still creating dangerous objects.

Roshan's acceptance of Dervis's job offer had her relocate to Karachi, a city she wasn't sure she was in love with in the same way she had been with Thatta. There had been a refined quality to her previous home, it being the first one she'd ever really had, along with the memories of her newfound freedom and friendship with Advi.

Karachi, in contrast, didn't have any of those sentimental connections for her. It was loud and cramped and overflowing with action every day, which is exactly why it was perfect for Dervis's purposes. There were merchants arriving and leaving constantly from the city's many ports, creating the ideal window for importing a product and exporting it rather seamlessly. If those avenues became too closely monitored by soldiers or spies – both equally as deadly for his trade – then there was a myriad of routes through the Kirthar Mountains which could maintain business over land.

A knock rang out and Roshan's head snapped up. She examined the shadows at her window, noting that they had grown long but not long enough. Dervis was early, which was rare for him. But he was also the only person who knew her address, Roshan having a small loft of her very own. She lived at the top of a high rising block of residences occupied by traveling salespeople and families, as well as shady characters who the less you knew about, the better. It wasn't in the good part of town, nor the bad, but rather wedged conveniently and inconspicuously between the two. Business happened at all hours given the proximity to the market so neither Dervis or Roshan ever stood out too much if they were coming or going.

Pushing away from her workbench, she grabbed the sword she kept near the door just in case. She had chosen this place because of the gorgeous light, all four walls fixed with huge windows that bathed the loft in a heavenly glow most hours of the day and – at sunset and sunrise – gave a breathtaking view of Karachi. These windows were also her exit route and Roshan gave her bag – prepped for any immediate escape – a cursory glance as she walked toward the sound of more knocks. She had a rope securely fastened and ready to throw out the window, meaning that if she had to she could flee in an instant.

Anyone coming for her would do so through the only obvious exit and entry point: the staircase. All she would need was a few seconds warning before she could fling herself out the window with enough crucial possessions to start again.

Of course, being a fence wasn't the only tradecraft she had picked up in the months under Dervis's employ. His ability to liquidate straight payments like coin and gold into other items of value that were more transportable was invaluable to her. Just like he had done for Maryam and the other women, she had him do the same for her. And she learned from Maryam's mistakes: no loans, no stakeholders, no one you were answerable to or who had power over you.

She had small stashes across the city, some with trusted bankers she paid for the privilege of keeping items secure for her. Others she dug deep into the earth, their position marked by stars she could read or landmarks only Roshan knew. She would never have to start again completely cold.

Gripping the hilt of her sword, she unlocked the door and positioned her body behind it so that if someone came through whom she didn't like, there was still the opportunity to throw her weight against the wood and knock them down.

"Oh, give it a rest, will you? No one here to hurt you is going to announce their presence with a knock."

That was Dervis's "greeting" as he strutted into the space with an annoyingly good point.

"You're forty-five minutes early," she countered. "You're never punctual. It's… suspicious."

He barked a laugh of amusement, flopping down onto one of the chairs she had positioned near her favorite viewing spot. He kicked his legs over the side of the arm, reaching toward the stack of books she had positioned there. He grabbed the one on top, catching the pieces of parchment that fell as he cracked open the spine.

"What are we learning today, I wonder?" he mused, eyes narrowing as he tried to decipher the marking there.

"Xiao'erjing," she said, snapping the text shut as she took it from him. Dervis had a great ear and a great tongue for language, able to switch confidently between dozens depending on the customer he was servicing. Yet unlike her he'd never had the luxury or time to learn further, his skill not transferring to the page.

"Touchy," he noted.

"Not touchy," Roshan huffed, touchily. "Concerned about where you obtained this particular piece."

She gestured to what was laid out on her workbench. Dervis's smug smirk didn't dip for a second as his eyes flashed toward it and back again.

"Does it matter?" he asked. "It never has before."

"I haven't recognized the handiwork before."

"Oh?"

She could see the curious glint in his eyes and that spelled danger for her. Dervis traded in secrets as much as he did coveted objects and jewels. He was protective of his operation, but she wasn't sure if that protection extended to her.

"Maryam worked with him," she said, adding her own layer of verbal protection in case she needed it.

"He made devices for her," Dervis said, a spark of remembrance in his eyes.

"You knew him, then?" Roshan asked, refusing to say Bakhit's name out loud.

"No, I stole one of the devices. Delivered it to a harem here in the city but they couldn't recreate it. I tried to get more, but I could never track the supply back to the source. Shame. That would have been a lucrative exchange."

"That's the source." She pointed to the device. "The copper used there and here is his handiwork I think."

She didn't think, she knew. But again, she was trying to walk back her connection to Bakhit with a pretend degree of uncertainty she didn't feel.

"Hmmm, let me follow it up. It wouldn't be hard to re-establish that connection with the harem if I could get more of what they truly desired." He smiled.

"They're solid customers," Roshan remarked. Many of the objects she cleaned and cleared went to them, with Dervis even recruiting her to deliver the items to the harem gates herself. The place was heavily guarded, meaning a woman approaching was much less of a threat.

"Prize jewels for the prize jewels," he'd said at the time, handing over a bundle of what looked like no more than dirt at first. As she'd picked through it, she'd realized the soil was to hide what was really being transported: rubies.

Today, however, Dervis had a different kind of delivery for her. Roshan passed off the device Bakhit had created to Dervis and examined an explicit painting of two princes making love to each other.

"What am I supposed to do with this?" she asked, tilting her head to try to better perceive the positions they were contorted into.

"Obviously I can't move it like this," he said, tapping the hardwood of the frame the picture was encased in. "It's going to a spicy bishop in Britannia, so I was thinking within a tapestry, perhaps? Two, probably, sewn together to explain the weight of the artwork and to protect it. Rolled into a cylinder and transported that way. Can you find something like that?"

"I'll visit the market this afternoon," she said, grabbing a ruler made from a stiff piece of wood she used to gauge an item's size. It had measurements etched down its length and she held it vertically, taking a note, then switched to horizontal. *Just like Bakhit taught you,* she thought. She added a margin on either side of the painting so it wouldn't be damaged by the stitches used to secure it.

"By tomorrow night."

She flashed Dervis an annoyed look. "And you need papers?"

"As legitimate as possible, please. I've bribed a monk to take it with him by sea, so I need a history of ownership."

She paused and took notes as he spoke, documentation she would burn once the job was done. It was unlikely a monk would be stopped and searched, but just in case, she had an old transaction parchment she had made handwritten copies of so there were blanks ready to go if an occasion like this arose. They often did, with Dervis's network of young spies always looking for opportunities amongst the preset jobs he assigned them.

Roshan ushered him out not long after that, feeling a pang as he took Bakhit's device with him. She thought of the old inventor from time to time, but it was only a fleeting consideration.

She had no physical token to remember him by, the only evidence of his existence being what she could do with her mind now: the reading, the writing, the memories. Watching

Dervis strut out the front door with a remnant of that life made her want to snatch it back. Yet she let it go.

As it turned out, it wouldn't be the last of the objects she would encounter crafted by Bakhit's skilled hands. The master thief tracked everything back to the source like he'd said he would, with a steady and constant supply of odd gadgets and unique inventions beginning to pass through Dervis's network and, therefore, Roshan herself.

She had done her own digging, figuring that if anyone would have a clue about what had happened to the old eccentric, it would be his own people. There was one major library in the city and a few smaller academies, which she frequented at first to learn and then to subtly ask questions about the inventor. It didn't take much: he was just as famous for his work as he was for evading the notoriety that followed him.

"Bakhit, ha!" barked a mathematician who seemed so old his skin had the pallor of a radish. "I once saw him tear an *infamous* philosopher to shreds, poking holes in that man's every belief until he fled the lecture hall in tears."

"My old mentor said he could have been one of the greats, but he was greedy," another young scholar remarked.

At first, she assumed he meant with money, because that had been her experience: his greed for more clients, more work, and therefore more funds had been his ultimate downfall. He hadn't known when to stop.

"He hoarded knowledge," the scholar continued. "He wouldn't share. He rarely taught. The things he learned and what he accomplished he kept to himself. Look where that got him."

She couldn't say she disagreed, after all, since the "where" turned out to be in the eternal employ of the prince who had once brought them to Thatta. The housekeeper had been killed and the guilt she felt over that was significant. Roshan had tried to warn her, tried to save her, but in the end it hadn't been enough. Bakhit had been imprisoned just like Advi had predicted. She learned that he had been kept in relative comfort, however, so he could continue working exclusively for the city's ruler like he had originally promised… at least for the first few years.

Because, eventually, the prince had seen the value of Bakhit's previous scheme. It was an earner. And for someone who had spent almost everything he had on overthrowing his family to gain control of the throne – then spent whatever he had left maintaining it – he was in desperate need of wealth. It was one thing to use Bakhit's inventions to protect and secure his rule, but it was another thing for him to use them to rebuild his riches. The prince didn't have to pay Bakhit now, as the reward was continuing to let Bakhit live. He had a direct line to the product he wanted and the only person who could make it, so everything else? Complete profit.

Roshan could almost track the precise moment the prince realized this potential goldmine – that was when Dervis had encountered the first object she had recognized with Bakhit's signature creation on it. Dervis didn't even need to create a secret channel to supply the harem, he was able to create one directly between them and an agent of the prince who negotiated price and quantity: Dervis merely became the go-between. She started to see more and more of Bakhit's work arrive amongst the erotic artworks, forbidden scrolls, precious stones and sacred weapons.

Some of them were no more than clever knickknacks that caused her to smirk, knowing how mad Bakhit would be, making something as simple as children's toys. *Beneath him,* she thought. Yet regardless, they were beautiful. She smiled as she tried to roll small balls into holes drilled into a hand-painted wooden surface. They were magnetized by a layer underneath the top level, which would see them drop inside then slide back down to the bottom so the game could repeat again. Others were rotating cubes with numbers, letters, and colors – little puzzle boxes that could keep you entertained for hours.

"There's a merchant obsessed with these," Dervis said, throwing one up in the air and catching it. "I can't acquire them fast enough to keep up with demand."

They were harmless entertainments. Much of what Bakhit was making was not. The first truly dangerous thing she came across looked like one of the puzzle boxes and she would have passed it off as one if not for the glow that emitted slightly as her fingers brushed over the numerals. Her ability flaring up.

Dervis had been looking over her shoulder when it happened and he didn't react, meaning that illumination was still hers and hers alone. When she had a moment, Roshan examined the puzzle box more closely and found a propulsive mechanism inside. It was fixed with shards of metal, nails, and other harmful scraps that could annihilate the flesh of anyone within the intended proximity. She couldn't decipher what set such an explosion off exactly, but she recognized the gunpowder held within a small glass cylinder at the center.

It would need to be ignited manually, she decided, meaning that this was useless until the intended owner decided otherwise.

Her immediate instinct was to destroy the object. But that would trap her in several ways. Dervis would know then that Roshan wasn't telling the whole truth about her interactions with the inventor. It would also tell him that she had the skills to identify what Bakhit was making and the objects' intended purposes. Information was once again her savior and her jailer.

Still, the damage this box could do… She checked its intended destination, breathing a sigh of relief when she saw it was an area of great conflict. A war zone rarely had innocents wielding spears and ordering custom weaponry. It had soldiers ordered into battle for the glory of rulers who wouldn't care about them otherwise, rulers who expected them to die.

When she slipped away for her daily training session, her choices weighed on her mind. Roshan didn't have Maryam's lovers or Advi anymore, so she trained alone. She jogged to the edge of the city, where buildings met the hard sand of the surrounding shore. She swirled her fighting stick through the air, bending and twisting herself as she performed tahtib solo, to an audience of no one. When she hacked away with her short sword, slashing at the trunk of a scorched old tree, she thought about some of the soldiers she had known. One had been a truly good person. A handful of others, too. Many were beasts. Did that mean they deserved to die the way she knew the puzzle box would kill them? Mortally injured and screaming in pain? Probably bleeding out and pleading to a god that had never existed to her?

Who was she to make the choice to value her life over theirs? If she had been born a man, she would have had no option but the military or farming like her father. Many were in that same position and yet... had she sealed their fates?

When she returned to her loft hours later, the freshly risen sun adding to her sweat-soaked body, Roshan had reckoned with the call. If she destroyed the puzzle box, she would have to run. She doubted she'd be able to get out of the city unseen given the extent of Dervis's rapidly expanding network. She'd have to fight, and she'd have to flee with a tail.

She was not ready to start all over again, not yet. She'd only been here a few months.

So, she stayed. She decided to send the box to its destination. She lived with the choice she made, hoping that the intended owner of the weapon would make a different one but knowing such a hope was extremely unlikely.

Later, when other items did come through from Bakhit, she always made sure to check where they were going. One was the present for a newly born heir to a faraway throne, the babe the intended victim of poison that would shift from granule to oxidized form when a chemical reaction was introduced. She disabled it, replacing the powder with sand and dyeing it until it matched the toxic pink of the original substance.

The once dangerous object would actually be just a gift now, with any number of explanations for why it didn't work possible. The routes were long and arduous. Dervis always warned potential customers of this: there could be no guarantee that objects would arrive perfectly intact. That wasn't his job. He only acquired and transported them, often creating the necessary fictions around their origin if required. Soon, other dangerous objects besides Bakhit's appeared on her workbench, and she did the same, assessing what would harm the greatest amount of innocent lives and then tinkering with the weapon's makeup.

There was someone from far up in the Tibetan mountains that had a true gift for jewelry laced with toxins. It took a lot of work and experimentation to determine how to neutralize that, her sensory skill helping her identify which item in a chest of treasures was not what it appeared to be. Her sabotage needed to be consistent and not just confined to Bakhit's weaponry so that such claims of "damages in transit" could be passed off as the cost of dealing with a network of professional thieves rather than specific intelligence.

All the while, she felt like she was having a wordless conversation with the first person who had ever offered her a taste of freedom. That meal had a bitter aftertaste, of course, yet it was weirdly comforting all the same. Bakhit's inventions would be sent her way and Roshan would use the skills he had taught her to make her old mentor's work impotent.

It was the only choice that allowed her any slumber.

Chapter Seventeen

Karachi, 824

When Azadeh and Roshan returned to the inn, things were calm and quiet. It made her nervous. Dias was posted by the window, so he'd seen them entering the inn. Francis sat in the corner, eyes closed, and Bible open on his lap. His lips were moving, gentle whispers coming from them as he recited a prayer to himself.

"Where are the twins?" Azadeh asked. It was so perfectly poised and phrased that if Roshan hadn't known otherwise, she wouldn't have picked up on Azadeh's deceit.

"I was hoping you'd know," Dias responded, nodding his head in Roshan's direction. "They followed her after all."

"Thanks for the heads up," she snarled, sitting down next to Nafanua. The warrior was fast asleep and Roshan tried to gently wake her. She didn't stir, so Roshan increased the effort. A groan of recognition came from the woman, but she seemed to struggle to full consciousness as she rolled over.

Roshan knew how she felt. They were all tired. The kind of tired felt deep down in the spirit, the tired that made every movement ache as you struggled to the next. She personally had been running on adrenaline for the past several days and it seemed as if she wasn't the only one.

"Tafesilafa'i," she mumbled. "Tafesil …"

Sāmoan wasn't a language Roshan had been exposed to before she met Nafanua and she struggled to understand what the women meant until she pointed. She retrieved the serrated fishhook weapon she'd seen her wield ferociously, its weight significant as she passed it to her.

"Thank you," Nafanua said, clutching it as she sat up.

"Are you all right?" Roshan asked. Nafanua did not look it. Her eyes were puffy, and a sheen of sweat formed at her forehead despite the conditions not being overwhelmingly hot.

"Ugh," she grunted in response. "I'll be fine. Just need to wake up, get moving."

"Let's do that then," Dias said, springing to his feet and paying little attention to Nafanua's condition. "Did you get the map?"

"I did," Roshan replied, laying out the first, most commonly used one for all to see. Azadeh didn't know about the local's map – no one did – and for the time being Roshan would keep it that way. "If we're rested enough, we should leave tonight."

"We can intercept here." Dias pointed. "Right at the point where the three borders intersect."

"If they're still traveling along the Silk Road that is," Azadeh noted.

"Well, we'll soon find out. Although if the twins don't show up soon, I say we leave without them," Dias said.

"Mmmmmm."

They all turned to face the unusual humming coming from Francis, whose eyes went from shut to wide open in a flash. *If he was doing his best to affect prophecy, he'd need to do a bit better than a slow blink,* Roshan thought.

"Mmmmm," he continued. "The Holy Spirit is divine, and it intervenes."

"In a useful way or…?" Roshan murmured, earning a smirk from Azadeh.

"We will find them at the point you speak of, Dias. And I know of the swiftest horses in the city. We will collide by morning." Francis smiled.

They assembled quickly, Roshan switching into the now-dry clothes the hooded stranger had first given her back in Fustat. Francis helpfully acquired fresh food supplies and water pouches for the group, even though Roshan and Azadeh had already picked up some of their own on the way back. His so-called prophetic visions led them to a stable which indeed did have the fastest horses in the city according to the owner they bought them off, who bowed his head in consultation with Francis to give them an even lower price.

"That makes terrible business sense," Nafanua mumbled as Roshan helped her on to the largest horse.

Roshan frowned. "Are you sure you're–"

"Fine," she snapped, cutting her off. "Just thirsty and famished. The food here is terrible. All the fish is overcooked."

"If your standard is raw then yes, I imagine it would be."

The woman gave her an exasperated smile before a gentle kick sent her horse forward. Onyx barked happily, trotting alongside Nafanua in a way that didn't seem to alarm the horses like last time. Maybe it was an animal thing. Francis rode with Dias, and Azadeh and Roshan together just like before, except so much had changed now.

Azadeh had her trust and Roshan had hers. They felt more like a team together compared to the hollow one formed on this mission. For a moment, Roshan felt the bonds of sisterhood forming, like the ones she'd felt between the wives and, later, the brothel. They trotted out of the city, the sky turning a curdling blood red as the sun set behind them.

"That's a bad omen," Azadeh whispered.

"Let's hope it's for them and not us," Roshan replied.

They set a rapid pace once they left the outskirts of Karachi, a pace that wasn't exactly safe for riding at this time of night, but what other choice did they have? They had climbed mountains and sailed seas to have this opportunity, so they *must* seize it.

They paused on the other side of midnight to let the horses cool down and take a brief reprieve for themselves. Roshan watched with concern as Nafanua stumbled off her horse. Francis attended to her with fresh water and some dry food that she immediately threw up. She barked that she was "fine" in between hurls, mumbling she just wasn't used to that much riding. They had little time to worry about it further as they mounted up again, their progress slower as they navigated the slopes around a mountain range which would bring them out directly at the point Dias had highlighted as ideal.

They were nearly on the other side of the range, with the faintest glow of sunrise up ahead, when Onyx slowed down next to them. The wolf had been racing beside Nafanua for most of the trip, never once letting up her barks and growls. She grew silent now, trotting beside Azadeh and Roshan. Roshan felt Azadeh straighten up next to her, the metallic sound of a sword slowly being drawn as Azadeh read the wolf's behavior.

"We're not alone," she whispered in Roshan's ear. The warning sent a tingle of fear down her spine. Onyx let out a low growl as her head and tail dropped defensively. Roshan's hand went immediately to the fighting stick at her side, her finger hovering over the button that would eject the weapon at a moment's notice. The others were partially illuminated ahead, and she tried to think of ways to warn them that wouldn't alert their attackers as well. But such actions were unnecessary as Nafanua sagged in her saddle, her hunched body slumping as she slid off the side of the horse. Dias tried to grab her, clearly thinking she'd been hit by something, when arrows started flying.

"Take cover!" Roshan cried. She and Azadeh spun off the side of their own animal and ducked to the ground. Nafanua's horse spooked and galloped away, creating confusion as she heard, rather than saw, arrows streaming after the horse. The attack came from above and whoever they were, they had the perfect vantage point for an ambush. Roshan cursed their superior position.

Azadeh placed her hands between her lips and whistled, the sharp sound signaling Onyx who sprinted off into the dark. The wolf blended so perfectly into the night that once the glow of her eyes was out of range, Roshan couldn't see her any longer. She heard when she made contact, however, as a man's pained scream split the night.

Onyx's growls mixed with the man's cries, and she saw Dias take a chance, leaving Francis unprotected as he ran toward the rocky outcrop where their attackers were more than likely firing from.

Roshan and Azadeh did the same, copying him as they used their horse for protection and half hung off their saddle to the side to ride up the outcrop. As soon as they were over the crest, they split apart. Onyx had torn one of the shooters to pieces and was already dragging another man by his leg, the archer shouting and his hands scrabbling at the ground for a grip or a weapon as he desperately tried to avoid becoming Onyx's next meal. He found a rock and spun around to hit Onyx with it, but the wolf was too quick – she leapt back with a bark.

Azadeh released her grip on the horse and dove, swinging her sword so that the man's arm was cut clean off. His yells were cut short as Onyx went for the jugular. Roshan did her own damage as she swung her fighting stick and batted away a series of arrows sent flying in her friend's direction. Dias leapt down on their other enemies from behind, stabbing and slashing wildly while Roshan continued to run defense by keeping her people protected with the best weapon for blocking an aerial assault. It felt like the whole thing was over as quick as it began, the cries of battle dying off as the victims did, too. Panting, the three of them stood, covered in carnage, looking at the bodies as sunrise bathed everything in a golden orange light.

"Where did they come from?" Dias panted.

Azadeh darted away, quickly descending to check on the others while Roshan counted the dead. Six men. They had been outnumbered and their foes had the element of surprise, but thanks to Onyx, they'd had the briefest of warnings. She watched the wolf tearing into the corpses, flinching at the wet sounds and *crack* of a bone snapping. Dias didn't seem repulsed as he plucked the bow free from the dead man, allowing Onyx better access.

"Have at it, mate," he said, analyzing the weapon. Roshan inched forward, frowning as she looked at the bow in his hands. "You recognize it?" he asked.

She did. The lower and upper limbs of this bow were distinctive and very unusual. They were longer than your standard weapon like this, almost comically so, when one settled into the correct stance for firing. Her fingers trailed the small design carved into the sight window before she turned away to pluck an arrow from the collection positioned next to one of the other dead shooters.

The arrows were thicker, too, which is why the bow was oversized to match their weight for firing. These weren't designed to simply harm or injure, they weren't designed for hunting animals, they were designed to cause a fatality on human targets. They were the same as what she'd seen a companion firing off the top of the Martyrs' caravan. They were also preferred by the famed Karachi archers, said to be some of the best in the world. *Allegedly*, Roshan thought.

"Is that a yes?" Dias called as she turned away from him, eyes scanning the ground as she searched for the tracks. She followed the marks in the dirt, dropping to all fours as she climbed higher up the slope. She had to be sure. A neigh as she approached confirmed her suspicions and several horses came into view, all tied to a tree hidden out of sight. Dias had followed and crouched down, clearly picking up on what she was thinking as he lifted the hooves of one of the horses.

"These look familiar," he said, tone dark as he looked up at her. "The fastest horses in the city, his vision said."

"These men came from Karachi," Roshan murmured, her hand running over the rump of one of the animals. They were still warm with exertion, and dirt and dust speckled their fur. "They would have left just after we did, but they knew the terrain better and knew exactly where we'd be. Again."

"Do you think that little prophet's vision might have told him to share information, perhaps?" Dias growled, springing to his feet. "And for what purpose?"

He wiped his sword on his thigh, cleaning it of fresh blood as he angrily stomped down the hill. She thought his rage was a bit much given he'd either killed or put members of the team in danger at various points, including her.

Yet he had asked the right question: for what purpose? Dias's motivation was clear. He was a pirate-soldier after all. Mutiny was in his nature. If he thought they were tracking some kind of treasure, then the fewer people to share it with at the end, the better. Francis on the other hand…

The sound of Azadeh's shout snapped her out of her musings, and Roshan sprinted down toward the others. Dias's sword was pointed directly at Francis' chest, whose hands were raised and his eyes wide as he protested his innocence. Azadeh was trying to intervene, putting herself in between them as Dias continued to yell.

"You sold us out!" Dias screamed.

"I would never! In the name of the Father–"

"Damn your father!"

Roshan opened her mouth to say something, but her words fell away as she observed Onyx sniffing at a mass she realized was Nafanua. Amidst the havoc, she had forgotten the woman falling from her horse, and she rushed over, skidding to her knees as she dropped down next to her.

"No, no, no," she whispered, seeing the arrowhead protruding from her back. As Roshan rolled her over, that fear was confirmed as Nafanua's lifeless eyes stared up at her. One of the huge arrows had cut right through her, the perfect shot piercing her heart. She closed her eyes for a moment, letting the anger and grief run through her. Onyx whimpered and she blinked away her unclear vision, focusing on the bloody snout of the wolf who sniffed at Nafanua's neck like she hadn't just been ripping into someone else's a second earlier. It caused Roshan to focus on the woman's face and the dried residue around her lips. At first, she thought it was vomit from earlier, but as she leaned in, she noticed it was a black, almost cakey substance.

She sniffed, her nose wrinkling in disgust as she jerked back. The veins on Nafanua's face had even become pronounced, snaking over her features like vines. *Poison,* she realized.

The arrow had struck an already dead target. The perfect cover for the true intentions of someone amongst them, someone who had been close enough to tamper with their food and drink unnoticed. Someone who didn't have the physical prowess to take on Nafanua otherwise; someone who could slip under the radar and shrink themselves amongst the louder, rowdier, and more dangerous members of their party.

Her head whipped toward the three who remained. The rage of the situation was still significant, but Francis and Dias were yelling at each other from a little way apart now. Azadeh was doing her best to mediate, but she leaned back against one of the horses with exhaustion. It was the mare Nafanua had been riding, the creature having circled back after it calmed down. The mare playfully breathed onto Azadeh's shoulder and she patted it idly, reaching into the knapsack hung over its side. Roshan leapt to her feet in a flash, sprinting toward Azadeh as she watched her part her lips and begin to pour the contents of Nafanua's canteen into her mouth.

Roshan pressed down on her fighting stick, ejecting its length, and used it to cover the distance she couldn't make in time by twisting her wrist. It flew from her hand, just enough of the edge of the tahtib tool brushing the container to knock it out of Azadeh's hand and on to the ground. She didn't stop until she reached Azadeh, grabbing her face in her hands as she felt a flash of fear and desperation that startled her.

"Did you swallow it? Even just a drop, did you swallow it?"

Azadeh was trying to speak, but her lips were mushed together as Roshan inspected her face.

"Spit it out, spit anything out! It's poison!"

Azadeh yanked herself away, spitting onto the dirt and Roshan's rapid heart rate began to slow as she realized Azadeh was all right. She hadn't drunk from Nafanua's canteen, and even if she had consumed a drop, it wasn't close to the same quantity that had no doubt killed the warrior.

"No," she said firmly to Onyx who was sniffing around the canister. The wolf glanced up at her, intelligence in those animal eyes that told Roshan she understood the order perfectly. Roshan twirled her fighting stick, extending it in a blur of movement so that it stopped less than an inch from Francis' throat. He was frozen in place, hands raised once more, but the innocence he'd worked so hard to project wasn't quite as convincing as last time.

"You killed her," she snarled.

"An a-arrow killed her," he replied. "If you look at–"

"She was sick before we left," Roshan snapped. "She could barely wake up and I pushed it aside, ignoring the symptoms because she told me to. But it was right there in front of us."

"Wait," Dias said. "Did he sell us out or kill–"

"Both," she answered. "Where did you grow up, Francis? With that blond hair and those blue eyes, do you hail from the Holy Roman Empire? Have you set sights on the Rhone Valley enroute to the Abbey of Saint-Maurice d'Agaune?"

There was a spark of something in his eyes and the faintest smirk tugged at the corner of his mouth. "The holy Martyrs made Agaunum illustrious with their blood," he said, that high-pitched voice grating on her nerves more than ever.

"You ba–"

Dias didn't get a moment to finish his curse as Francis threw some kind of object at him while kicking up the dirt in Roshan's face. Roshan spun to shield her eyes while Dias yelled, pulling at his shirt desperately. A sizzling sound was soon explained by the fabric disappearing before her very eyes. Dias tore his shirt off, his fingertips bubbling with blisters as he made contact. One of the horses neighed and Roshan looked up to see Francis struggling to mount it even as he urged it forward. Dias reached for an arrow, drawing his elbow wide just as Francis got on the horse fully and began to ride away as fast as he could. Dias was just about to let the arrow fly, Roshan trusting that Dias's aim and anger were true, when she pushed the weapon away.

"What are you doing?" he hissed. "I had the perfect shot!"

"Shoot wide," she said. "Let him see and hear the arrow whistle past his head. Let him think you missed."

Rage was etched into every feature of Dias's expression, but with a shake of his head he did as she said. They watched as Francis' figure ducked, the projectile falling wide of its target.

"That little white rat has been working against us the whole time," Dias snarled. "He signaled Wei too early on purpose, screwed us then. Screwed us now by sending us into the middle of nowhere while killers waited in the dark. He killed our second best fighter the way a coward would, with poison."

"And you used a woman as a human shield," Azadeh snapped. "Be careful positioning yourself as the new holy man of the group."

"I'm holy furious, how about that?" he responded. "I hope you have a good reason for why I didn't kill that fair-skinned devil?"

"I do," Roshan replied, voice calm as she faced Azadeh. "How did you find me in Karachi? You've never been there before. That city's a maze to strangers."

"Her," she said, nodding at Onyx. "I'm a great tracker, but I can't compete with her abilities."

"Good," Roshan sighed, a smile playing on her face. "That's what I was hoping you would say."

"Why?" Dias snorted.

"Because who do you think that blue-eyed bastard is fleeing to? He's a puppet at best. And he's going to lead us right to his masters."

There was a loaded pause as they stood there, battle-worn and blood splattered. A sharp whistle cut through the silence and Azadeh gestured forward with her hand, pointing off in the direction Francis had fled. He was still visible to them, his figure much smaller now as he shrank into the distance. Onyx's head snapped up and after a moment, the wolf was gone. She dashed after him like a streak of black, showing them the path toward their target and toward vengeance.

Roshan hated where Onyx was going. She hated the vistas around her becoming more familiar, the surrounds and the climate evoking terrifying recollections of the past. They had been tracking Francis for a week. He was a terrible rider and they had made such solid progress – led by Onyx who would run forward then double back to make sure they were following the correct trail – that they had to keep hanging back so he wouldn't spot them.

When they made camp for the night Roshan knew she

was close to the village where she had spent her childhood. The facts could not be denied any longer.

They were heading to Baghdad. Whether that was always the destination, or the Martyrs had abandoned their route along the Silk Road once Francis told them they were on their trail, she couldn't be sure. Regardless, the reality did not sit well with her. They were less than an hour behind Francis and that evening in particular felt like the lull before a massive set of waves.

Roshan kept watch while the others slept… or at least they were supposed to. Instead, Dias was sharpening his sword on a flat stone, his brow furrowed with concentration. Azadeh was practicing her words, a ritual she had fallen into each day as Roshan would give her a new set of letters and lessons. Roshan had been serious about her literacy and as she watched her, the younger woman's head jerked up, as if sensing Roshan's gaze. She smiled, and Roshan glanced away, thinking about how these lessons with Azadeh promised a future that could not exist. Historically, hope and friendship proved a dangerous thing for her to entertain, so she pushed it down, suppressed it deep within herself. She repressed the joy that flared as Azadeh moved to take a seat next to her, dreading the time when she would be on her own again.

Onyx had returned to them during their rest, and the wolf relaxed at Roshan's feet, recognizing her as Azadeh's ally. She'd been feeding the wolf pieces of jerky that Onyx seemed to enjoy the texture of rather than the taste. Onyx lifted her head before flopping back down and over.

"You've done so well, my dark girl," Azadeh said, rubbing

Onyx's belly until her tongue lolled out. "Not much longer now."

"How did you and Onyx come to be?" Roshan asked, voicing a question she might not have much more time to get an answer for.

"In my tribe, dogs are as much a part of our everyday existence as goats or cattle for some people. They live with us, they sleep with us, they work with us, they guard us. My father believed that any animal could be trained, so long as you were respectful, patient, and never undervalued the spirit that resided within."

"I like how that sounds," Roshan murmured.

"When I was a little girl, our village would frequently get attacked by raiders who were getting pushed south. We would fight back with our dogs, but it wasn't enough. My father started training wolves, in part to discourage them from taking small children from town but also as a form of defense. Onyx was the runt of the last litter my father's wolf ever had. I'd trained a few by then, but with her it was… different."

"You had a connection," she said.

Azadeh's stare was loaded as she looked at Roshan. Roshan broke the gaze, regretting it. Azadeh nudged the fishhook resting next to Roshan. "What do you plan on doing with that?"

"She said she had a brother," Roshan remarked. "If we make it through this, the Tafesilafa'i should be returned to him and I can tell him where we buried her body."

"Is that why you took Wei's charm?"

Roshan was surprised she had noticed. "It is."

Azadeh nodded, as if that was the answer she expected. "You're a good person."

"I didn't take anything from the twins," she countered. "So… not that good."

"You took their lives," her friend replied, earning an amused snort.

Roshan felt the smile on her face fade, her tone growing serious. "You should try to rest," she cautioned.

Azadeh shrugged. "We're almost there. I can feel it. Why waste the minutes sleeping?"

"Because we don't know what waits for us in Baghdad," Roshan replied, grave. "But I can guarantee you… it's not good."

Chapter Eighteen

Fustat, 824

Roshan had her eye on a crocodile.

It was huge and could gobble her up in two snaps of its massive jaws if it wanted to. It was also on the far bank of the river and the felucca she needed to reach was much closer, just a short swim away. Of course, it wasn't the crocodiles you could see that were the problem: it was the ones you never knew were there until it was too late.

There had been an attack recently, a mother and son dragged from the banks of the city and into the Nile so fast they'd barely had a chance to scream. Only parts of them had been found. Roshan didn't want that fate for herself, but she had no choice as she slipped into the cool water. She tried to steady her breathing as she slowly, carefully swam. Erratic movements would attract the predators, so she was trying to project a calm that she did not feel.

She kept her eyes on the big reptile far across the way,

who either hadn't spotted her or wasn't interested in her presence. Roshan hoped it would stay that way as she navigated around the hull of the felucca that was her target. A very mean couple lived on board the boat and they frequently traveled, which meant the vessel had been the ideal location for one of her personal stashes. They had no idea, of course, and she hadn't intended to return to this one so soon, but it was a matter of life and death.

She gripped the edge of the boat, heaving herself up on the starboard side and moving quietly. The *splish splashes* of water dripping from her person wouldn't be enough to wake the residents in the same way entering from the bow would have. Swimming had been the only option and as she carefully lifted one of the loosened wooden slates, she sighed with relief as she spotted her items below.

There was a beautiful breast piece lighter than any armor she'd ever seen and designed specifically for a woman, which she had slipped out of a stolen order for herself. Small parcels of jewels and fabric that were easier to move. An elaborate series of documents for a woman who looked just like her but went by the name Elaleh and, ah, *there it was*. She lifted the tiny, wooden box free from the other treasures, slipping everything else back inside the case she had designed to look just like the rest of the felucca. Roshan moved the wood to seal her hiding place and slipped back into the water once more. She kept the object held above her, needing it to stay dry.

As she slowly paddled toward the shore, she felt something brush against her foot. She froze, trying to resist the urge not to panic. Those kind of movements would draw attention she did not want. Roshan continued to swim, pushing thoughts of those knife-like crocodile teeth ripping into her flesh and her body twisting in a death roll far, far from her mind. She exhaled as her feet touched sand and she turned back, intending to smile at the large crocodile she had no doubt was still lounging on the other side. It wasn't there.

A ripple was her only warning. She leapt forward just as the huge beast erupted from under the surface in a spray of water to her left. She had no choice but to veer right, throwing her legs up as high as she could as she waded through the shallows, knowing the crocodile was still behind her. She didn't slow once she hit the shore and instead she kept running. She had seen those creatures move just as deathly fast on land.

The commotion had caused the occupants of the felucca to wake, along with dozens of other residents who lined the nearby banks. Roshan couldn't worry about that now, zigzagging so that her route was more difficult for the creature's log of a body. She hurdled over the edge of the nearby dock wall, not pausing until her feet hit stone and she was shielded from view.

There was a small herd of cattle nearby, far enough from the water's edge to be safe, but she had essentially led the crocodile right to them. The cows mooed loudly, bucking and kicking against each other as the creature gave up on her with an annoyed hiss. There was a much more appealing prospect nearby after all.

She peered over the dock edge, watching as those who lived on the water emerged from their homes – lanterns and weapons in hand – in an attempt to protect their livestock.

They were shouting, thrusting long spears at the crocodile to drive it back into the water while not getting too close.

Perfect, she thought, watching the scene unfold. The havoc had inadvertently cloaked her presence and, with a cursory glance, she slowly walked away. She had left Karachi three months ago, briefly working out of Sanaa before setting up more solid roots in Fustat after Dervis identified the city as ideal for their operations, given recent political turmoil. Roshan only had a passing understanding of what that meant; the only information she really needed was where she was going and when.

Fustat was similar to Karachi in its stifling heat during the summer and its melting pot of different cultures and ethnicities and religions all colliding in the one place. There was also a rich history here, the huge pyramids rising in the background of the cityscape being the most obvious example. There were also the remnants of centuries of scholarship and learning that had largely been destroyed following the destruction of the Library of Alexandria, but still remained in the echoes of things that were learned and taught, as well as the books that were saved and scrolls that were smuggled.

She had felt a sense of exhaustion when she arrived. She was tired of moving and searching for something she couldn't quite put her finger on. Fustat had felt like a small piece of reassurance to her, simply because of how much it reminded her of Advi at first, and then because of the value the city had for academic pursuits. Her quest that night had been one such academic pursuit, albeit with a slightly demented origin.

As she returned to the villa she called home – at least for the moment – Roshan stripped off her soaking clothes. The small, wooden box she'd taken from her stash looked perfectly dry, but just to be sure, she placed it in a bowl of rice to soak up any additional moisture.

She cleaned up quickly, not having the luxury of time as she changed into a more comfortable sleeping robe and tied the sash around her waist. At this time of night, any reasonable person would be deep in slumber. Yet Roshan had been kept awake the past two nights with worries. She lifted the source of her concern from under her workbench, lighting several candles and positioning them near reflective surfaces so the illumination was as bright as could be. If she'd had the time, she would have waited until dawn.

She couldn't risk it. Dervis was coming in the morning to collect what looked like a rather plain music box. She wasn't sure who the intended customer had been, but they were little more than a mark as it was Dervis who had stolen said music box. It was testament to its importance that he had performed the thievery himself, a lucrative bid coming in for the superficial invention. It had been delivered to Roshan with the express instruction to forge legitimate papers and wrap the object like a treasured gift with which a father would reward a daughter. *There was something to that analogy*, she thought, lifting the smaller music box from the bowl of rice until they were side by side.

They were both Bahkit inventions, with Roshan not sure why she had kept the smaller of the pair when it had passed through her hands almost a year ago now. As her eyes scanned both objects, she was glad she had kept it hidden in her stash, because the answer about how to disable one lay within the makeup of the other. The new buyer, she had learned, was a rising Mamluk general. He had grand ambitions and grotesque ways of achieving them, his method of warfare being less concerned with the battlefield and more with the amount of fear one could inflict with mass casualties. She had heard of the carnage he had spread through small towns then larger ones, the bloodshed only matched by the brutality.

He gained power over his enemies by letting them know *what* he could do to them before they died, this horror directed not only at soldiers but anyone in his path. Citizens were the best collateral and the weapon Bahkit had created was the perfect tool. She couldn't allow this general to have it. As she carefully unscrewed the false bottom, she understood why this music box was much larger than the other: it was designed for maximum impact. Potential fatalities could be anywhere in the hundreds, and she let a flash of anger toward her old mentor course through her for a moment. *How could you do this?* she thought. *How could you let this get into the hands of anybody?*

Nobody should have a weapon like this, and it was within Bakhit's power to construct something that could have just fizzled out. He could have built a safety mechanism or made it look like it did something grand when really it was just an illusion. He had more power than anyone to do the right thing and yet he made these objects and dusted his hands with a sense of nihilism that disgusted her. It was mere fate that had given her the skills to disable his destruction and she was grateful for it, even though no one would ever know. *That was fine,* she thought. She knew. And that was enough.

There was a small handle at the side and when you turned it, lifting the wooden lid, a sweet tune would play as various mechanics knocked notes into place. The song depended on what had been programmed on to a rotating drum inside, with little protrusions visible that – as it spun – would pluck the teeth of a steel comb. The lengths of the comb's teeth varied, longer ones playing lower notes and shorter teeth playing higher so that it worked much like a tuning fork she'd seen musicians use back when she'd spent the night dancing with Maryam.

The teeth vibrated at different speeds and when a certain speed was reached, the true intent of Bakhit's mechanism would kick into place. There were small cylinders underneath that would combust once the ignition thread that connected them was ignited. All she had to do, in principle, was sever it. She'd risked her life and almost been a crocodile's meal in order to test this theory on Bakhit's older music box, the proposed impact being only enough to hurt a family pet if she was wrong.

Crouching out of the way, she used the handle to crank the smaller music box faster and faster, desperate to get through the annoying tune and prove her theory. It didn't explode. It had worked. She double- and triple-checked the design on both, making sure that Bahkit hadn't embedded multiple ignitions as she repeated the process and used the smallest blade she'd ever owned to snip the connection. She trimmed it right back, so there was never any visual clue that something had been disabled if you opened the inner workings of the music box.

It was now just that: wood, steel, cogs and bolts spinning together for someone's audible pleasure rather than their doom. When Dervis arrived in the morning, the music box was packaged up exactly to his specifications and he trotted off happily to deliver it to the *new* new customer.

Did Dervis know what these inventions did? He must have had some clue, yet clearly he didn't feel the kind of responsibility she did when it came to intervening. He had mouths to feed other than his own, with the network of thieves he established in each city slightly larger than the last. Many of these children and teenagers would have starved without Dervis's employment and she wondered if that had been the fate he was destined for when he was young. With each urchin he sculpted into a criminal, he diverted not just their grim reality and future but the one he'd lived himself. It was a nice thought, and as the music box left her possession, so did the tension.

Roshan barely had the energy for her daily training when she returned to her villa well on the other side of dusk the next day, taking time to soak in a long, hot bath that had been prepared for her. When she finally emerged from the waters, her fingertips had pruned and the warmth had made her lightheaded. Fustat was overrun with cats and as much as she had tried to ignore them as they skipped alongside her on daily errands, there was one that kept coming back.

She had been sitting on the balcony outside, long since finished with her dinner of hamam mahshi when the cat sprang up on to the ledge nearby. Roshan recognized it, the ginger creature a return customer. She watched as he prowled toward her coolly, not wanting to look too keen even though his skinny frame told her he was in desperate need of the scraps she'd begun feeding him daily. He jumped up onto her lap eyeing the remnants of the cooked pigeon she'd mostly finished.

"Better than the wild ones, aye?" she asked, getting a cursory meow in return. The bird had been stuffed with couscous and herbs and she flicked them loose with her nails, knowing that he hated anything except the meat. He greedily nibbled at the morsel she fed him, a hearty chunk of roasted bird first and then the more challenging tendrils that he had to work off the bone.

"Alsada," she said, scratching under the rusty colored cat's chin.

He wasn't interested in the slice of basbousa she'd saved for dessert, sniffing at the cake before deciding it wasn't to his liking.

"No sweet tooth, hmm," Roshan murmured, licking the citrus from her own fingertips. She usually shooed the cat away before she went to bed, it being the second to last thing she did before she locked up. Maybe it was because she felt deflated, having thwarted an evil man from doing evil things yet having no one to celebrate her victory with. Maybe she was just lonely. But she let the cat stay that night, lying in bed as she watched him make biscuits on the blanket, tiny paws pushing against her stomach, urging the tough muscles underneath to yield.

Roshan had an early start the next morning, needing to be at the market before sunrise to get materials before customers crowded in and took note of what she was purchasing and why. She dressed in exactly what she would need to leave the villa, ensuring she wasted no time fumbling in the dark to put on her clothing and pin her head covering in the morning. The cat didn't seem to mind her going to bed fully clothed, as long as he could curl up on her chest, her fingers running through his fur and a weight seemingly lifted off her shoulders.

Perhaps that's why she didn't hear them coming. She had her first deep, immersive sleep in weeks, so the usual clues alerting her to trouble slipped by unnoticed. Her first warning was her ginger friend, the cat's hisses stirring her to consciousness. He was standing to attention, his spine curved and tail straight in alarm at something she couldn't see.

Her mind was still foggy as she blinked awake, trying to understand what was happening seconds too late. Sleep evaporated the moment her door was kicked in, a boot slamming against the wood and the frame splintering with the impact. Roshan woke in an instant. She flipped on to her stomach, hands reaching for the set of fighting sticks under her pillow just as she felt fingertips clasp around her ankle.

She was tugged backward and out of bed, landing with an ungrateful *oomph* on the hard, stone floor. The impact dazed her, and she had a moment to comprehend the dozens of soldiers filing into her villa.

Seems a bit much for little old me, she thought, curious about which one of her crimes had led them here. Roshan didn't have to wait long for an answer.

"You're under arrest, thief!" the man in charge spat.

Well, that was a relief. Theft wasn't murder and theft wasn't going to reveal her true identity. The crime was most likely still a death sentence, depending on what they thought she'd stolen, but it was a fate that would be restricted to just her and wouldn't include her family. More than she could hope for.

"What's your name, thief?"

This question surprised her. "You're arresting me for theft, but you don't know my name? What am I even accused of stealing?"

"Gold!" a soldier at the back croaked, holding up a handful of nuggets from a pouch. Part of her had wondered if Dervis had sold her out to spare himself. If it was a question of his life over hers, she'd always known he'd choose his. There had been a comfortable truth to that kind of certainty. Besides Dervis, Roshan was the most valuable player in Dervis's operation and further up on the hierarchy than anyone else in his employ. He'd give up almost everyone else before her. The gold nuggets, however, said everything.

That was nothing like the gold she had helped transport in the past. She'd never seen such gold pieces as those the soldier held up. Someone – a very skilled someone – had snuck in while she slumbered, somehow been able to not disturb her or the cat, and planted that evidence. She'd been set up. But by whom?

A question for later. All she could do now was fight.

Roshan kicked out, using both legs to thrust the lead soldier away from her and into a crowd of his colleagues. She rocked backward in a somersault and used her hands to spring upright. She was barely standing before a punch collided with the side of her face. Roshan watched as spit, mixed with her own blood, flew from her mouth. She dropped low, ducking the next blow and delivering an elbow, followed by a half-dozen body hits, to the man who'd punched her.

There was the metallic *schwick* of a sword being pulled from a sheath and swung. Roshan narrowly slid under the blade, rolling onto the bed where she had elevation. She thought she'd missed the blade but soon realized that she'd been cut just above her eyebrow. She hadn't even felt it. The rush of blood partially clouded her vision as she used the spring of her bed to leap above another sword blow and bring her heel down on a man's head. The impact shuddered through her leg as she kneed another soldier, knowing that she was never going to be able to best this crowd in hand to hand combat without permanent injuries to herself.

They had more hands. More weapons. She lunged toward the window and the balcony, to make it look like she was trying to escape. A few took the bait, but she feinted back at the last moment and dove for the pillows again. If she could just get to her fighting sticks, if she could put some distance between herself and these bastards, then she could make it out of here and start searching for the new enemy she'd made. The enemy who dared frame her with measly gold nuggets. Delight flashed through her like lightning as she felt her fingers connect with the hard, wooden cylinders. Her grip was closing on them just as she was kicked in the side, the force so hard she retched.

Someone else dove on her, throwing her back, and she lost contact with her fighting sticks. *No!* she thought, eyes wide and hands desperate as she tried to scramble her way back to them. Another devastating blow to her head made the room cloudy, the layout fading in and out of the fog of her consciousness. She was about to pass out, she knew it, and Roshan heard her own pained groan as she reached out one last time. Her hand was kicked out of the way by the lead soldier, who crouched down until her entire view was taken up with his ugly face.

"You're going to hell," he snarled, those words the last thing she heard before darkness closed in.

Chapter Nineteen

Baghdad, 824

When they rode into Baghdad, Roshan ignored the instinct to turn the horse around and race in the opposite direction. She'd lived here, but never really *lived* here. The scents and sounds felt more familiar to her than any of the sights, the city holding more trauma and horror in her memory than anything else. Dias, Azadeh, and Roshan left their horses at an inner city stable, hoping there would be the possibility to come back for them as they took their last chance to check their weapons and ready themselves for what was to come.

Onyx waited out on the street and as soon as she caught sight of them, she loped off. She set a casual pace, one easy enough for them to follow at a brisk walk. Roshan pulled her hood down low, just like Dias and Azadeh, staying disguised as night began to consume the city. The Roman pirate spotted Francis first, not making any verbal cue but his reaction was obvious when his hand shot to the hilt of his sword.

Roshan followed the direction of his glare – a look so sharp she wasn't sure how Francis didn't feel it piercing his back like an arrow.

But the young man had proven smarter than any of the others up until that point, working against them from within. He'd taken out Nafanua when she could have crushed him with one hand. He was smug, thinking himself better than them.

That was exactly what Roshan was counting on.

Francis never once looked over his shoulder or showed any signs of self-consciousness as he crossed a bridge, the still waters of the Tigris river beneath him. *Just like you did once,* she thought, shaking her head slightly to ditch the thought. He confidently marched right toward the center of the city and into, she realized with a gasp, the one place in Baghdad she really, truly knew inside and out.

"The House of Wisdom," she whispered, lingering in the shadows as she watched him disappear inside.

"Never heard of it," Dias muttered.

"Why would you?" Azadeh countered. "You're not particularly wise."

Roshan blocked out their bickering as she glanced at the guards at the door. The place was open to everyone usually, but not tonight. It appeared this evening it was closed for a private function and the guests of honor were six annoyingly resilient cult members.

"Enough," she snapped, cutting them off. "I know a way in. Follow me."

The Grand Library seemed to be the focus of the guards' attention as she skirted the perimeter of the building, with the remaining wings open and operating as she watched scholars come and go as usual. She took Dias and Azadeh in through one of the side entrances to the east wing, which led to the courtyard and would be quiet on a cloudy evening like tonight. There was little to see. She halted their progress at a lattice that had vines creeping up toward the sky, telling them to wait for her here. She wanted to check where the first guard would be stationed and from there she'd be able to work out where they needed to go. She climbed, feeling the structure underneath her struggle with the additional weight and she considered tossing her cloak free.

Roshan was glad she didn't as she crouched on the sill of an upper window, peering inside and seeing a guard biting at his fingernails in the corridor extending out below her. He looked bored and young and like someone who was hired for this rather than a Martyr who lived and died for it. She gestured down at the others to follow her, Azadeh climbing up first and Dias waiting. Onyx paced at the bottom of the garden, clearly uneasy about being left behind. A soft whistle echoed, and Roshan wondered what that command meant as she leapt into the corridor.

She was soundless, the young guard not hearing her progress and not realizing she was there until it was too late. Roshan knocked him out with a swirling blow from her fighting stick, and the man's skull made an uncomfortable *thunk* as her weapon connected. She caught him before his body noisily fell to the ground, lowering him carefully as she held her hand in front of his nose to check if he was still breathing. He was, but he'd be in a lot of pain tomorrow.

Voices floated up to them and Roshan walked forward, realizing the corridor was actually a huge balcony looking down into the large grandiose room below. She didn't have a chance to check who the voices belonged to as she was joined by the others. There was a dark mass next to her and she turned to find Onyx watching, the wolf licking her lips as she scrutinized the man's exposed flesh. This young guard had never been in more danger in his life and he had no idea. She held up her hand in what she hoped looked like a firm warning gesture. She mouthed the word "no" and Onyx backed away, but didn't look any less hungry. The whistled order Azadeh had given her was clearly to find a way up unseen. The adrenaline bubbling between all of them wasn't restricted to the humans.

"They're here," Dias whispered, hunched next to her. Roshan's gaze followed his, looking down through the pillars of the upper balcony and into what was frequently used as one of the main lecture locations. She had seen hundreds of bodies packed into this viewing area, looking down on the great men of their generation as they spoke about everything from algebra to astronomy. There was another level above them that held less space and she glanced up, not seeing any guards but sensing something. Her vision bloomed slightly, and she had to blink away the glow to focus on the present situation because below them, things were getting interesting.

All six members of the Martyrs of Agaunum stood in a circle and she was able to get a better view of their robes now, the dark maroon color glinting with that same golden trim. On their chests, directly over their hearts, was the symbol she had sketched for Azadeh in the Karachi library.

"The six-pointed cross," Azadeh whispered near her neck, joining them.

At the very center of their group lay the case in question, positioned perfectly on a platform. Roshan's eyes were once again drawn to the weird markings on its surface. Below, Francis entered the space with another colleague who was just as white and blond as him. They took up positions behind the Martyrs and bowed their heads.

"What are they waiting for?" Dias questioned.

"The customer," Roshan realized. "This is a delivery."

No sooner had she said the words than an additional person entered the space. This person was also cloaked head to toe, but in nothing as garish as the Martyrs. Their fabric was a deep, midnight blue and dragged behind them across the marble floor like an otherworldly bride. Although she couldn't make out their features, this person was almost impossibly tall and lithe. As tall as the twins, almost, but their body seemingly skeletal under the rich silks cloaking them.

"That person doesn't leave here with that case," she whispered, turning to the others. They all nodded silently. Roshan watched for a moment as Dias and Azadeh crept off so that they could surround the Martyrs. Onyx slunk down the stairs, no doubt to find a much better angle from which to strike. The Martyrs began reciting a prayer as the new figure – *the customer,* Roshan thought – moved to the center of the group, hands extended toward the case. One by one, each of the Martyrs dropped to their knees and bowed their heads.

Roshan got to her feet, pressing her back to the shadows as she waited for the whistle she knew Azadeh would make. Climbing up onto the railing, she crouched and used the length of her fighting stick to maintain balance. The customer went to open the case, their long fingers bracing on the handle as it lifted apart and opened–

The tall newcomer hissed. Leaping back in pain, the customer cut off the Martyrs' prayers with an angry response. A Martyr had risen to his feet, responding in a language she didn't understand. Roshan frowned, realizing that she might not know the words, but the brief glimpse of the case's interior made for a whole different vocabulary – and it was one she knew very well. Her flash of recognition was pushed aside as Azadeh seized upon the confusion. A whistle cut through the Martyrs' verbal argument, sharp and piercing as her friend signaled them to attack.

The Martyrs spun around at the sound, struggling to pinpoint the exact location as the arched ceilings created the perfect echo. The literal wolf in their midst lunged for Francis first in a move Roshan appreciated. The voice that so annoyed her when he spoke wasn't that annoying now when he was crying out in pain, blood spraying from his jugular as the wolf pulled him to the ground.

Dias flew in from above, his sword raised above his head as he landed on the shoulders of a Martyr. He used gravity to increase his downward power and the blade sank deep into the man's skull, effectively slicing his head in half. The Martyr dropped to his knees and didn't get up, his limbs still twitching as his nervous system reacted.

Interesting, Roshan thought, springing into action herself.

She dove from the balcony, using a different Martyr to break her fall as she landed on his back. His own skull collided with the unforgiving floor, cracking like an egg. Just like Dias's target, this man didn't get up. Her moment to evaluate that was pushed aside when a Martyr threw her to the side as he crouched down to examine his colleague. He let out a pained cry as if heartbroken by the loss, something else she found intriguing as she threw her legs in rotation, utilizing the momentum to get back on her feet.

Another Martyr sprinted directly at her and she took them both on at the same time, using her fighting stick to keep them at a distance until the others could help. She saw Azadeh enter the fray, sprinting toward her to provide assistance. Her friend drew her sword, striking at the back of one assailant and barely making a dent.

"The head!" she screamed. "Aim for their heads!"

"What?!" Azadeh shouted back, confused. Roshan cursed herself for creating a distraction and she cried out as she saw a dagger flying directly toward Azadeh. She yelled as the blade made contact. It should have killed her, landing in her neck, but she'd thrown her hand up at the last moment. Azadeh squealed as the blade embedded deep in her flesh. She grunted as she dropped her sword, needing her free hand to yank the dagger loose – a move that left her exposed.

Roshan fought harder, faster, slipping into the rhythm where she found herself not thinking, just reacting. She focused on the dull *thunk thunk thunk* as she lashed out and pivoted, reshuffling to position herself next to Azadeh so she could defend both of them simultaneously. It took everything she had to keep the Martyrs at bay. The wood of her fighting stick reverberated through her hands as it counteracted the sword blows. She tossed a glance behind her, searching for Dias. He hadn't misheard her call of warning to Azadeh and his sword slashed through the face of one of the Martyrs. His eyes connected with hers and she understood immediately that he wouldn't be coming to help them.

Wood splintered and dug in her hands and Roshan's attention sliced back to the present, watching as her beloved weapon took the last blow it would ever take. It was a miracle the fighting stick had lasted this long but she felt her heart break as it exploded into a cloud of splinters. She ducked the swing of a Martyr's sword, dropping down to try to grab her own sword. Her fingers slipped amongst the blood. She felt Azadeh attempt to snatch it for her as the two Martyrs loomed, but she was certain this was it.

This was the moment she would die. *How nice,* she thought for a fleeting second. *How nice to not die alone like you always thought you would, pressed flesh to flesh with someone fighting by your side, someone who cares, someone loyal.* The shine of the blade's metal was interrupted by a flash of black colliding with the closest Martyr to her. She blinked, belatedly understanding that Onyx had just saved them. The Martyr's hands fought to toss the wolf off him, punching and slashing until she heard the wolf whimper.

There were splashes of sticky red swirled amongst the black fur now, and Azadeh's cry mixed with the wolf's as she jumped forward. With the dagger that had pierced her own skin, she pulled Onyx's body off the Martyr and stabbed him, the motion repeated again and again. Roshan's own attacker was diving down on her and she had just enough time to get her sword angled upright.

The blade glanced off the maroon robes, sliding up toward the high cut of his hood where it slipped between his neck. It wasn't a fatal cut, but there was enough blood rapidly pouring from the wound that he clutched desperately at the gash. It would take both hands pressed to his flesh rather than his sword to stay alive.

She saw the choice dance in his eyes – his life or take hers – only for the decision to be made for him. A figure fell from the ceiling, arms extended in an expert fall that should have killed a regular person. But this was no regular person. The hooded stranger landed like gravity was merely an inconvenience, swinging his arm as he passed the bleeding Martyr. The hidden blade ejected as he spun, decapitating the Martyr in a perfect circle. If she thought he was there to save her, she was wrong. He barely slowed his pace and strolled right past.

The customer was nearby, frozen in the middle of the havoc, taking a step forward and a step back as they tried to find a route to flee. There was nowhere to go among the chaos. Roshan watched as the customer drew a sword, and it appeared uncomfortable in their hands, despite the clear mastery they had over the weapon. In contrast, the hooded stranger's blade looked like an extension of their soul, the way she felt when she performed tahtib. She couldn't look away as the stranger engaged the customer in battle, fighting so fast and so fiercely her eyes could barely track it. He moved like a demon, or an angel, she couldn't decide.

Watching this battle felt like she was intruding on

something intimate, like Roshan should divert her gaze. It seemed like an ancient feud finally being brought into the light, even if she couldn't understand it as the customer and the hooded stranger engaged each other in combat.

Her eyes darted to Azadeh, clutching Onyx and crying. Her head was buried in the wolf's fur, the animal whimpering as she bled out. A Martyr could have been creeping up behind Azadeh, but Roshan knew the woman wouldn't care. Azadeh's soul was fracturing as the wolf who'd spent her entire life by her side died.

To her right, Dias wiped blood on his thigh as he paced toward the case still on the pedestal. There were no more Martyrs left, no more Francis. The hired guards had been killed or had fled. There was just the case they had been sent to chase after, and Roshan opened her mouth to tell Dias to stop, to not take it, to not open it.

She swallowed the words. The pirate ripped open the case. Roshan heard the mechanisms kick in, listened to the weights shift and the cogs connect as Dias triggered the device. It exploded in his face, shards of metal and debris exploding out of the box.

The customer had barely opened the box, had only ejected some of the gunpowder. Dias received the full force of the case's destructive power. Roshan closed her eyes, sparing herself the sight of the result for a moment. She had helped create such destruction enough times, and she had tested it on melons and animal carcasses.

When she reopened her eyes, not much remained. Roshan staggered up, using her sword as an aid. The hooded stranger was using his own blade in a much more practical fashion, withdrawing it from the body of the customer the Martyrs had been serving. The customer dropped in a flutter of fabric; Roshan half expected the person to disappear like magic. The customer landed and they landed *hard* instead. The hooded stranger attacked again, quickly using his hidden blade to deliver two more blows. He then checked the body, and only when he was satisfied did he stand back up. He caught her staring, Roshan refusing to look away.

"That's what you wanted the whole time, wasn't it?" she said, her voice little more than a croak. "It was never about the case. It was about *who* the Martyrs were delivering it to."

The hooded stranger walked toward her with that deathly gait. He paused, pulling back his hood so she could properly see his face in the light of the library. She guessed people only really saw him when they were about to die. Even better if they never saw him at all.

"I could sense you," Roshan continued. "Waiting up there for your target to arrive. Waiting for us to cause enough confusion so you could strike."

"Where?" he asked, titling his head with interest. "Where was I?"

"Up there," she pointed. There was no reason to lie if he was going to kill her anyway.

"You have a knack for that, don't you? Knowing where things should be, what they are…"

Roshan didn't respond. Clearly, he knew the answer.

He moved past her, toward the case. "And you're partially right, partially wrong. It was about the case: I needed what was inside it and I needed someone who could disable it. You were the more promising one of the two individuals."

He looked down, inspecting what was left of Dias.

"But what I really wanted was the Martyrs of Agaunum exposed, along with the person who hired them. Your team got me both, albeit at immense cost."

"That's why you wanted murderers, thieves, warrior princesses… there would be no guilt if we died because we deserved it."

"Do you feel like you deserve it?" he pushed. "You have killed precisely one person. Anyone would describe that person as a heinous excuse for a human being. You've let others die, certainly, but by your hand? Your intent? Just one."

He raised his finger.

"Are you absolving me of guilt?" Roshan questioned, confused.

"No, but I could. You've been directionless your whole life, *Roshan.* I could give you the purpose you've been searching for and a mission that would make your every breath matter."

Her heart thudded against her chest, the lure of his words tugging at her very being. She could taste the promise, practically smell the potential. She wanted it.

"That sounds like a life of service," a voice said, cutting through her thoughts. She turned to find Azadeh stumbling to her feet, clutching her injured arm. She was soaked in Onyx's blood, the loyal wolf dead behind her. The pain etched across her face was palpable.

"And sacrifice," the hooded stranger pressed, not denying it. "But what is freedom if we don't fight for it?"

"That doesn't sound like freedom," Azadeh argued. "That sounds like a prison with different bars. That sounds like a cult. You know, like the supposedly immortal Martyrs of Agaunum."

"They look very dead for a cult of immortals," Roshan murmured, her eyes scanning the various carcasses.

The hooded stranger snorted. "They were not immortal. They were gifted with technology that made any blow not directly above the neck useless."

He bent down, lifting back the robes of one to reveal what looked like another layer of that fine, glittering gold.

"You could still drown them, set them on fire, blow them up, but in hand to hand combat... well, you experienced the difficulties of eliminating them firsthand."

"This technology was from the person you killed," Roshan theorized. "The Martyr's customer. Is that what the symbols mean? The ones on the case?"

"I imagine that would interest you," he mused. "A new language to pick apart. But no, the symbols tell you who is in the box."

"Who?" Azadeh prompted. "Not what?"

The hooded stranger stared at her hard. He had not misspoken.

Azadeh shook her head, backing away cautiously. "I do not want this," she muttered. "Everything that has happened from the moment I said yes to this mission has been a mistake."

"Then leave," he said. "My word is my bond. Your payment will be waiting for you, as discussed. Your father is healed."

Azadeh nodded, half turning away as she gestured at Roshan. "Come on, let's go." She extended her good hand, waiting and expecting Roshan to take it.

Roshan remained where she was. Her legs were rooted to the ground as if her soul had made the choice for her. A new world was opening before her, and Azadeh wanted her to leave it.

Azadeh raised her eyebrows, surprise and hurt crossing her features. "Don't do this, don't go with him," she begged.

"I'm tired of running," Roshan replied, stepping toward her and taking her hand. "I'm tired of chasing something always out of my reach. I want to matter. I can tell *this* matters."

"You matter," Azadeh countered. "As an individual, *you.* We could matter."

She gripped Azadeh's hand tighter, wishing that she could go with her. In another life, maybe. But all Roshan had was this one. She planted a kiss on Azadeh's forehead, holding her lips there for a moment longer before pulling away.

"Live the life you've earned," she whispered. "And don't look for me, dear friend."

Azadeh blinked, tears streaking down her face. To her credit, she listened. She backed away from Roshan slowly before spinning on her heels and sprinting off into the depths of the library. Roshan knew she'd never see Azadeh again. Her heart ached, but she put her feelings to the side. She could make peace with her feelings in time. When she turned back around, she could feel the hooded stranger's eyes burning into her.

She kept her own gaze lowered as she marched back toward him, not wanting him to see what was in her heart playing across her face. Debris crunched under her feet, and she paused, recognizing something amongst the smashed wood and blood and shattered ceramics.

It was a bead, once bright purple but now a muted lilac. Her sister Masha's favorite color. She crouched down, examining the small sphere in her hand and rolling it around to see where the glass was cracked. She hadn't even felt the bracelet break, hadn't sensed it cut from her wrist with the incidental slash of a blade.

Roshan imagined crawling around, desperately looking for the remaining beads that Bolour had selected as well, hoarding them all and recreating the gift which was so special to her. The bracelet had been her token as a girl and had traveled so far with her as a woman, enduring so much until… this. It had not survived this fight. There was something tragic about that.

"You made the right decision," the hooded stranger said, his words cutting into her grief.

"Shut up," she mumbled, rising and gently pushing him to the side as she went to approach the case. "Be careful. The range on that is bigger than you think. Bakhit always went for maximum impact."

"Can you disable it?"

"Yes," Roshan replied, crouching low as she examined the bottom. "This case doesn't belong to Bakhit, does it? It belonged to your…"

"Target," he offered. "Your old mentor was hired to create a device that could sit within it and still protect the contents when activated."

"Depending on how quickly you need what – sorry – *who*'s inside, then I need time to disable it."

"As long as it's protected, that's what matters."

She frowned, thinking deeply. "Shut it and seal it back up.

We can transport it as is and the contents will be safe until you reach your destination. Which is where exactly?"

"Alamut," he responded. "The fortress city."

She scoffed. "There's no fortress there."

"Not yet, no..."

She narrowed her eyes, trying to deduce the meaning behind his mysterious words but feeling like she had come in halfway through a play that was being spoken backward.

"Will you ever give me a straight answer, or do I just have to trust you?"

"Of course," he replied. "Both."

Roshan cashed in on the promise right away, testing him as she pointed at the body of the customer she'd seen him annihilate. "Who hired the Martyrs?"

"The Order of the Ancients." He said the words with weight that she felt in her bones.

"Which is who the deceased worked for?"

"Correct," he confirmed.

She held his gaze, the answers coming from not just his lips but the windows to his soul. He cloaked so much of himself, but he was letting her see the truth in his answers.

Roshan nodded, there being approximately six thousand, six hundred and sixty-six other questions she wanted to ask. Yet that would have to do for now. She moved around the back of the case, closing it from behind and listening carefully as all of the mechanics clicked back into place. Only when the busy whirring stopped did she lean back and exhale deeply.

"There's probably three impacts in this," she said. "Dias used one. It resets every time you close the lid, so be careful on the remaining two."

"Thank you," the hooded stranger said, taking it carefully from the platform.

"What now?" she asked. "Where do we even begin?"

He smirked; that gesture was never followed by anything good, but in this case, maybe she would be wrong. The world flared just a little bit brighter around him, her sense blooming around this man as he threw his hood over his head and shifted the weight of the case against his hip.

"How about an introduction?" he said, extending a hand. "My name is Fuladh Al Haami. Welcome to the Hidden Ones, Roshan."

Acknowledgments

Daughter of No One was probably the hardest book I've ever had to write, which is saying something eleven novels deep. In part, it was because I'm such a huge *Assassin's Creed* fan and felt a lot of self-imposed pressure when it came to writing something that would live up to the depth and complexity so many incredible storytellers have created within this world and across decades.

There's a huge number of people who helped me climb that mountain of conflict, starting with Blake Howard who dialed down my freak out about this project being so massive and told me to concentrate "on writing something you love, like Ronin."

The best editor I've ever had, Gwendolyn Nix, which is somehow a real name. She pitched this project to me as "hey, so you like history, right?" and fought for me to tackle this in the first place by seeing the connection between Roshan and myself. Would 10,000% bunker down in the House of Wisdom with ya.

Jeffrey Yohalem, who I'm so, so grateful for his time and his generosity when it comes to helping shepherd others into a world he helped sculpt. A personal and professional lifeline in the building of *Daughter of No One* and the inspo for many of my favorite elements about it. Alissa Ralph for bringing the AC mantra "nothing is true and everything is permitted" to life with her insights and invaluable perspectives.

Assassin's Creed's biggest fan within Canadian time zones, Tim Hanley, research curator and the only person I've known to ever fall into an open manhole, Daniel O'Malley, and Baghdad's babe, Dr Mayada Zaki.

Finally, Ed Wilson. Always, for encouraging me to say yes to mad shit.

About the Author

MARIA LEWIS is a screenwriter, bestselling author, film curator, and pop culture etymologist currently based in Australia. Over the past eighteen years of her career, she has built an international reputation as a storyteller across a diverse range of mediums including the award-winning *Supernatural Sisters* series of eight novels. In the film and television space, she has worked on projects for Netflix, AMC, BBC, Ubisoft, DC Comics, ABC, Marvel and many more. She is also the writer, researcher, presenter and producer of audio documentaries *Josie and the Podcats* and *The Phantom Never Dies,* about the world's first superhero. In 2022, she made her directorial debut with *The House That Hungers,* based on her award-winning short story of the same name. With Aconyte Books, she is also the author of *Marvel Heroines: Mockingbird Strike Out.*

marialewis.com.au // twitter.com/moviemazz

UBISOFT
ASSASSIN'S CREED
BASED ON A UBISOFT CREATION
ASSASSIN'S CREED
THE GOLDEN CITY
NEW YORK TIMES BESTSELLING AUTHOR
JALEIGH JOHNSON
A YOUNG EMPEROR'S LIFE HANGS IN THE BALANCE IN ANCIENT CONSTANTINOPLE, AND ONLY THE BROTHERHOOD OF ASSASSINS CAN SAVE HIM.
THE MING DYNASTY BECOMES THE LATEST BATTLEGROUND IN THE WAR BETWEEN ASSASSINS AND TEMPLARS.
ASSASSIN'S CREED
THE MING STORM
YAN LEISHENG
BASED ON A UBISOFT CREATION
ASSASSIN'S CREED
THE DESERT THREAT
YAN LEISHENG
ACONYTEBOOKS.COM
ACONYTE